THE MATCH TRICK

TRICK

by Don Zacharia

The Linden Press/Simon & Schuster
New York, 1982

This novel is a work of fiction. Names, characters, places and incidents
either are the product of the author's imagination or are used fictitiously.
Any resemblance to actual events or locales or persons, living or dead, is
entirely coincidental.

Published by The Linden Press/Simon & Schuster
A Simon & Schuster Division of Gulf & Western Corporation
Simon & Schuster Building
Rockefeller Center
1230 Avenue of the Americas
New York, New York 10020
THE LINDEN PRESS/SIMON & SCHUSTER and colophon
are trademarks of Simon & Schuster
Designed by Ed Carenza
Manufactured in the United States of America

1   2   3   4   5   6   7   8   9   10

Library of Congress Cataloging in Publication Data

Zacharia, Don.
The match trick.

I. Title.
PS3576.A17M3   813'.54   81-20808
AACR2
ISBN 0-671-44017-9

*Lyrics from "So Long, Frank Lloyd Wright" © 1969, 1970
Paul Simon. Used by permission*

Portions of this book originally appeared in *The Partisan Review* in 1974.

FOR JUDY AND ZACHY

NEVERS

This diary is all about Nevers. If there wasn't a Nevers, there wouldn't be a diary.

Nevers is her name. Nevers _____. She doesn't like it when I use her last name: either verbally or in print. Yes, I know, Nevers is a very peculiar name. She told me she was named after a small town in Virginia where her mother used to summer. I don't know. She lies a great deal. I looked it up in the Atlas and there is no Nevers in Virginia. There is a Nevers, but it is in northern France. When I mentioned this to her she threw a fit and did something to me I don't feel like going into.

Nevers is the most beautiful woman in the world. That I am involved with her gives me extraordinary pleasure and fills me with unexplained contentment. Just walking in public with Nevers gives

Don Zacharia

me a keen awareness of myself, brings a rush of blood to my head. Every turned head is a boon; every stare a pat on the back; every open-mouth look a macho smack on the arm. Oh, is Nevers a crowd stopper. She appears to be unaware of it all; but I'm not. Her eyes avoid everyone. My eyes catch everyone. I count every turned head, register it on my imaginary meter, grade it for future reference and store it away to savor. Men stare, women stare, old people, young people, gays give appreciative glances, blacks whistle, Puerto Ricans snap their fingers, taxi drivers honk their horns, policemen give long glowing looks, and Nevers walks among them oblivious. She is the total beauty. Everyman's fantasy. A match-up of the most exquisite face with the most sensual body, and I, I am hers. But strangers don't know that. The only people who know that are Nevers, myself, and a black teenager she sometimes uses. Strangers might think that she is mine. I wonder what goes through their minds as we sally about Manhattan. I would love to ask someone, anyone, but I think I would make a fool of myself.

I always like to walk somewhat in back of Nevers. She approves of that. It gives me a better opportunity to witness the commotion she causes. Christ, is she exquisite. As we approach men nudge each other. People crane their necks from passing cars. Men will cross the street to get a better look, and more than once I have seen them, having passed us once, turn around, walk by us in the same direction, and then turn around again just to get a second wonderful look at Nevers. There must be an army of men fantasizing nightly about making love to her. Their fantasy is my reality. Do they know?

Nevers doesn't tower over me the way she says she does. With heels on, which she always wears, she is six feet, about two inches taller than me. She likes that. She puts her arm around my shoulders, as if she were the man, and with her beautiful red hair flashing about, we walk down the street creating a minor riot. She calls me her little man at times like that, which is ridiculous considering that I used to play basketball and was pretty good at it (holding the all-county record for consecutive baskets).

I can't wait to introduce Nevers to my buddy Phil. I can't wait. A pipe dream. Phil is always checking out good-looking asses and he would flip over Nevers. I am sure he would appreciate her as much as I do. I haven't told Phil about Nevers. For that matter I haven't told anyone about Nevers. She is a secret. My secret. My secret. Mine. Mine. All mine. The whole situation is impossible. What I am doing to my family, especially Beth, is awful. What anguish my behavior creates. But right now there is nothing I can do about it. It is hopeless. It is beyond my control. I am out of control. My life *is out of control. I am speeding down an endless hill. I remember all those old gangster movies where they would strap the opposing mobster in a car and send him down a mountainside. That is me. That is how I feel. I don't always feel strapped in (ha ha), but sometimes I feel the car doesn't have a steering wheel. How I can be doing this to my daughter is something that I cannot think of now.*

Frieda Bloom, my therapist, is aware of the fact that there is something going on in my life that is impossible for me to talk about. It has come out in our private sessions and once in the group session with Beth and David. I back off, like a horse rearing at a jump. A couple of times I have almost talked about Nevers to Mrs. Bloom, but so far, no go. As far as Phil goes, I don't think I can do that. I don't think Phil would understand my relationship with her. It was Mrs. Bloom's idea for this diary. She told me if I can't talk about it, perhaps I could write about it. So I am. I think so far it's a pretty good idea. Feeling better about everything already.

Phil is the closest friend I have ever had, yet I find it impossible to talk about Nevers with him. I get the feeling that Phil would do anything for me, I mean anything, *and it bothers me that I have held back on him on Nevers. I feel I have betrayed him. I have enough to be guilty about, and by not telling Phil I am only doing something that will create further guilt. Well, I will tell him. Or even better, maybe some day the three of us could have dinner together. Ah, Noelie, you're just kidding yourself. I couldn't do that. There is absolutely no containing Nevers, and she would do something to me in front of Phil that would be intolerable. Phil just wouldn't understand. His head just isn't into that. Poor straight Phil. Nevers might*

Don Zacharia

create a situation where I would have to pick between her and Phil, and as terrible as it sounds, at this point in my life I just don't trust myself in that kind of a scene. So, good old pal, old buddy, old friend, just hang in there. I'm sorry. You know I have always felt that I would trust you with anything, or I would do anything for you, but I guess Nevers is the exception. No hard feelings, buddy.

Nevers is so beautiful. I tell her she could easily become a top model. She scoffs at my suggestion. Nevers doesn't work; to my knowledge never has. It is amazing, considering how much time I spend with her, how little I know about her background. She has an income from somewhere, but I haven't the vaguest. She certainly doesn't need from money as she always has large quantities of it stuffed about, in coat pockets, in desk drawers, floating around the bottom of pocketbooks. Despite this, or in spite of it, I give her money. There is no pattern—sometimes as much as five hundred dollars and sometimes less, but never less than two hundred. She started it. She said she wasn't going to see me unless I gave her money. She said she wasn't going to make an issue of it or bring it up again, but she expected it. That's the way it is. I'd rather not think about it.

I am constantly in a state of sexual arousal with Nevers. Part of it has to do with the way she looks, the way she dresses. No matter what she is wearing, there is always the hint that if you keep looking, within ten seconds you will see more. Nevers spends a great deal of money on clothing. She dresses for the most part simply, classic chic—Halston, Armani—innocent sundresses, sexy silk V-necked blouses, tailored pants, suits that she looks wonderful in, a minimum of jewelry but always a thin gold necklace, boots that make men's hearts flutter, and if she wants to really knock everyone out, a wide-brimmed hat. Nevers in a hat would create a traffic jam in Wyoming. Nevers is one of those women who would look exquisite in a housedress from Alexander's. She doesn't shop in Alexander's. She buys all of her clothing in Madison Avenue boutiques, with occasional forays to First Avenue. She always pays cash, and being in the clothing business, let me tell you, Nevers is a hell of a customer. She takes me with her many times. We waltz around those boutiques and the women in those stores eye me very curiously. Well, I can't

The Match Trick

blame them. Ours is a very curious relationship. In those situations Nevers knows just how far to go with me, and I love it. *She acts as if I am her servant while she breezes about, picking out half a dozen dresses, and then when she is in the dressing room she will call out in a voice loud enough for everyone to hear for me to come in and help her change. It is a routine I have become proficient at. There is nothing routine about my feelings, though. I unbutton her dress, help her off with it, hang it up, and then help her into whatever she is trying on. Many times she will have me wait in the dressing room while she goes outside to see how she looks and then comes back with something else to try on. This can go on for hours. I don't mind a bit. Once in a boutique on First Avenue I remained in a dressing room for two hours while Nevers tried on dozens of outfits. She spent three thousand dollars there, cash peeled out from her purse in hundred-dollar bills, so no one seemed to care. It's a good thing we are in New York. I think if we were in Cleveland we would be arrested.*

I am always terribly aroused by this scene. Nevers realizes it and toys with me. She doesn't wear a bra, and depending, I guess, upon her mood in the morning, sometimes doesn't wear panties. Dressing and undressing her drive me mad. As I slip her dress off she will fondle her nipples. My hands glide over her sides, her stomach, her buttocks. She smiles encouragingly but I don't dare do anything unless she tells me first. Sometimes in between changing she lets me lick her for just moments. "Suck my cunt for just thirty seconds, Noelie," she will say. She gets aroused in those impossible situations. I feel her juices flow into my mouth. I am aware of her excitement. "Five more seconds," she moans, and then, "enough," she whispers, pulling me up. She kisses my mouth, once, twice. I help her into another outfit, her face aglow, her breasts pushing against the fabric of the dress. The odor from her cunt overpowers my nostrils, my mouth, the tiny dressing room we both share. I am sure that when she goes out everyone will be aware of what took place. I am dizzy from excitement, my head ablaze, and shut my eyes. "Wait here," she says and floats into the store.

When we leave we get plenty of stares, but I don't care about that anymore.

WAITING FOR SUSU

When Noel came home Monday night, his wife, Susan, wasn't there. "Hello, hello, I'm home, sweetheart." Noel tried to remember something, but he was damned if he knew what. "Susan?" He squinted, confused by the darkness in his home. It was a summer evening, and only six-thirty. "Susan," he called out again. How odd, Noel thought, Susan was *always* there.

His children were at camp. His thirteen-year-old daughter, Beth, was a rock when she left, but his son, David, only eleven, cried when boarding the bus. That moment tortured him. "Susan," again, *"Susan?"* He moved into the kitchen and looked around. There was no note. A milk bill hung on the refrigerator door held there by a little round magnet. Noel studied it, shaking his head, convinced the milkman was padding the bill. He opened the refrigerator and closed it. He snapped on a light and shut it off. The house was still. It bothered him. He couldn't remember the last time he came home to an empty house. Noel clapped his hands twice for the dog to come to him. Nothing happened because there wasn't a dog. I'm going wacky, Noel thought. Nutsville.

Once the Roths had a dog—a smelly springer named Sam that would jump on Noel whenever he came home. The dog was forever killing rabbits and squirrels and triumphantly carrying them into the house between his jaws. When it first happened, his wife and his daughter, who were both very concerned about killing *any-thing*, became hysterical. Noel, unnerved by their hysteria, not knowing what to do, picked up a newspaper and hit the springer. The dog, confused, dropped his kill on the rug and began to whimper. Beth began to scream. Susan clutched her daughter, cupping her face into her shoulder.

"I don't believe you, Noel. Why don't you get a hammer and hit him with that?"

Noel got a shovel, picked up the dead squirrel and, walking deep into the woods in back of his home, scooped out a shallow grave, and with the "killer" looking on, buried the squirrel.

"You don't give a shit," Noel said. The dog pawed at the ground. Noel patted him.

The scene was repeated. Noel came to the defense of the springer. "It is the balance of nature," he said eloquently.

"It is unwarranted murder," his daughter cried out.

"The balance of nature," Susan sneered. "That's what Goebbels used to say about the Jews."

Noel, who was a sensitive person, couldn't take it. His son's allergist came to the rescue when he suggested that David's wheezing might get better if they got rid of the dog. It was a snap decision. The next day Noel gave the springer to a trucker he knew who lived in Connecticut. That was in June.

Tonight. As Noel wandered about his home without direction, wondering where Susan was, turning on a light, turning off a light, opening and closing the refrigerator twice, checking the gas burners, tonight, he missed the dog, Sam.

· · ·

Don Zacharia

Noel put his sneakers on and went outside to shoot some baskets. Dribbling to the right, he banked the ball in. Two long jumps from the corner find their mark. Dribbling across the key, a right-handed hook doesn't even touch the rim and goes cleanly through the net. He toes the foul line and bounces the ball four, five, six times, and shoots. It hits the front rim and bounces back. Noel readjusts the arch of the ball but misses again. He tries three more shots from the foul line, missing them all. His high-school coach, Ray Warren, a stubby man who saw shadows everywhere, talking to Noel about his foul shooting, once told him, "It's mental. It's a psychological block. You understand, Noel?"

"Like Wilt the Stilt?" Noel asked.

"Yes. Exactly. I'm sorry for you." He punched him in the arm.

It was ten after seven. Noel got a beer and sat on the back lawn facing the house. He studied his hands. They were small. That was the problem. That always was the problem. Harry Gallatin, who once played for the New York Knicks, had hands like hams. Harry was a customer of Noel's and bought most of his clothing at Noel's store.

"My hands are really small," Noel once told him, "that's why I quit basketball. I couldn't make foul shots. I couldn't grip the ball right. Look." He held both of his hands up.

"They look normal to me."

"Baloney. On a piano I can't even reach from C to C."

"Ronnie Costello had small hands."

"Ronnie Costello? Who's he?"

"Played for Utica, 'fifty-two and 'fifty-three. Used to drive me crazy."

"Ah, come on, Harry, you're kidding."

Noel liked Harry, liked talking to him. He gave him a discount on everything he bought, and always steered the conversation around to basketball. Noel spoke to Susan more than once about having the Gallatins over for dinner, but nothing ever came of it.

At seven-thirty Noel went up to the bedroom and looked around. There was no note. Everything was in place. He went into the bathroom. Susan used to leave him messages on the bathroom mirror, but there was nothing there either. He wondered where Susan was. How unlike her. How out of context. He studied his reflection in the bathroom mirror. His reflection was his reflection. How stupid. Why couldn't it be something else?

He looked exactly the way he looked. I am what I am. A thirty-six-year-old haberdasher. Shit. He pulled his stomach in. Brown hair, brown eyes, a quick, heavy beard, handsome, a broken nose over forgotten issues, an almost-athlete with just the beginning of a bald spot. Women look at me, but I have never broken eighty on a golf course. At nighttime, when I can't sleep I fantasize about playing professional basketball. Ahh, how sweet, Noelie. An Ivy League graduate could be so many things. Noel opened his mouth and studied his tongue. He looked at himself for a long time. He touched his hair and then his face. He ran his hands along the outside of his thighs, pleased by the hardness. I should have been taller—six inches—is that so goddamn much to ask for? I should have been—what? What I would like to do for a living is be a manufacturer. Yes. I'd like to manufacture little round magnets. No kidding. Hi, my name is Roth. No kidding. No kidding. Whatcha do for a living, Mr. Roth? What is your current form of employment? What is your occupation? How do you bring the bucks home? Well, I'll tell you, it's like this, I manufacture these little round magnets. No kidding.

They had almost always lived there. A fine house in a valley with deep woods behind it. At first they lived in an apartment, but Noel made a lot of money quickly, and they bought the house two years after they were married. How pleased they both were with their lives. How very perfect the first months in the house were. The day they moved in Susan walked all about with Beth snug in a backpack. Susan looked radiant, her hair in a loose knot, feeling the finest she had felt in a long time. She drew a picture of a tree on an unpainted wall. "Tree," she said to Beth, who was sleeping, "with lots and lots of roots."

It was raining hard that first day and Noel came back from a

Don Zacharia

tour of the house. "Not a drop of water inside." He was pleased.

"It was predestined," Susan said.

Noel was angry. They fought very little in those days, but somehow, in his mind, something other than "predestined" should have been her comment.

Noel was working six days a week, and on Sundays would sleep late, dreaming stuff that his life wasn't. Susan, letting him sleep, would take Beth for a bike ride. After, she would come to Noel, a ribbon in her hair, the faintest touch of lipstick, smelling of oranges, talcum powder, the lingering remains of last night's perfume.

"We saw the newspaper man. He waved to us and we waved back. Beth liked that." Noel, pretending sleep, didn't answer. Susan kissed him awake, and Noel smiled at her.

"My teeth feel sandy," he said. They had steamers the night before.

"Let's go to the beach today."

Noel nodded yes. He lifted up the covers and motioned for Susan to come in.

"Tonight." She kissed him again. "The seat of the bike hurts my cunt."

"You can't have everything," Noel mumbled.

They went to the beach. Beth, only two, was happiest about that. Susan would sun herself while reading the Sunday *Times*. Noel would sift sand through his fingers, go to the hot-dog stand and bring hot dogs and Cokes back for everyone, and read the sport pages. It was almost September and Roger Maris had only nineteen home runs. Incredible. All the sports writers were calling him a fake—after hitting sixty-one home runs the year before—but Noel wasn't so sure. In the afternoon the three of them built a sand castle. It was some sand castle. Actually, it was a series of castles, close to the water's edge, complete with moats, bridges, towers, and little people represented by sticks. It took half the afternoon to finish it and when completed they all sat back with legs crossed and chins tucked in and watched the incoming tide wash it away.

They were so sure of their love in those days. The day John F.

16

Kennedy was killed they both cried and made love quietly in the late afternoon under the covers with Beth sleeping next to them.

"Doctor Spock would vomit," Susan whispered.

"I love you so much," Noel said. "I feel so sad. So sad."

Susan started to cry again as Noel was coming. "What kind of a country do we live in?" she sobbed.

"I think Beth is waking."

Both of them still.

"It's all right," Susan said. "Did you come?"

"Yes."

"Stinker. I'm still hot. I feel so sad. So sad. I liked that man so much."

It was seven forty-five. Noel opened up the trunk of Susan's car. Susan wasn't there. The mere presence of her car puzzled Noel. Susan wouldn't go around the corner without driving. Someone could have picked her up? Noel was uncomfortable with that. He went outside and shot some more baskets. He walked around the house twice and then went back inside. He looked in all the closets in the house. Susan wasn't in any of them.

"Do you know where Susan is?" Noel was talking on the phone to his best friend and lawyer, Phil Radcliff.

"Why?"

"She's not home."

"Did you look all over the house?"

"I looked in the closets and I looked in the trunk of Susan's car."

"Did you look in the attic? Did you look in her studio?"

"No. Is Phoebe there?"

"Did you call just before you called?"

"Jesus!"

"Just before you called the phone rang and when they heard my voice they hung up."

Defensively, "It wasn't me."

Don Zacharia

"I think Phoebe has a lover."

"It *wasn't* me."

"Hiyuh, Noelie," Phoebe came on an extension. "I'm eating a carrot."

"Hi, Phoebe. Do you know where Susan is?"

"Isn't she home?"

"I definitely think you should look in the attic," Phil said.

"Get off the phone, Phil."

"I got my new graphite woods, Noel—"

"Get the fuck off the phone, Phil."

"The ball jumps off the clubhead—"

"I'm hanging up," Phoebe interrupted.

Noel was sorry he called.

Phil slammed the phone down.

"You want a sandwich, Noel? You want to come over for a sandwich?"

"No. Did you speak to Susan?"

Ignoring the question, "Did you look for a note?"

"There isn't any."

"Are you sure?"

"Yes, I'm *sure.*"

"You're worried."

"*I am not worried.*"

"How sweet. Noel is worried. Wait until I tell Susan."

"Jesus Christ, Phoebe—"

"I bet Susan told you what she was doing and you forgot."

Exasperated, "I didn't call you for this."

"You are worried. I can tell by your voice."

"Goddamn it, I am not worried," he shouted. "Susan's car is in the garage and Susan is not home and there is *no* note and I don't want a sandwich."

"I spoke to her this morning. Right after you left for work she called."

"Why didn't you tell me that in the first place?"

"I didn't hear you ask."

"Did she tell you what she was doing this afternoon?"

"No."

"Was she upset?"

"Yes. She told me the two of you had a fight at breakfast."

"It wasn't a fight."

"Forget it. Just forget it. Susan didn't go into details, and I don't want to know. Despite what you and Phil think, we don't tell each other everything. Besides, you know damn well what was bothering her."

"The party?" Noel said, referring to the surprise party given for Meyer Meyerson Saturday night.

"Yes, the party. Susan told me that Saturday night was the worst night of her life. She called the entire evening a fraud, and seeing the match trick again a revulsion. The way you men reacted to Meyer coming home, you would think the Messiah had arrived."

Noel smiled at Phoebe's remark. At breakfast Susan had said the same thing to him using the identical phrase, "the Messiah had arrived." There was something very special about having Meyer back after being gone ten years. Noel tried to explain it to Susan, but it was impossible. She wouldn't listen, or didn't want to listen.

"I could talk until I was blue in the face," he told Phil on the golf course the morning after Meyer's party, "and she wouldn't understand. What pisses me off is that she won't even *try* to understand. Her feminism gets in the way. If you tell Susan I said that, I'll deny it. Meyer, to me, to many of us who knew him, represented what could have been a breakout, a getaway. We lived through what he was, and now we live through what he could have been. Better he didn't try. Better he quit the way he did. I saw the game when he quit. They were playing N.Y.U. in the old Garden. He was guarding Happy Hairston and was eating him up. There must have been fifteen thousand people watching. Toward the end of the first half, Meyer took himself out of the game, walked off the court into the locker room and never came out for the second half. The next thing I heard he quit college and was living in Dayton, Ohio. Just like that. Nobody could believe it. Here's this guy who was all-county baseball four years, all-county basketball and football three years, and all-state baseball and basketball three years. That's really unheard of, Phil. Every college in America was after his ass; he gets a four-year scholarship to Dartmouth, and in the third basketball game of his college career, quits, just like that. No indication, no warning, just quits. Do you know why I think he did it? So we could all go on living with *our* Meyer. Who needs reality when you can have illusion in its place? Can you imagine what it was like for me growing up with Meyer? He was everything I wasn't. I used to think Meyer was going to play three professional sports. How fantastic. Am I happy with what I'm doing? Am I happy selling the latest Cardin pants? How come I go to Madison Square Garden to watch the Knicks when they don't come to my store and watch me take inventory?"

"I'll make some phone calls and get back to you," Phoebe told Noel. It was a compromise on her part. She knew that Susan was with Meyer. "In the meantime, stop worrying, Noelie. I can tell by the tone of your voice that you're worrying. Do you hear me? Stop worrying. Tell Susan to call me when she gets home."

Phoebe hung up. She drummed her fingers on the table and smiled at Phil. She touched her hair, enjoying the way it felt. "I wonder," she spoke slowly, stringing the sentence out, "if Meyer fucks as well as he played football? If he does, lucky Susu."

The attic was hot, stifling, at least 120 degrees. Noel could barely breathe. He looked around quickly, feeling anxious. Ridiculous, Noel thought, to have come up here. Susan wasn't there, but everything else was. Every piece of furniture they had ever bought and stopped using; every piece of clothing Susan had ever worn. Every picture, every book, cribs, dishes, silverware from their home, from Susan's mother's home, everything that two people could possibly amass in fourteen years of marriage, and all in total disarray. There wasn't even the beginning, the semblance of order. To Noel, who prided himself on organization, it was a quagmire. They had

The Match Trick

more than one fight about it. He left the attic in a panic and rushed to Susan's studio in the basement. It was impossible to breathe up there.

There were three "No Smoking" signs in Susan's studio. Noel had insisted upon it. He lived in fear of Susan's blowing up the house. "My wife," he told his friends, "manufactures dynamite for a living." Each night when he came home and saw his home still standing, it brought a moment of relief to him. Susan was an artist, a successful one, and for the last few years was working with metal. Noel looked around the studio and shook his head in despair. Like the attic, Susan's studio was in total disarray. Everything was haphazardly strewn about: recent work, some finished, some half finished, some never to be touched again (Noel's problem by his own admission was that he couldn't tell one from the other), Susan's tools, a bale of barbed wire, goggles, an acetylene torch, and two gas tanks with the words DANGER—COMBUSTIBLE printed on each.

It wasn't always Susan's studio. Originally, when they first bought the house, it was a playroom, its walls filled with posters, an old neon sign from Noel's store, and some early paintings of Susan's. He wouldn't say so, but Noel liked Susan's paintings better than her sculpture. The furniture in the room in those days was leftovers, an old sofa and a black and white television set that gave a distorted picture. The people were very long and stretched out and no one would put up with it except Noel. He liked to watch late-night basketball games from the West Coast. Sprawled out on the old sofa, the fact that Walt Frazier looked twelve feet long didn't mean a thing to Noel. He liked it down there and sometimes would fall asleep, the deepest of sleeps, and wake up at three in the morning feeling, for reasons he couldn't understand, very fine. For his thirtieth birthday, Susan surprised Noel and bought him a pool table for the playroom. It was the kind that had a ping-pong top if you wanted to use it for that. It brought a little more traffic to the downstairs playroom, but besides that, changed the character of the room. For one thing, when they moved the table in, they

Don Zacharia

had to move the television and the old sofa out. Noel didn't seem to mind. Sometimes the four of them would play ping-pong; and some nights Phil would come over and he and Noel would play serious straight pool. They both were pretty good players and their games had a quiet competitive edge they both enjoyed.

A year after Susan's gift, she took it back. One day she called the Salvation Army and had them take out the pool table (they were very pleased with that) and all the remaining furniture. It was the first, but certainly not the last, unilateral decision that Susan was to make. That night when Noel came home, Susan told him what she had done—that the downstairs room was going to become *her* studio, and that she had gotten a lock for the door and was going to *keep* it locked, and that she hoped he understood. Noel understood all right. He hit her in the face for the first and last time, not as hard as he could have, but hard enough to make her nose bleed. Susan was remarkably calm; she didn't become hysterical, she didn't walk out of the room, she didn't hit back.

"If I had done it any other way," she said, holding a washcloth to her nose, tilting her head upward, "it never would have happened."

Susan wasn't in her studio.

At twenty after eight Noel was sitting on the toilet, wondering where Susan was, trying not to worry, and taking his pulse, when someone came into his home. His pulse was one hundred and ten. "*Susan,*" he called out. He rushed to the stairs, buttoning his pants. "*Susan, Susan,* you're home. Where the hell have you been?"

"It's us, Noel." It was Phoebe and Phil.

Noel, standing on top of the stairs, was stunned. He cleared his throat. His chest was pounding. "I thought you were Susan," he finally said.

"We rang the bell," Phil said apologetically, "four or five times."

"It stopped working the other day." Noel came down the stairs.

"Are you OK, buddy? You look kinda—"

"I'm OK. You gave me a start—I thought you were Susan."

"Sorry."

"Did you eat?" Phoebe asked. "I'll make you a sandwich."

"No. I'm not hungry. Come on, let's go in the den." Phil and Phoebe sat on opposite ends of the sofa, Noel in a chair across from them. Phoebe tucked her legs under her, pulling her skirt up over her knees. Phil, who was a string of a man, six feet three and one hundred and sixty pounds, stretched his bare legs halfway into the middle of the room. "I'll get some drinks in a minute," Noel said.

"Did Susan call?" Phoebe asked.

"No, she didn't. Did you speak to anyone?"

"I called Lois Fruned. She didn't know anything, of course. She told me to tell you that she was sure that Susan was all right and that she had spoken to her this morning. I didn't call anyone else, Noel, because that would start a lot of ridiculous gossip, and besides, if I don't know where Susan is—" She didn't finish the sentence. She didn't have to. Phoebe, who was Susan's best friend, and was right about *everything*, knew where Susan was. The only problem, as she saw it, was Noel. "I think," Phoebe went on, feeling comfortable in what she was saying, covering for her friend the way she knew Susan would cover for her, "that Susan is all right. I think, for her reasons, Susan is at a movie, or taking a walk, or talking to some friends, or having dinner, or resting in a park. Susan is doing what *you men* like to call a number. She will come home when she is ready to come home, in five minutes or in five hours. Your little *girl*—" Phoebe's voice had an edge to it—"or your image of your little *girl*, isn't home at the prescribed hour, and Noel is in a panic. The worry shows on your face, and it's not a worry for Susan, it's a worry for Noel. You're overreacting for your own reasons; your own problems; your own fears; your own insecurities. Nothing has happened to Susan." Phoebe sat back, pleased. "Stop worrying." It was an order.

Noel, listening intently to Phoebe, wondered why his hands were suddenly so cold. "Do you feel the same way?" he asked Phil.

"Yes, he does," Phoebe interrupted.

"Will you shut up, Phoebe. If you're going to talk for me, I might as well go home."

"Please," Noel said, "please."

Don Zacharia

"I really want a drink," Phoebe announced.

"In a second. You know once when I was a kid I couldn't find my basketball and after a while I began looking in the dumbest places for it, like the refrigerator and the oven; that's what I've been doing so far tonight. I've actually looked in the refrigerator for Susan." Noel shook his head and smiled. "I'm glad you two are here. I think if you called and asked if you should come over I would have said no, but now that you're here, I'm glad." He hesitated, took a deep breath and plunged ahead. "I'm worried about Susan. I don't feel what you feel, Phoebe. I think something has happened to her, and I feel like I should do something, but I don't know what. I just have this feeling; I can't explain it. I feel I should call someone, but I don't know who. Should I call all the local hospitals? What should I ask them? Should I call the police—?"

"Jesus Christ," Phoebe gasped, "don't call the cops, Noel. Get me a drink instead."

"What do you think, Phil?"

"I think you're overreacting. Susan is a couple of hours late, I know you're concerned, but you *are* overreacting."

"How about a drink?" Phoebe beamed.

"One more question, Phil. If two or three hours from now Susan is still not home, what do I do then? Will you still feel the same way?"

"That's crazy. You know she'll be back."

"But if she's not—come on, Phil—what then?"

"I suppose," Phil said, choosing his words carefully, "using your scenario, that at some point, three hours from now or so, if Susan isn't home, calling the police is something we can think about."

"Phil," Phoebe said, shaking her head in disbelief, "if I'm ever a couple of hours late and when I get home I find the local fuzz there, I'll cut your balls off."

"That's very comforting, darling. Some people think you already have."

"Come home, Susan," Phoebe wailed, "where ever the hell you are, before they call out the National Guard."

Noel couldn't help but laugh. Following Phoebe's advice, trying not to worry, he went into the kitchen to make drinks.

As soon as Noel was gone, Phoebe began speaking quietly to Phil. "Are you crazy, Phil? If Susan isn't home by midnight are you really going to let him call the police? Phil, Susan is with Meyer—"

"Did she tell you that?" he interrupted.

"No, she didn't tell me that," Phoebe said disdainfully. "It's not the kind of thing she has to tell me. I know, can't you understand that? Susan is with Meyer. It's as plain as the nose on your face. She's getting her ashes hauled. You understand that, don't you? This is going to be tough enough on Noel without the Crownhill police force poking around."

"I'm not so sure you're right, Phoebe," was all Phil had a chance to say before Noel came back with the drinks.

Noel poured white wine for Phoebe, a scotch on the rocks for himself, and a scotch and water for Phil. Phoebe took one sip of the wine, wrinkled up her nose and asked if she could have a scotch too. Noel poured her a scotch, put some records on and sat down. The scotch made him immediately dizzy. He had forgotten he hadn't eaten. He leaned back, fighting the dizzy feeling. He looked about. There was something wrong. Just like when he first came into the house and something seemed wrong, but he couldn't put his finger on it. Perhaps a picture on the wall needed straightening? There was a glass table top sitting on a steel cube, an ashtray that Noel liked—

So long Frank Lloyd Wright / I can't believe your song is gone so soon / I barely heard the tune / So soon / So soon

What was it—ah—one of those three-way lamps. Noel leaned over and put it on, click-click-click. A tree was dying from lack of light. Susan had bought it in a nursery in Hartsdale; he remembered the day she shlepped it home. "A bargain," she said. The ashtray came from Jensen's, the table and chair came from Pace.

Don Zacharia

What could it be—the crookedness of the picture? The death of the tree?

I'll remember Frank Lloyd Wright / All of the nights we'd har- monized till dawn / I never laughed so long / So long / So long

Jesus, how dumb, how dumb. Noel sipped his scotch and cupped his head with his hand. How dumb, how dumb. Susan wasn't here! Of course, that's it. That's what was missing. If Susan was here she would be sitting on the floor opposite Phil, drinking scotch, wearing dungarees and a cotton sleeveless T-shirt. (She had nice small breasts that she liked Noel to play with through the fabric of the shirt.) Noel was beginning to feel mellower.

Phil, according to Phoebe, was nothing more than a thirty-six-year-old jock. That's what she labeled him a long time ago, and Phil never argued the point. To Phoebe's distraction, Phil's favorite casual outfit, which he was wearing while they were waiting for Susan to come home, was cut-offs and an old athletic sweatshirt from college with the letter G on the sleeve, and the faded letters "Stick," his nickname, printed across the back. The shirt, whenever he put it on, alienated Phoebe no end. "Phil's wearing his cock outside of his pants again," she would say. Phil played varsity soccer three years for Yale. His senior year he was second-string all-American, beat out by the goalie from Georgetown.

"In the world of soccer, I was legendary," Phil said.

"I once went to a game," Phoebe added. "There were eighteen people there."

They fought a lot and had very little in common. Most people who knew them in the early days of their marriage gave them a year at best before a divorce. The years passed by, and all the people who gave *them* a year got divorced, but Phil and Phoebe stayed married. They had two sons, Eric and Mark. Phil was a partner in a successful New York law firm. He met Noel Roth in an elevator, soon after they were both married.

Noel, who in those days didn't like talking to anybody, particularly in elevators, looked at his shoes, aware of and uncomfortable with the fact that there was a gaunt, distressingly tall man in the elevator with him who was wearing glasses. They lived in the same building, and Noel had seen him before and knew in advance that he *didn't* want to meet him.

"You want a lift to the city?" he asked Noel. "I'm driving today."

Noel, who thought he was comfortable with his solitude, was dismayed that this gawky-looking man who always seemed to be in a hurry had spoken to him. If they had been in that elevator for ten years, he told Phil later, he wouldn't have spoken first. He would have preferred, in those days, forever silence. You mind your business, and I'll mind mine.

"I'm not going to the city," Noel mumbled, thinking his noninterest was evident. The elevator stopped on the third floor and someone else got in. Noel thought he was going to have a nervous breakdown. From now on, I walk down eight flights. It will keep me in shape.

"I'm Phil Radcliff. We've been neighbors for nine months, and I think it's time we met." He held his hand out to Noel. The other person in the elevator seemed to be reading the *Times*.

What do you do with an absurd stringbean of a man who you don't want to meet who offers his hand to you on a descending elevator? You take it. "I'm Noel Roth," weakly, touching his throat with his other hand. They were out of the elevator. Noel took a deep breath. He was only twenty-three and recently had his first electrocardiogram, and his chest had felt peculiar ever since.

"How come you don't go to the city?" Phil asked Noel. "Everybody goes to the city."

I will never lose him, Noel thought. He wants to know my life history by the time we reach the street. Where should I start? When I was six I played reform school with a girl named Dorothy Rollins. "I own a men's clothing store in White Plains." Noel said it quickly, spewing the words out. It was something, in a world filled with lawyers, doctors, dentists, Wall Street brokers, that he was not happy about, and this particular morning he was unhappier

Don Zacharia

about it than at any other time. Noel was walking to his car, and this stranger, who minutes ago was someone he had hoped he would never have to speak to, was walking alongside him.

"That's terrific," Phil said.

I think he intends to spend the day with me, Noel thought.

"How about dinner tonight?" He had stopped and grabbed Noel's arm.

I knew it, Noel thought. I knew it. I will never get in an elevator again. "I'm married. My wife makes the plans—"

"So am I," Phil interrupted. "I'll have my wife call yours. I bet we have a lot in common."

He left with a wave of his hand and that strange lope of his. A thin wind, Noel thought, would blow him to pieces. Noel escaped. The first thing he did when he got to his store was call Susan. "Look," he said, "I have a favor—do me this favor—no questions asked—and I'll take you south this winter even though I'm on the verge of bankruptcy. You're going to receive a call from a lady whose last name is Radcliff. I think they live on the sixth floor. I don't know what her first name is, probably Shirley. She's going to ask you and me to have dinner with them tonight. Tell her whatever you wanna tell her, but tell her *no*. Blame it on me. Tell her your husband is an Orthodox Jew and won't eat anywhere but in his own house. What's tonight? Is tonight Friday?"

"She's already called."

"*What?*"

"She's already called, and I've accepted. Come on, Noel, it will be fun meeting some new people for a change."

Noel hung up. That cocksucker. That skinny cocksucker stopped at a phone booth within minutes after he left me.

They had dinner that night in Phoebe and Phil's apartment. She made some kind of a Spanish dish that wasn't bad. Phoebe sat across from Noel and crossed and uncrossed her legs all night. She certainly has nice legs, Noel thought.

They all became good friends. Phil and Susan, Susan and Phoebe, Noel and Phoebe, Noel and Phil. The four of them became inseparable. Weekday dinners in either Susan's or Phoebe's apartment became commonplace. Weekends and vacations were always spent together. It became an accepted fact that if you invited the Roths to a party, you'd better invite the Radcliffs if you wanted the Roths to come, and of course, the reverse was true. Susan and Phoebe became pregnant within months of each other and their children, Beth and Mark, as infants shared the same crib many a night. They bought homes at the same time, and in the same neighborhood. Considering the closeness of the two couples, there was a remarkable lack of friction over the years of their friendship.

At the beginning, to Noel, who had never had a male friend in his life, it was an exhilarating but confusing experience. At first he tried holding Phil at arm's length, but Phil with his boundless enthusiasm cut through Noel's rebuffs as if they were nonexistent. If Phil and Phoebe, and to a lesser extent, Noel and Susan, as married couples, had nothing or very little in common, Phil and Noel, as friends, had everything in common—both athletes, both Ivy League graduates, both married to attractive, bright women, and both making it in the business world, Phil as a lawyer and Noel as a retailer.

Phil became the one person Noel could turn to with any problem and get some kind of a sensible answer or direction and, most important, not feel obligated afterward. The two men developed a special relationship: an honesty with each other that to a stranger (and certain friends) was disarming—a constant sarcastic ribbing that many people were suspicious of, and oddly enough, a gentleness at certain times, never around other people, and never around their wives. That would be an admission of something they'd rather not admit. But it was there and they both knew it.

As their friendship grew stronger and stronger, in the darkest recesses of Noel's mind he sometimes felt that if a physical disaster ever befell him, if he lost his sight, became paralyzed, a paraplegic, it would be Phil who would stand by him, not Susan. He never discussed this with anyone. He never even thought about it, but he was aware of it. To Noel Phil was the Rock of Gibraltar. He knew that if the reverse ever happened, *if Phil ever needed him*, he would be there, but somehow, when he thought about it, when Noel

Don Zacharia

played the picture out, it was always Phil who was saving Noel.

Back in the middle sixties, he and Phil had tickets to the Giant football games. Before each game, hundreds of men in wheelchairs, each with an attendant, were wheeled into the left-center-field area where they could watch the game. World War Two, Korea, Vietnam, Noel thought. A pang of guilt. There is nothing romantic about dying, being permanently maimed. Poor guys in your wheelchairs. They were always wheeled out in the middle of the last quarter no matter how close the game was. Noel didn't understand that. Watching them leave through his binoculars, he asked Phil why that was. "The crowds?" Phil shrugged. Noel still didn't understand it. He remembered one man, head turned toward the field, arms pushing against his chair, raising himself up, straining to see whatever part of the game he could see as he was wheeled out. Noel thought about it, but didn't think about it. He was convinced that if anything like that ever happened to him, Susan would leave, but Phil wouldn't. Phil would wheel him into the game and stay until the *end*. So what do you do with information like that? Noel thought. Nothing. That's what.

When Noel's father died in 1972 watching a doubleheader at Yankee Stadium, it was Phil who visited Noel every night long after everyone else stopped. Noel, who for twenty years had only indifferent thoughts about his father, found his death to be the most traumatic moment of his life. His mother had died when he was a teenager. "I'm an orphan," he told Phil. "A thirty-five-year-old orphan, but an orphan." Phil would come over after dinner, or sometimes have dinner with them. Most of the time the two of them would take walks to get away from Susan. "She's all right. She really is," Noel said. "It's just she's so damn hard on everything and everyone. Pathos they weren't giving out when Susan was born. To her, my father was an ignorant man who spent the last ten years of his life going to dirty movies, and reading dirty books."

• • •

The Match Trick

Itchy had lived on the West Side of Manhattan and used to come up to their home on weekends and take the children to Yankee Stadium. It was a regular production. To Noel, it was as if time stood still. As if it were 1948. The two children, Beth and David, loved it. His father, Itchy, lived for it. When they went to the stadium, the three of them would leave at ten in the morning and catch a local Central train to Melrose Station in the Bronx. There they would take a Number Seven bus to the courthouse, walk to the stadium; usually they got there around noontime, sit in the bleachers and eat a lunch prepared by Susan, tunafish sandwiches and hard-boiled eggs, watch the Yankees play two and listen to Itchy tell them how it used to be.

"You see where that kid Murcer is playing? Well, before him there was Mantle. He was fast like a speeding bullet, and before him—" he paused here, a moment of silence— "Di–Mag–gi–o." When Itchy said DiMaggio it became a nine-syllable name. "What can I tell you kids? You're watching that shmo Murcer, it's a crime you didn't see the great ones."

After the game, they stayed until the last out in the last inning, none of that beating-the-crowd stuff (what crowds?), and they made the reverse trip home. When they finally got to Crownhill, Melrose Station wasn't exactly a regular stop and sometimes they would have to wait an hour for a train, Itchy would call the house and Noel would come to the station and pick them up. The whole day cost tops six bucks. Noel would offer his father a ten-dollar bill for the day, but Itchy would wave his hand away. "On me," he would say. "Put it in the kids' bank."

By the time Noel picked them up, everybody was starved, and they would rush home and eat while Susan fumed—supposedly because it was so late at night, but it was much more involved than that. One night she broke the ice.

"Why don't you do something different one Sunday?" she said to Itchy. "Why don't you take the children to the Museum of Natural History for a change?"

Itchy looked at her like she was dropped from Mars. The most incredulous proposition he had ever heard in his life. He looked at his son, waiting for help.

"We'll talk about it later," Noel said.

Itchy left the room without saying a word.

"You're the worst cunt that ever lived."

"A haberdasher," Susan said. "I married a haberdasher."

They had some fight. Noel told Susan that she was killing his father. That she was putting him in the grave. That was too much for Susan. She told Noel what was bothering her.

"Look," she said, "I think we are getting into an unhealthy pattern. For two years now, every Sunday Itchy takes the children to a baseball game; you spend the entire day at the club playing golf with Phil; and I spend the entire day either reading the *Times* or talking to Phoebe. Would it be so terrible to break that pattern and do something different? To do something *together*? The children have never been to Chinatown; to Orchard Street. They went to the UN because the school took them."

"My father won't do that." Noel was confused by Susan's argument. "My father asked me the other day how come we don't join him on Sunday at Yankee Stadium. 'Try it,' he said. 'You'll like it.' "

Things went on as if nothing happened. Itchy continued to take the children to baseball games, Noel played golf with Phil, and Susan fumed. She made Noel very aware of her unhappiness with the situation. Beth and David, unaware of what they were being deprived of, unaware of the great DiMagg, the great Mantle, began to root for Murcer, White and Blomberg.

Finally, one day in August Noel gave in to Susan. He told his father that next Sunday they were all going to go down to the city together, to the Lower East Side; that the kids had never seen the Lower East Side and they would like it very much if he would join them.

"Next Sunday," Itchy said slowly, "is a very important set. Baltimore is in town. I don't think we should miss it."

"Pops, the Yankees are in seventh place; what kind of important?"

"I wouldn't miss the Orioles," his father said, "for anything. I saw Nick Etten play. Have a nice time on the Lower East Side. I'll be seeing you." He left.

The following Sunday Noel and Susan and Beth and David all piled into Susan's station wagon and went down to Orchard Street. They ate pickles and knishes from a street-corner stand. Susan bought a hat. Beth bought a sweater. David bought a sweat shirt, and Noel bought a cane. They went to a movie in the afternoon and had dinner in Chinatown. The day, including tolls and tips, cost Noel one hundred twelve dollars and fifty cents.

When they got home Phil and Phoebe were waiting for them, and Noel could tell by the look on Phil's face that something was wrong. Phil came right out with it.

"We've been trying to reach you all day. Your father died in Yankee Stadium. I'm sorry, Noel."

"Oh, my God," Susan cried out.

"Do you know what my father's estate was?" Noel and Phil were walking. It was two weeks after Noel's father had died. "A savings account with eight hundred dollars in it, his personal belongings, and about one thousand pornographic books."

Phil shrugged. "Listen, I liked your father. I don't think that just because he got off on porno to such an extent you should be so hard on him. He was a decent man, a lot more decent than most of the people we know."

"His life was such an empty one. Is it fair for his son to make that statement? What a way to die. What a place to die. Watching the Yankees lose nine to three. Susan says he did it on purpose. She doesn't really mean that, but I think I know what she means. My mother died seventeen years ago. I was eighteen. That's almost my whole adult life. In that time my father never saw another woman that I know about, never went out to dinner, went to a movie once with us and didn't like it, never did anything, Phil, but stay in his room and read those fuck books and come up to us on weekends and talk about how great the Yankees used to be. Nick Etten was his hero. I wonder if he read those books two times? Three times? Four times? I wonder if he had favorites?"

Phil didn't say anything. He wondered why his friend was doing this to himself. They walked in silence.

"You know what?" Noel finally said. "We've been walking for about five minutes and neither one of us has said a word to each other. When I first married Susan, on our honeymoon that same thing happened, and she said to me, 'What's the matter? You bored with me already?' And I said, no, I was just thinking, and she said that she was very insecure, and when that happened she felt that I was thinking of another girl, or I wasn't in love with her. That put a lot of pressure on me. I felt I always had to have something to say, and lots of times I didn't. Susan has changed a lot from those days."

They stopped for a moment to look at an old chestnut tree that hadn't thrown off any chestnuts in five years. "Why do you think that is?" Phil asked.

"I don't know. Our pear tree is doing the same thing. Do you ever think of getting a divorce? Splitting from Phoebe?" Noel asked out of the blue.

"No. I can't honestly say that I do. Do you?"

"Yes. The last year or so. I don't know—I think I'm too much of a romantic—and one thing our marriage doesn't have anymore is any semblance of romance. Susan spends so much time with her sculpture, eight, nine, ten hours a day, that I just revolve around it. I fit in. If I fit in. I'm sure she feels that her work is more important than our marriage."

"Oh, come on," Phil interrupted.

"No. I mean it."

"I think you're reacting to a lot of things, Noel. Your father's death for one."

"You wanna jog?" Noel asked.

"Let's go."

The two men started off in a slow jog, both old athletes, both still aware of their bodies; the jogging came easy. Phil was tall and skinny as a rail. His college nickname, Stick, still fit him; he hadn't put on a pound from his Yale soccer days. Noel was perhaps ten pounds heavier.

"In high school," Noel said, "I once did a mile in five-twelve."

"Five-twelve. Jesus. Who'd you beat?"

"I beat a lot of guys. I think I came in fifth."

"It must have been a white man's race."

"Nah. I was pretty good. No shit. I had this terrific kick."

"You had this terrific kick and you ran a five-twelve?"

"I probably was fifteenth in the stretch, passing all those guys—" Noel picked up the pace. "I felt like—what's his name—that guy from Africa?"

"Kip Kenno?"

"Yeah."

"Except he walks faster."

"Track was a dumb sport. I only went out for track to stay in shape for basketball. Originally I went out for the dashes, but forget it. Those black guys would be crossing the finish line, and I'd still be on the blocks."

"A long-distance runner. My pal is a long-distance runner."

"I have heavily muscled legs."

"Oh, my God."

Both men were getting a little winded, but neither one wanted to quit first. Finally Phil panted, "That tree is the finish line. Let's see your kick." Noel sprinted to the tree and waited for Phil. They were both breathing heavily. The two men walked down the darkened street, gasping for air, shaking their wrists. Phil grabbed Noel's hand and held it aloft, and they went into a long slow victory jog. No one saw them.

"Before we get home," Phil said, "there's one more thing I want to say about your father. I know how you feel about your father, I know and imagine how Susan feels about your father. I know how Phoebe feels about your father—"

"How?" Noel interrupted.

Don Zacharia

"Well," Phil was sorry he asked, "she feels pretty much the way Susan feels, I suppose. She's not so close to it but she said that he died having never accomplished. I don't even know what she meant by that. But I think there's something you should be aware of. Your two children, Beth and David—forget that they love him, forget the tears at his funeral, the important thing is that they don't feel about Itchy—" Phil hesitated, using his first name that way caught him up short—"they don't feel about Itchy the way Susan, Phoebe and you do. They think, and if you don't believe me, ask them, that your father was the most accomplished, fulfilled guy in the whole world. That's not the way they would phrase it—but that's what they feel, and twenty years from now, when they are our age and talk about their grandfather, they will talk about him with a kind of respect and feeling and love and will be telling their friends about all their legendary days at Yankee Stadium. My sons have always envied your children and the relationship they had with their grandfather. They would switch with them in a minute."

Ten-thirty came and went. Perhaps it was the scotch, or just being with Phil and Phoebe, but many of the fears and anxieties that Noel felt before about Susan's absence seemed far removed from him now. These were his two best friends, and it was good to have them over under any circumstances. Susan was doing a number, Noel decided. She had done enough of them the last few years, and this was just one more. He talked about it briefly with Phoebe, and she agreed with him. There was a lot of drinking going on, and Noel suddenly became hungry. Phoebe made him a bacon sandwich on an English muffin. Noel was starved and devoured it. Phoebe's OK, he thought.

"I've got some story to tell you later," Phoebe said.

Phil rubbed his hands together. Noel felt a tightening in his stomach. Phoebe's stories were always titillating. Phil wanted to play a little game, trying to guess what the story was about, but Phoebe wouldn't cooperate.

The Match Trick

Susan, Phoebe thought, was quite a girl, having an affair with Meyer so blatantly. She envied her. Phoebe had one-half of an affair once. It was never consummated. He was a professor at N.Y.U., and they would meet in Washington Square Park. They had known each other for three months when one day he got a room in the Fifth Avenue Hotel without telling Phoebe. They were sitting in the park, like always, and he pressed something into her hand. It was the hotel key. Phoebe panicked. She said no. He was very hurt. He had spent a lot of time with Phoebe talking about her intellectual fulfillment and all that crap. She couldn't. She just couldn't. They had a fight. He told her that all she was capable of was an intellectual fuck; that if a physical relationship was so frightening to her she should see a psychiatrist. He called her an elitist. He apologized. He said he was sorry. He said he would be gentle. He said he was a terrific lover. He said he had spent twenty-seven bucks for a fancy room in the Fifth Avenue Hotel and now what was he supposed to do with it?

Phoebe said that she was sorry, and she really was. She left him, took a cab back to Grand Central, caught an afternoon train back to Crownhill, and went to Susan's and told her what happened. Phoebe really was sorry. She would have liked nothing better than to have gone to bed with her professor. "There is nobody," she told Susan that day, "who wants to have an affair more than I do. What's wrong with me? Why can't I just *do it*?"

Everyone thought Phoebe was the hottest piece of ass in the whole world. That is, everyone except Phil and the professor sitting glumly in the park wondering how he could get his money back for the room. Noel thought Phoebe was one step away from nymphomania. He used to kid Phil about it, and Phil never said anything to make him think otherwise. Noel did a lot of fantasizing about Phoebe. Sometimes when he was making love to Susan he imagined he was with Phoebe, slipping off the panties that she had provided him glimpses of a thousand times.

Phoebe was a fine-looking girl; short-cropped black hair, a good body, a little too round in the hips but the greatest legs in the world. She always wore skirts or dresses showing off those wonderful tapered legs, sitting more often than not with her legs slightly open. "Let them look," she told Phil when he once complained about it.

That's all the professor could think of that day in the park. Those fine legs that he had seen so much of—crossing and uncrossing, opening and shutting—wrapped around his back, pumping straight up in the air, shaking that old hotel. Phoebe was sorry. She would have loved to have been a lover. She and Phil tried most things. They read books, she spoke to her doctor, they even tried a vibrator, but Phoebe told Phil it did nothing but tickle her. Phil lived with it. Too bad. You can't have everything, I guess, Phil thought. If I had everything, I would have weighed two hundred and twenty-five pounds instead of one hundred and fifty and been second-string all-American in football instead of soccer.

They all had three scotches more or less. Phoebe was not a good drinker, got high quickly, and when that happened began slurring her words and sometimes would get sick. Noel was careful, for when he got drunk he got anxious and it wasn't worth it. Phil was a good boozer. He cut his scotch with water. He told Noel to do that but Noel liked the taste of scotch. Susan was the best of them, though. She could really put it away, seven or eight drinks in an evening, and feel nothing but high and then sleep so heavily that nothing could wake her.

"Do your eyes ever overblink?" Noel asked Phoebe. "My eyes are overblinking. I think it comes from overdrinking. Look at me. I can't stop them."

Phoebe studied them. "They're not overblinking at all."

"Bullshit, Phoebe. They're blinking so fast you can't even see them. It's psychedelic."

"Let's play twenty questions," Phoebe said to Noel.

"Look at my eyes."

"I can't look at your eyes. You're looking at my legs again."

"Oh, you have great legs, Phoebe, now look at my eyes."

"They're not blinking at all."

"She's not sensitive," Phil said.

"Okay, boys, listen to this: I was at the beauty parlor Friday afternoon." Phoebe had started her story. "I really should wait for Susan, but I'll tell her another time. I was at the beauty parlor Friday, and sitting across the room was Nina Campanella. She has eyebrows that join in the middle and she was getting them plucked. I was getting the shakes just sitting next to her. You know her, Phil. We met her at the town picnic, and she was at the pool a couple of times." Phil looked confused. "She has short, black ratty hair that she streaks, kind of dumpy, those eyebrows, Christ, how could anybody forget those eyebrows. She's married to the town engineer, Dominic Campanella—everybody calls him Campy for short—that's what she told me anyhow."

Phil nodded his head in recognition.

"I know her, too," Noel said softly. They both looked at him—the way he said it, there was an implication that caught them by surprise. "I knew her in high school."

"Did you screw her?" Phoebe asked. "If you screwed her, Noelie, I'm not going to tell you the story. I'm going to forget the whole thing." Phoebe seemed hurt.

"No, I dry-humped her in the back of the high school. How clearly I remember that."

Everyone had another drink. A plane came by overhead, very low, its noise filling the house. They didn't know it when they bought the house, but they were on a secondary landing pattern for LaGuardia. "That damn builder," Susan said when she first found out.

Phoebe went on with her story. "Okay, I'm in the beauty parlor reading *The First Circle*. I'm up to the scene where it's Christmas and Solzhenitsyn is telling us about a Jewish Communist named Rubin who in a sense was collaborating with the Germans. Dino, the beautician, is rapping with Nina in Italian. It's all a very greasy scene. The dryer is over my head, and Estelle, the girl who

Don Zacharia

does my nails, hands me a note. The note was from Nina, it was written on her own personal stationery. I thought that was very strange, I mean, I don't know anybody who walks around with their own stationery in their pocketbook. The stationery was pink with little designs in each corner and printed all in lower case across the top was: *a note from nina c.* The note said—I have it—wait a minute." Phoebe reached into her purse, pulled it out and read, " 'Dear Phoebe, I would like very much to talk with you after. Would it be possible for us to have a drink? Fondly, Nina.' She prints very well, by the way."

Phoebe passed the note to Phil, who sailed it to Noel.

"It was impossible to get her attention. When Dino plucks your eyebrows, he wraps up your whole face with hot towels. He thinks he's a surgeon. I jotted OK on the envelope and handed it to Estelle who handed it to Nina. She was finished before me, and she left without even *looking* at me. I had no idea what was going on, but I must say I was getting interested. When I finished, she was waiting for me in her car. A new Buick convertible. Pretty snazzy for the town engineer. She motioned for me to get in and asked if I wanted her to put the top up. No, I said—this is fine. 'Your hair will get messed,' she said. 'There's a babushka in the glove compartment.' She waited until I put it on. 'I'll drive you back to your car,' she said as we drove off. We went to La Shack. Nina ordered a dry martini, and I had a glass of Mountain White. We sat there shmoozing about everything: PTA and town politics and all that crap. She told me that she was sure that Dominic was having an affair. On Thursday nights he was supposed to be bowling, but he hadn't bowled in three years. But she said she didn't care. 'What's good for the goose is good for the gander.' That's the phrase she used. Swear. I was waiting, not saying much, I *knew* she didn't bring me there for this. Nina orders another drink, it's not even noontime. I told her that if I ever had two martinis, I'd be flat on my face. She apologized and said it's all a question of what you get used to. Some people can drink a lot and never show. Well, I said, you are one of those persons. Then she hits me with it. 'What are your feelings about swinging?' she asks. I'm very cool, not knowing where this is going. I just smile. You know, I have an idea, but I'm very cool. 'Dominic and I have tried it a couple of times,' she tells me. 'We belong to a loose kind of group. Once with a couple in Brewster, it was awful, and once with a doctor and his wife and friends of the doctor's in Danbury. It was fantastic. We had some great sessions, but they moved to Cleveland.' I don't say a word. I am very very cool. She doesn't say anything either for a while. Finally she said that she had heard rumors about me and Phil and the Roths. That's not the way she phrased it. 'There's always been a lot of talk about you and your old man and the Roths,' she says." Phoebe paused here, catching her breath. "Do you want me to go on?" She smiled.

Phil slid to the floor. "I can't stand it. A ménage à six." Noel was making himself another drink. He looked at Phil and made a panting motion.

"You haven't heard the best part yet," Phoebe said.

Neither Phil nor Noel was shocked by Nina's suggestion to Phoebe. They had heard these rumors about themselves before. No one had approached them like this, but they knew there was talk about sexual switching between the Roths and the Radcliffs, and, if anything, they encouraged the rumors. It was exciting; it was something to do at a party; it made them different. To them, it was just a game. But that's all it was, just a game. It was not uncommon at a party to see Noel and Phoebe off in a corner, touching each other. Phoebe casually would put her hand on the inside of Noel's thigh; Noel would touch her breast; they would giggle and sometimes kiss. While this was going on, Phil and Susan would be dancing, their bodies so intertwined that just looking at them you knew *something* had to be going on. Well, nothing was. They were all much too straight for that. Once, just once, Susan, half drunk and half stoned (she was not only the biggest drinker, but the biggest pot smoker among them), dancing a slow number with Phil, aware of his hard-on, rubbed against him in such a way that Phil came. It was a breaking of the rules, and nothing was ever said about it, and it never happened again.

"At this point," Phoebe went on, "Nina put me on the spot. She

Don Zacharia

asked me point-blank if she should continue. I said, kinda easy, it's a very delicate situation, and whereas I couldn't really speak for everyone, I'm pretty sure that Phil and Susan and Noel would be interested. But, I said, it's very delicate. Nina smiled and grabbed my hand. 'Let me tell you where Dominic and I are at. Do you mind if I speak frankly with you?' I said I thought she had been pretty frank up to now. 'No—no, I want to tell you where we're at in plain four-letter words. Cunnilingus is all right sometimes, but that's not where we're at.' OK, I said, go ahead. I thought my heart was going to explode out of my chest. I know my hands were shaking. 'Dominic and I like to be ass-fucked at the same time. We really get off on that. That's where we're at. The scene as we see it—listen—if the four of you have something else in mind—we're swingers—anything goes except animals, that's filthy—but this is our scene. While your old man and Susan's old man are ass-fucking my old man and me, we'll be going down on you girls.' Nina finished her martini by this time. I was no longer cool. I was having the biggest anxiety attack of my life. I thought I was going to pass out on the spot. 'Are you all right?' she asked me. 'Yes, I'm just excited,' I said. She smiled. 'I don't blame you.' She drove me back to my car. 'You're not saying much.' 'I'm just excited, kinda nervous.' 'I understand,' she said. 'Supposing you speak to your people, and I'll call you in a week.' End of story."

Phoebe grinned and shook her head. "How did I do?" She took a gulp of scotch and slapped Noel. "How did I do, Noelie?" she hollered, excited by her story.

Phil collapsed on the floor, having an asthma attack. "I got Nina," he gasped. He punched Noel in the leg. "You got Dominic. Oh, God—oh, God." With one hand he clutched his groin, and with another his throat. "Get me my inhaler." He was barely audible. "Get me my inhaler," he whispered to Phoebe.

Noel was laughing so hard tears were coming to his eyes and his insides hurt. Phoebe sat there, not moving, watching Phil and Noel. She was pleased.

. . .

The Match Trick

It wasn't that Lois and George Fruned just barged in. Lois was the last person in the world to do something like that. They rang and rang the bell, and when no one answered, hearing a terrific amount of noise from inside the Roth home, they tried the front door—it was open—and walked in. They went into the den, and this is what they saw: Noel Roth was on his hands and knees, his back arched, his posterior elevated, his pants were down around his knees, and he had on a pair of bikini jockey shorts, white with blue trim. His eyes were tightly shut, his mouth open, with his tongue darting in and out of his mouth, and his body rocking back and forth. Phoebe Radcliff was sitting on the floor directly in front of Noel, her legs wide apart, her knees drawn up, her skirt pulled up around her hips. She was rocking back and forth in the direction of Noel Roth's mouth, and was also wearing bikini panties, but they were satin and all in white. Philip Radcliff was standing, standing is not exactly the right word, he was hunched over Noel's elevated posterior and was resting his hands on Noel's shoulders. His eyes were also shut tight and he was moving back and forth in what can best be described as a humping motion. Phil's cut-offs were down around his bony knees, and he had on a pair of plain white jockey shorts. Everyone was shouting at everyone else:

Phil: How's it *feel*, Dominic?
Noel: (Moans and mumbles something unintelligible)
Phil: I'm giving it to you good, Dom.
Phoebe: I'm getting it good from Dominic.
Phil: It's a doubleheader.
Phoebe: It's a triple play.
Noel: Cunnilingus is for the birds.
Phoebe: You're talking too much, Dom.
Phil: Are you close?
Noel: Who? Is who close?
Phil: Nina. Are you close?
Phoebe: Oh, yes. I am sooo close.
Phil: I am close tooooo.

Don Zacharia

Noel: I'm not sooooo close.
Phoebe: Go faster, Dominic.
Phil: Go faster, Nina.
Noel: Everybody's going too fast.

Phil, who was a lawyer and trained in sensing problems, opened his eyes and saw Lois and George Fruned standing there. He stood up, pulled his cut-offs up, buttoned them, and kicked Noel in the ass. Phil had taken ephedrine for his asthma, before, and between that and the physical activity and suddenly seeing the Fruneds, his heart was beating so rapidly he was sure he was going to have a coronary. "Hi," he wheezed as he kicked Noel in the ass again. Noel got up and pulled up his pants. Phoebe got up and went into the bathroom. Lois looked very composed. George looked like he was going to faint. Lois spoke. She seemed, considering the circumstances, quite calm. "We were coming home from the movies, and Phoebe had called before about Susan, so when we saw all the lights on, we thought we would stop in. We rang the bell." She was talking directly to Noel, who deep down was the sorriest of the three of them that the Fruneds had barged in that way. Phoebe, still in the bathroom peeing, was embarrassed somewhat, but loved the idea of being caught. Phil, if his heart would ever beat normally again, thought the whole thing was worth it just for the look on George's face. Poor Noel, he was so hot that for the moment he only wanted to sit down. He was mortified that Lois or George or Phil would notice. He had such an erection, how could anyone miss it? "It's only a charade," Phoebe said at the beginning. It was Phoebe's idea. "I'm drunk," she said. "That's the only reason I'm doing this. Noel and Phil were feeling pretty good, too. It's only a charade."

When Phoebe had pulled her skirt up over her hips—"Shut your eyes, Noelie, don't you dare look at Phoebe's panties"—what he had been half seeing, half dreaming about for years was suddenly thrust into his face, inches from his mouth, his nose, his eyes.

44

The Match Trick

White satin panties, skimpily cut at the hips, crowding the crevice of her ass, the crotch slightly discolored. Aware of Phil's hands on his shoulders; once or twice Phil grazed his buttocks with his thighs. Noel had his eyes tightly shut. He had visually taken in all that was possible. His mouth open, Phoebe's odors overpowered him. His groin exploded. He had a small but evident (to him) emission. Noel was stunned by his excitement in playing the role of Dominic. (You be Dominic, Phoebe said, I'll be Nina.) He played on, despite the emission, feeling no relief. (Could they know?)

"We heard a lot of noise." Lois, still looking directly at Noel, smiled, "so we came in. I'm sorry."

Phoebe came out of the bathroom. Noel wanted to go upstairs and change his underpants, but sat down and made himself another scotch. Positively the last one, he thought.

"Sit down. What do you want to drink?" Phil said, taking over the role of host.

George sat down and held his hands up and shook his head. George looked like he might never speak again.

"I'll take some wine if you have it," Lois said.

"Sangría? When I came over tonight, I said, Phoebe, make a pitcher of sangría because it's going to be a party."

Phil gave Phoebe a hard look. When she began talking about herself in the third person it was always a sign that she had too much to drink.

"Sangría would be fine."

"Phoebe didn't make sangrías. Phoebe has been drinking scotch with the boys."

Noel liked being with Lois, although tonight wasn't one of those nights. She was the only person in the world who could walk into a scene like she did and not say a word. She had long brown hair parted in the middle that she was constantly pushing back from her face, showing off her fine, high cheekbones. When she was younger, she was a local gymnast of some renown, coming in third in the Eastern finals for the 1956 Olympic tryouts, but failing to make the team. "The parallel bars did me in," she told Susan. Her body

45

Don Zacharia

still retained that litheness, and clothes seemed to flow about her as she moved. She was a classically beautiful woman, better-looking than Phoebe, but Phoebe always seemed to get more attention from men.

Her marriage was a disaster. At least Noel and Phil, both of whom liked Lois, thought so. They had one child, a boy who unfortunately looked more like George than Lois, and the three of them got on. They seemed to have no real close friends. Lois was a friend of Susan's, and through Susan became a friend of Phoebe's. The Roths and the Fruneds would occasionally get together for dinner or a movie.

"How do you stand him?" Phil asked Noel.

"I don't. When we go to the movies, Susan sits on one side of me and Lois on the other. It's not such a bad deal." Dinners with the Fruneds were a problem. "Please," Noel asked Susan, "if we have dinner with them, can't we at least have Phil and Phoebe join us?"

"Look, it's one night," Susan countered. "You're going out to dinner one night with a man you feel uncomfortable with. I think," turning the problem back to Noel, "it is your neurosis."

The fact of the matter was that Lois told Susan that George wouldn't go out with them if the Radcliffs were there. "Noel and Phil do such a number together. You know how I feel about Noel— I don't have to preface this—but when he is with Phil, and George is there, there is—" she paused, searching for the word.

"Adolescence?" Susan interjected.

"No, that's not quite what I mean—homosexual bitchiness." She looked at Susan, wondering if she had gone too far.

Susan nodded her head.

"I'm sure George doesn't think of it that way." Lois smiled. "George just feels uncomfortable with the two of them."

It was difficult to understand why Phil and Noel disliked George so. He had no fewer or no more qualifications than many people who were their friends. George went to high school with Noel and Susan and Meyer. When Noel was reminded of this, he always said that for the life of him he couldn't remember George in high school.

46

The Match Trick

"If he was in *my* high school," Noel said, "he should change his name to Mr. Obscure." Two years out of dental school George recognized that his talent was limited, and he opened up a small practice in Mamaroneck. He rarely did anything but fillings and an occasional crown. He was cheap, painless; his average patient was in and out in twenty minutes. And all the local cops, firemen, laborers, storekeepers and, particularly, blacks thought he was the greatest. Blacks because he was nice to them, fixed them up as best he could with his limited skills, kidded with them, didn't hurt them and charged damn little money.

So what was it about this man that bothered Phil and, especially, Noel? The fact that he won every bridge tournament in the area? That once when the four of them played Scrabble he spotted Noel fifty points to a game of seventy-five and beat him easily? Noel had spent his life competing and losing most of the time. What made George different? To Noel, it was George's appearance—he was an absurdity, an object of ridicule. Noel was embarrassed to be seen with him. Legs and arms that looked like they belonged to a scarecrow, a circular face with sunken eyes, a small nondescript mouth which was a wonder, considering how much food it took in, and bald—no, not bald—almost bald. George shaved his head once a week to make sure he was bald. When everybody else was using a Gillette Techmatic on their face, George was using one on his scalp. Bald like a baboon's ass. His stomach? An enormous oval, an obese tumorlike object that hung to some point below his groin. How did a woman as beautiful as Lois ever marry a man who looked like George? Someday, Noel thought, he would ask her point-blank. It seemed arrogant to Noel: George was so nonchalant with her, as if he owned her, as if it was his *due* to have a woman like that. It bothered the hell out of Noel.

George belonged to the same country club as Noel and Phil. His *golf* game was a joke. The golf swing, which in the hands of a competent golfer was a smooth, precise, seemingly effortless movement, in the hands of George became an erratic, herky-jerky thrust at the ball. After the shot, no matter what the result,

47

Don Zacharia

George would flip the club to the caddy and waddle off down the fairway *like he was pleased with himself.* "He might be able to do a Double-Crostic faster than God," Noel told Susan once while having breakfast, "but he can't hit a golf ball worth a shit. I have no idea why a man like that joins a golf club, and what's more, I have no idea how he got in." Susan, who had been to the club three times in four years, added some sugar to her blueberries.

Shortly after George joined the club, Noel became obsessed with the idea of viewing George's sexual apparatus. Noel was convinced, he told Phil, that it was missing, which made his relationship with Lois even more mysterious. After two weeks of failure, Phil joined the hunt. The two of them tried for over a month without success. "I have never in my life tried so hard to see a man's cock, and all I ever come up with is his lousy stomach." Noel and Phil would sit in the sauna, nude, legs apart, their organs nicely hanging for anyone to see. When George came in, he was wearing one of those faggoty terry-cloth robes tucked about his middle. They would wait. What the fuck was wrong with George? What was he hiding? How come he never took that fag robe off like everyone else? When George went to the urinal, Noel went to the next one and made small talk. "Pee comes out. Pee definitely comes out—I mean, when the man stands at the urinal, pee definitely comes—but if you ask me from where?" Noel shrugged.

"Why don't you just finally ask him," Phil said. "Just say, 'George, can I look at your cock?'"

The breakthrough came one day when George was taking a massage. Noel walked by the massage room three times before he walked in. George was on his back getting his neck worked on.

"Hi, George, excuse me for a second." Noel didn't look at him. "I pulled this muscle in my shoulder," Noel said, talking to the masseur while swinging his arm around. "Anything you can recommend?"

"Hot baths, Mr. Roth, and lots of them. The hotter the better."

"Thanks," Noel said, cutting him short. "Say hello to Lois, George."

His eyes swept down George's body. Ahhh—so there you are, you little bastard. He left.

Phil was waiting for him. "Well?"

"Later."

"I'll break your head."

"Well, he was lying down, on his back—Phil, the man has the smallest prick you have ever seen in your life. It's inverted. It's hidden within the magnitude of his balls, and for a second I couldn't even see it. It's a speck, a dot, a particle, a pinpoint. Jesus, Phil, I feel sorry for that guy. He's got no shmuck."

From that day on George's nickname became shmuck. Never to his face, but whenever Phil or Noel referred to George, it was always, "You want to fill in for the shmuck," or "I'm going out to dinner tonight with the shmuck."

When Susan heard about the incident, she didn't speak to Noel for two weeks. The whole thing, in Susan's mind, was very difficult to understand—almost incomprehensible. Difficult because her husband, Noel Roth, who appeared to be the instigator, was not a cruel man, and George Fruned, who appeared to be the victim, was not a shmuck.

"Where is Susan?" Lois asked.

"She's upstairs sleeping," Phoebe said.

Noel stood up. He looked at Phil, who was staring wide-eyed at Phoebe. Susan. Susan. It was ten of twelve. What to do? The thought of calling the police was suddenly ludicrous. Susan. The apprehension that he felt before seemed distant. It was dark out, but if he put the garage lights on he could shoot some baskets. Who the hell was Ronnie Costello? Someday I'm going to hit her. I've already done that. Susan. Meyer. Maybe I should leave? She gives the appearance of not minding. I wouldn't mind going to bed with Lois. She's so cool. Her body is so supple. I bet she's double-jointed. I bet she can do marvelous things in bed.

"Susan hasn't come home yet," Phil said. "She hasn't called either. Her car is in the garage, and we think she might be on the last train, which is due in at twelve-thirty."

"I've one question," George finally spoke, his hands folded over his stomach. "Who's Dominic? Who's Nina? I want to tell you I've walked in on some peculiar situations before, but this was the *crème de la crème*. Who the hell is Dominic?"

Phoebe stood up, holding a hand to her mouth. She looked ashen. "I'm sick, oh, God,—" She dashed from the room. "Phil—Phil—" It was a cry, a wail. Phil ran after her. There was a slamming of doors; the toilet was flushed repeatedly; muffled cries and gasps could be heard. Noel hadn't been aware how easily, sitting in the den, you could hear sounds from the guest bathroom, which was at the other end of the house. They were all listening.

Phil came back into the room looking unhappy. "Phoebe had a bit too much to drink. She extends her apologies and went upstairs to brush her teeth and take a nap." He sat down.

"If Susan were on that train," Lois was talking to Noel, "don't you think she would have called by now?" Lois spoke so evenly, each word balanced next to the other, that sometimes Noel wasn't sure when she finished a sentence.

"Yes," Noel said, "I do."

"Well, if you're not alarmed, I suppose it's ridiculous for me to be alarmed."

"I didn't realize it was so late," Noel said. "I don't know what happened to the night."

"I spoke to Susan," Lois said. "I spoke to Susan this morning—"

"When?" Phil interrupted.

"About nine-thirty."

"That's odd," Noel said. "Susan was to work first thing this morning with old man Blum in his studio."

"She didn't go today," Lois said. "She told me she wasn't going."

"Did she say why?" Phil asked. "Did she say where she was going?"

"No. Just that she was canceling."

"Did you ask her why?"

50

"Of course not."

"What did she talk about? Did she give any hint of where she was going? What she was doing?"

"We talked about a lot of things."

"Can't you be more specific?"

"It has no bearing on Susan's absence. If she told me where she was going, don't you think I would have told you?"

"What did you talk about?"

"I won't tell you that."

Phil was incredulous. "Why not?"

"I'm not in a courtroom, Phil."

"Susan is six hours overdue and you were the last person to have spoken to her and you won't tell us what you talked about?"

"Why haven't you called the police?" Lois ignored him, directing her question to Noel.

Noel shook his head. "I don't know. Phoebe didn't think it was such a good idea. I brought it up a long time ago. It seems like a long time ago." Noel looked at his watch. It was almost midnight. "I suppose I've waited this long, I might just as well wait until twelve-thirty. She might be on that train." Noel knew he didn't sound very convincing.

"She's not on that train, Noel." Lois spoke gently, aware of Noel's confusion. "Susan wouldn't come walking in like that. She would call first. Have you lost sight of who she is? It's not her style, Noel, not in a million years. Maybe it's my style, maybe it's Phoebe's style, but it's not Susan's. It's not in her character to do something like this. If I can understand that as her friend, how could you possibly think differently as her husband?"

Noel was troubled by what Lois said. He didn't know what to answer. Finally he turned toward Phil: "What do you think I should do?"

Phil took a deep breath before answering. "She might be right, Noel. Why don't you call them? We're probably making a big deal out of nothing. If Susan comes waltzing in with the fuzz here, so what? A year from now we'll laugh ourselves silly about it."

Noel nodded. He felt drawn out, fatigued, down. He left the room

Don Zacharia

feeling a certain amount of humiliation in what he was about to do.

"Lois—" Phil glanced at George, wishing he were out of the room—"Phoebe thinks that Susan is with Meyer Meyerson. She thinks that Meyer picked Susan up this morning, and they are spending the day, and it looks like the night, together."

"Did Susan tell her this?"

"No. She's assuming it."

"Do you believe it?"

"I don't know. I did for a while. I don't know what to believe. If it's true, it's a hell of a way to get her message across."

"What message? Phil, listen to me; if Susan wanted to give Noel a message, she wouldn't do it this way. I'm not saying that she's not capable of having an affair, or spending the day with Meyer, but she wouldn't do this."

"Where do you think she is then?"

The question, as obvious as it was, threw Lois off guard. "I—I don't know. I suppose there's the possibility that something happened to—her. God." The significance of what she had said jolted her. "I hope not."

Noel came back into the room.

"What happened?" Phil asked him.

"Not a hell of a lot. They transferred me to a detective. A Sergeant somebody. I forget his name. He's coming over."

"I probably know him," George said, looking up for the first time. "I have a lot of cops who are patients."

Phil stared at him. Every word, Phil thought. He probably is taking in every word that is being said. The shmuck.

In a few minutes the doorbell rang. Phil got up to answer it.

Walter Rudd. He reached into his inside jacket pocket and handed Noel a card. That's what it said on the card: Walter Rudd. He sat down next to Lois, across from Noel. Noel smiled, uncomfortable. When his son went to camp, Noel knocked on the bus window as it was pulling out; his son looked at him, a frozen expression of fear on his face. Why? Walter Rudd. He reminded Noel of someone. He seemed awfully young, under twenty-five. Impossible, Noel thought, how could this man find Susan? Short with a semi-crew cut, paunchy for his age, a round, red face (a boozer), wearing a sports jacket with corduroy pants that seemed to end at least four inches above his plaid socks. He was not the kind of person that Noel or Susan would ever choose to have in their home.

"This is Detective Sergeant Walter Rudd." Phil introduced him around.

Oh, Susan, Harry Gallatin you wouldn't have in your den, but this shlimazel of a cop sits here. He had an attaché case tucked between his legs like he was riding a subway. A cop with an attaché case and plaid socks. Someday I will come home and find my house blown up. As George predicted, they knew each other and were exchanging a story about a mutual friend. Noel couldn't listen.

"My wife has been missing since six P.M.," Noel interrupted.

The sergeant looked first at Noel and then at Phil. "Now hold on a s–e–c. You're Mr. Roth?" pointing a finger at Noel, obviously confused. Noel looked at him blankly. "And you?" pointing to Phil.

"I'm Phil Radcliff. I'm Noel's, Mr. Roth's, best friend and attorney. I let you in."

"*Right.* For a s–e–c I got confused between the two of you. And you're the d–o–c's wife?" Lois nodded. "Least I got the players on the right bases." He smiled.

Noel wanted to cry. He wondered if he could call up the police and ask them to send another man, older, for chrissakes. Someone who looked more representative. Someone who didn't spell out loud. This man couldn't even find Noel in the den.

"My wife," he started again, "has been missing since six P.M." Lois was sitting very straight in her chair, nodding her head occasionally. She seemed intimidated by the presence of a policeman. Phil was slumped down in his chair, legs stretched out halfway to the sofa. "I know that on the surface that might not seem significant to you, but it is not the kind of thing my wife would ever do. I'm sure there are many people who do that kind of thing, but if my wife is missing for six hours, I have to believe something happened to her."

Don Zacharia

"Mr. Roth, are you worried? Sure you're worried. If I was you, I'd be worried. Let me tell you something that will make you stop worrying. They say self-praise s–t–i–n–k–s, but I have become the department's expert in missing persons. If you called yesterday, my day off, you would have gotten Gallenta, and then you would have something to worry about. There's a theory I espouse. It's called Rudd's Theory of Mathematical Alternatives. I doubt you've ever heard of it. It's simple. Anyone can understand it. And when I explain it to you you'll stop worrying. There is no such thing as missing persons, Mr. Roth. You got me?"

Noel looked at Phil, who rolled his eyes upward. He had an urge to ask this fucking moron to get out of his house.

"People aren't missing, Mr. Roth, they're just someplace else for the time being. They do their thing, and then they come home. Some people come home in an hour, a day, a week, a month, but they all come home. Do you know why that is? Because there're no mathematical alternatives. That's why." Sergeant Rudd sat back, pleased.

Am I stupid? Noel thought. He looked at Phil again but Phil purposely had his head turned.

"Hey," Rudd spoke, "any chance of me getting a brew?"

"Sit right there, Sergeant," Phil said, jumping up. "Heineken o–k–a–y?"

"Great."

Phil came back with the beer. "You wanna glass?" Phil said, hovering over him.

"Thanks, yes."

"Do you like a head?" he asked, pouring it carefully.

"That's fine. Thanks." He took a long drink of beer. "Boy, that sure hits the spot. You have to understand something," looking at his watch. "It's midnight for you people but for me it's noontime." He took another drink of beer and ran his tongue over his lips. "Mr. Roth, you gotta recent picture of the Mrs.?"

"The who?"

"The Mrs."

"Susan? You mean Susan? I have a self-portrait of her done in lead pipe and barbed wire."

"What?"

"Yes, I have a number of photos of Mrs. Roth." Years ago he had taken nude Polaroid shots of Susan. She was very provocative, playing with her breasts. They hid the pictures well so that the children wouldn't find them, and now Noel wondered where they were.

"Sergeant," Phil interrupted, "you were telling us about mathematical alternatives."

"In missing-person cases there's an old motto—no news is good news. If the Mrs. was killed in an accident this afternoon, don't you think you would have been notified? Don't you know hospitals and morgues don't do nothin' till they notify the next of. I mean they don't do *nothin'!* If she was mugged, r–a–p–e–d, murdered, anything like that, you'd know it while the body was still warm. You people ain't Mafia; nobody's going to kidnap her. That's what I mean by mathematical alternatives. If she ain't here, and nobody has notified you, where could she be? Get me? Mathematical alternatives. Doesn't that make sense?"

Phoebe was right, Noel realized. Phoebe was always right. Calling the cops was a dumb move. The dumbest of dumb moves. Noel stood up. "Phil, can I speak to you for a minute?"

"Would you excuse us, Officer?" Phil said.

"S–u–r–e. I could go for another brew on your way back."

In the kitchen Noel spoke quietly to Phil. "You gotta get rid of him, Phil. He's a fucking idiot."

"Jesus, how?"

"I don't know. Susan will croak when she comes home and sees him. Just get rid of him."

"Noel, for chrissakes, I just can't go over to him and ask him to *leave!* Do you know what Phoebe really thinks?"

"What?"

"She thinks Susan is with Meyer."

"Yes. I've thought of that also."

Don Zacharia

"Do you think it's a possibility?"

"I don't know. I just don't know, Phil." Noel shook his head sadly. "It's all so out of context. Do you know what I mean? Suddenly, Friday, Meyer blows into town after not hearing a word from him in ten years. Saturday the welcome home party, and two days later there's a cop sitting in my living room because Susan is missing."

"Has Susan ever done anything like this before?"

Noel thought of the time Susan unilaterally made the playroom into her studio. "Not really. Not like this."

"What happened Saturday night after the party?"

"Nothing. Susan and Meyer came here before me. She was showing him her work when I came home a few minutes later, and then the three of us had coffee and cake."

"Any comments yesterday?"

"About Meyer?"

"Yeah. About anything."

"No. I mean nothing that means anything. Nothing that I could interpret into an explanation of Susan's absence. Just a lot of flak about the match trick."

"I got that too." Noel looked tired but Phil, protective, didn't say anything more about it. "Do you know where Meyer is staying?"

"The Rye Hilton."

"Why don't you call there and I'll see what I can do about Rudd." Phil put a half-dozen beers into an ice bucket.

"OK. What are you going to do?"

"Get him drunk." Phil winked. "Buddy, I can only imagine what you're feeling. Somehow it will all work out. You'll see." He gave him a friendly punch in the arm.

Noel called the Rye Hilton and asked them to ring Mr. Meyerson's room. No one answered. He asked them to page him in the bar and the lobby; no luck there either. "Do you have a check-out time for Mr. Meyerson?" "One minute, please. Tuesday morning," the answer came back. "Would you like to leave a message?" "No, thanks."

Back in the living room, Rudd was talking to Lois and had a pad and a pencil out.

"Mr. Roth," Rudd said, "you're lookin' better already. You don't look so worried. Rudd's Theory of Mathematical Alternatives at work." He hiccupped. "There's a couple of exceptions to my theory. The first is suicide and the second is a romantic angle. Taking suicide first, do you think your wife is the type? Did she ever talk about it? Do you know what kinda pills she took? Was she seeing a psychiatrist?"

Noel stared at him. Oh, Sergeant, what kind of a fucking question is that? Pills? She took so many pills Noel couldn't keep track of them. She took Seconal, Consequental, Darvon, Miltown and half a dozen other things. Yes, Susan talked about suicide; she did a major sculpture and called it "Suicide." And yes, she went to a psychiatrist for five years. Who the hell doesn't? What else do you want to know? She fantasized about her work constantly. What else? She insisted that their son go away to a sleep-away camp this summer, against Noel's wishes. "I need this summer," she told Noel. "I need it for my work. For once in my life I want to have one head, one single direction. I don't want to think about anything. You, the children, anything. I don't want to be a housewife, I don't want to be a mother; I want to work within the framework of my art for two months out of my life. Is that so much to ask?"

Noel didn't say any of these things to Sergeant Rudd. "My wife didn't commit suicide, Sergeant."

"I didn't mean to imply she did, Mr. Roth. I'm just spelling out the f–a–c–t–s. How about the second part, the romantic angle? About seventy-five percent of all missing persons have a romantic angle. Do you think the Mrs. could be off with someone? Another m–a–n?"

Noel looked at Phil wildly. If I punch a cop, he wanted to say, what will happen to me?

Phil, sensing trouble, jumped up. "Sergeant, how about a shot of Seagram Seven with your beer?"

"Hey, Mr. Radcliff, you crazy? This is my lunchtime."

"One can't hurt, Sarge."

"You twisted my arm."

Phil poured a generous shot for him and opened another beer.

Don Zacharia

"Mr. Radcliff, if I didn't know better, I'd say you're tryin' to get me drunk."

"You gotta be kiddin' Sarge. Three or four beers and some whiskey! You gotta be kiddin'. How about you, Noel, wanna beer?"

Noel, who had stopped drinking an hour ago, felt thirsty. "OK."

"How about you, Lois?"

"All right."

"Four brews comin' up."

"You don't say much, Mrs. Fruned."

Lois smiled. "Can I get you something to eat?"

"Now you're sayin' plenty. You know," looking at his watch, "this is my lunchtime."

"In about fifteen minutes I'll make some bacon and eggs."

George suddenly woke up. "That's a terrific idea."

A party, Noel thought. My wife is fulfilling her childhood dream, her most blatant fantasies. My wife is with another man, he is touching her where I touch her, he is licking her neck, her breasts, her belly, her cunt; she is going down on him (you'll be disappointed in the way she does that, Meyer), and we're having a party. She takes forever to come, Meyer. You're going to be exhausted. I hope you carry a vibrator in your back pocket or you're going to feel like your wrist is falling off. And she gets very uptight when you change hands. "Are you tired? If you're tired, you can stop. It's not important if I come," she'll tell you. You gotta be in shape, Meyer. It's like going both ways—playing offense and defense in a football game—like running the mile and then the relays. You really have to be in shape, Meyer, to get your just reward.

They were all drinking beer. It was ten after one. Noel was getting tired. It was a long evening. If the children were home, Susan wouldn't have done this. Strange—fate, chance, life, being in the right place at the right time, meeting people, direction, getting on a bus. If I was born a fish I could swim, if I was born a seagull I could fly—I was born a man so first I crawled—now I walk—only to crawl again—oh—dear—God—Noel wished everybody would go. Why did the world have to know that Susan was fucking Meyer, that Meyer was fucking Susan. What now—do I leave after fourteen years of marriage—what now—to humiliate me like this—this moron of a cop with his attaché case and plaid socks—oh, Susan—why does the world have to know our business—if you had to have an affair, couldn't you do it like other people—quietly in the afternoon, come home in time and take a bath and then make dinner? Does everything you do have to be so loud, so pronounced, so sculptured, so on display, so in view? Has our sex become a piece of your total environment? Are you going to put us on display in a gallery and let people view us and whatever they get out of it, they get? If one in a thousand, Susan said, gets out of a piece of sculpture what I have put into it, I have succeeded as an artist. Well, everybody is getting this, Susu. George is getting it, Lois is getting it, Sergeant Rudd is getting it, Phoebe and Phil are getting it, and I'm getting it, Noel Roth, your poor fucking husband, a haberdasher made good, a miracle, they said, that he should make so much money selling men's underwear. Better I should have been a lot of things. Better I should have been a writer, a teacher, a lawyer, a designer, an architect. A builder of buildings, a planter of trees, a farmer, a maker of magnets, anything—but a haberdasher! I measure men's crotches. On my hands and knees I put pins in their pants to make their asses tighter. Sometimes my hands graze their thighs and they shudder. (I don't do that anymore. I have three Italian tailors who do it for me. But I used to. I wasn't born with three tailors.) I am a retailer. I belong to the Chamber of Commerce. I am a haberdasher, that's all. I do so much volume that Barney's is aware of my presence. But I, a simple tailor, a Columbia graduate, I'm getting it too, Susan. You have finally reached the masses, Susu, with your art. Everybody's getting it. I'm not even sure you would be pleased by that.

"Mr. Roth," Rudd's nasal voice cut into his thoughts, "I was just telling Mr. Radcliff here that if the Mrs. doesn't come home by morning, and I'm bettin' she does, I'm bettin' another brew here with your buddy that any minute she's gonna walk through that front door and give you a smooch like nothin' happened. But if I'm wrong, and she doesn't come home, and if you think there might be a romantic angle, you would be ahead of the game if you hired a private detective. My brother-in-law is a private detective, and if this should become a matrimonial case, my brother-in-law is to matrimony what I am to missing persons."

Oh, my God, Noel thought, standing up, I'm going to hit him.

Phil, sensing trouble, stood up also and handed Noel a beer. "Take it easy," he whispered to Noel.

"Who was the last person to speak to Mrs. Roth?" Rudd asked, touching the tip of his pencil to his tongue.

"Lois was," Phil said. "Mrs. Fruned spoke to her at nine-thirty this morning. Isn't that right?"

"Yes, that's right."

"How would you describe her mood this morning?" Rudd asked.

"Susan had a million moods. They shifted depending upon what she was talking about."

"Would you describe one of her moods as being despondent?"

"Yes."

Rudd wrote something in his note pad. "Do you think Mrs. Roth is capable of suicide?"

"Yes. I think in the scheme of things Susan is capable of suicide. So am I. So are a lot of people. Do I think Susan committed suicide today? No."

"Did she talk about it today?"

"Did she talk about what?"

"About committing suicide."

"Of course not."

"Can you tell me what she did talk about?"

"Yes," Phil added, "what did you talk about?"

"I rather not say."

"Do you want to tell me privately?"

"No. Sergeant, what we talked about has nothing to do with Susan's absence. Nothing whatsoever."

"Mrs. Fruned, why don't you let me make that decision?"

60

The Match Trick

"I'm sorry."

"Lois," Phil said, "I just can't imagine what it is you talked about that under these circumstances you feel you can't discuss with us. You might not think it's relevant, but supposing it is? Supposing Susan said something to you this morning that would be an indication—?"

"Phil," Lois interrupted him, her voice flaring out, "if you really want to know what we talked about, I'll be happy to tell you. We talked for the entire thirty minutes about the match trick. She said that Saturday night was the singular worst night of her life. She said that it was the fourth time she had seen the match trick in seven years and she remembered each time with total clarity the events surrounding it, who was there, the moments before, the moments after, the reaction of the people. She said that watching it Saturday night her body, she kept repeating that phrase, my body, she said, not my mind, but my body, she must have repeated it ten times, my body was being debauched, defiled. She kept saying it and saying it. She said that you and Noel are scatological twins, and it's taken her years to realize it. That's what Susan told me this morning. Does it help you, Phil? Does it help you, Sergeant? I'm sorry, Noel. I was pushed into that."

There was a stillness in the room. No one seemed willing to speak.

"What's the match trick?" Sergeant Rudd finally asked.

"Forget it," Phil said hoarsely.

"Hey," the sergeant said, feeling his authority dwindling, "I think it's important for me to put all the pieces together—"

"I said, Forget it, Sergeant. I'm Mr. Roth's friend and attorney and I'm making the decision that it's irrelevant."

Phoebe saved the day. She suddenly appeared in the room, looking not so hot, pallid, drawn around the eyes, her hair pressed down where she had been sleeping.

Sergeant Rudd was the first to see her. He stood up.

Don Zacharia

"Well, well, well." He smiled at her and then smiled at Noel. *"Well, well, look who has come home."* He looked around the room with a broad grin. "Well, like I said, mathematical alternatives come home to r–o–o–s–t." He looked around the room again, obviously pleased with himself. "Mrs. Roth, Mrs. Susan Roth, Mrs. Susan R–o–t–h, I'm Sergeant Walter Rudd—R–u–d–d of the Crownhill PD. We've been waiting for you." Sergeant Rudd extended his hand. "How do you feel? Are you all right? Do you want me to call a doctor? Your husband has been quite worried. See, Mr. Roth—I told you not to worry."

Phoebe looked at him like he was a madman. "Phil," she said shakily, staring with disbelief at Sergeant Rudd's extended hand, "get this crazy cocksucker out of here before I vomit again."

"Ahh—Sergeant, I think you made an error. This is my wife, Phoebe Radcliff. She has been upstairs napping. Phoebe this is Sergeant Rudd. He's here to help us find Susan."

Phoebe sat down next to Phil, clinging to his arm, staring at the sergeant. Noel caught Phil's eye but had to look away; trying not to burst out in laughter, he bit his lip.

Rudd was too shocked to say anything at first. He stared at Phoebe with disbelief, then at Phil, then back at Phoebe. "OK." He finally spoke, nodding his head. "This little game you people are playing has gone far enough. You wanna play games, play them elsewhere, but don't play them with Walter R–U–D–D. There's something going on here that doesn't meet my eye. I mean, it doesn't meet my eye. Got me?" He was talking directly to Phil. "First things first, what the hell is the match trick?"

THE MATCH TRICK

"A dumb move," Noel said to Susan Saturday afternoon. "A real dumb move." If Noel and Susan had their way, they would have invited Meyer to a small dinner party at their home, a dozen old friends, a sit-down affair, with good music, good wine, and barbecued steaks. Steve Moser, who was the all-county center on the championship football team with Meyer, made all the arrangements. Steve had been so vehement in having a welcome home surprise party for Meyer the way *he* wanted to do it that by the time Noel heard about Meyer's being back in town, it was too late to do anything. "I spoke to Hogjaw," Noel said, calling Steve by his high-school nickname, "and I got the feeling that he had been planning this party for fifteen years. I can't believe everything he has done in just a few hours. He contacted the entire 1953 football team plus another fifty assorted people. He's even got Coach Warren down from New Hampshire. I haven't seen that old bastard in a decade. It's going to be a cast of thousands. This is your life—Meyer Meyerson."

Susan, who once thought she was in love with Meyer, shuddered.

The last time anyone had seen Meyer was 1954 at the N.Y.U.-Dartmouth basketball game nineteen years ago. At half time, Meyer quietly got dressed, told the coach, who was too shocked to say anything, that he was quitting, and left.

He went home and told his parents that he was leaving school and going to Dayton, Ohio, where he had a friend he would be staying with. His parents, who were two small, very old, extremely religious Jews, and had long since stopped trying to understand their son, accepted the news stoically. "Have a glass of tea with us before you go, Meyer," his mother said. They had never understood the wild adulation that Meyer received from the first time he picked up a bat in a Little League game. The three of them sat down to have tea. It was a bizarre scene: Meyer, who weighed 195 pounds, was six feet four inches tall and *still growing*, some people thought, sitting with his two feeble parents, neither of whom was five feet tall and *together* didn't weigh as much as their son. Mrs. Meyerson's hands were shaking so badly from a palsied condition that she couldn't drop her sugar into the glass. Meyer steadied her hand. She was telling Meyer's father in Yiddish what Meyer's new plans were. Not that Meyer's father didn't understand English. He had been in America for fifty years and understood English perfectly, but this was the way it was always done. When she finished her explanation, Meyer's father shrugged. As far as Meyer was concerned, that's all his father ever did in relationship to him: shrug. Meyer's father didn't speak ten words a week to Meyer. When people would talk to him about Meyer's achievements or show him newspaper stories or headlines about his son doing everything that other fathers dreamed about, Meyer's father would glance at the stories and then shrug. He never criticized Meyer, but then he never applauded him either. He once told his wife in

Yiddish, who translated it back to Meyer, that there was more to life than catching a ball and someday he would find this out.

"Ask him what he wants me to be?" Meyer cracked. "Would he be satisfied if I became a rabbi?"

"Rabbis," his father said in Yiddish, "don't grow so tall."

Meyer's father was a floor waxer. He earned a modest amount of money and they got by. Some days Meyer would help his father out. Mr. Meyerson would never let Meyer use the waxing machine. "It takes years and years and great skills to use the big machine properly," he told his wife. Meyer seethed. It was Meyer's job to do all the corners the waxing machine couldn't get into. On his hands and knees he would first steel-wool the area, apply the wax, and then with a chamois hand rub it until the area he was working on looked like the rest of the floor.

"You got some son, Mr. Meyerson," his customers would tell him. "That a boy as famous as he should take the time off to help his father in this day and age—it must make you a proud man."

Meyer's father would shrug. At the end of the week he gave Meyer eight dollars. That's what he gave him the first time he worked for him, and that's what he gave him the last time, which was the summer before Meyer went to college.

Meyer, in his high-school years, often thought about becoming a professional baseball player. He wasn't crazy about the contact in football, and in basketball he felt he was a step too slow, but baseball, he and a lot of other people thought he couldn't miss. When the time comes, he thought, he would buy his parents a home on the right side of town, like he always heard athletes who made it did. Meyer could picture the scene: his parents being interviewed on TV in their new home and Mel Allen asks his father what he thinks of his son and his brand-new home. His father looks blankly until his mother *in Yiddish* on *national TV* tells him what Mr. Allen said. His father shrugs. "And that's the story from the Meyerson home," Mel Allen says. "The elder Mr. Meyerson is obviously too overcome with emotion to comment on what is *obviously* the happiest day of his life."

Don Zacharia

. . .

Getting ready for M.M.

The evening of the party the Radcliffs and the Fruneds went to the Roth home for drinks before they went to Meyer's homecoming. Noel, Susan, and George Fruned knew Meyer from high school. For the Radcliffs and Lois Fruned, it was to be their first meeting.

"I think," Phoebe, already on her second scotch, said to everyone, "the only way I can handle this evening is stone drunk."

"At the rate you're going I'm sure you'll be there," Phil said.

"Meeting M.M.—" Phoebe rolled her eyes up—"after ten years of hearing his revered name, I'm finally going to meet the great M.M.—a floor waxer from Dayton—"

"I hope you won't be disappointed," Noel said.

"Maybe he's become fat like a tub of lard."

"I doubt it."

"Maybe he smokes a cigar and picks his nose and slams people on the back when he talks to them."

"Jesus." Phil seemed upset. "Are you going to be this way the whole evening? You're acting like someone stuck a thorn up your ass."

"Phil," Phoebe said, taking out a pocket compact and studying herself, "shut the fuck up. How do I look?" She brushed her lower lip. "I look marvelous," she answered her own question. "Will there be Italians there?" she asked Noel.

"Yes. Plenty of them," Noel said, grinning.

"Italians. The place will be swarming with Italians. An Italian beer party in Tuckahoe. How terrific."

Susan came into the room. George Fruned whistled. She looked quite beautiful, Noel thought, taking more time in putting herself together than she usually did. "What are you all saying about my Meyer?"

"He's my Meyer," Phoebe said.

"He's my Meyer," George squeaked.

"Do you think Meyer will remember who you are?" Noel asked him.

"I think so."

"If he saw you on the street, do you think Meyer would remember your name?"

"I think so." George seemed unsure. "We traveled in different circles, but I think so."

"I'll bet you fifty, George, he doesn't. When we get there, I'll go up to Meyer and after we're finished saying hello to each other and shaking each other's hands and going over old times, I'll say, 'Meyer, what's this man's name?' and you know what Meyer will say? He'll say, 'What man? I don't see no man. Who? What? Where?' I'll bet you fifty, George."

"That's not fair." George, who normally took Noel's sarcasm in stride, seemed off balance.

Lois stood up. "Can we go now?" She stared at Noel.

"Let's have another round first," Phoebe said, holding out her empty glass. The party for Meyer was called for seven-thirty and it was already eight-fifteen, but Susan and Phoebe both wanted to be *very* late.

"Can I see you for a second, Noel?" Susan stood up and Noel followed her into the kitchen. "I want you to lay off George this evening."

"I'm just kidding around," Noel protested.

"Well, stop kidding."

"You look gorgeous." Noel leaned over and kissed her. Susan pushed him away.

"You're messing me up."

"I haven't seen you in a dress so long I forget what your legs look like."

Susan lifted her dress up to above her hips. She had nothing on underneath. "How do they look?"

"Jesus." Noel moved toward her, but Susan handed him an hors d'oeuvre tray.

"Please behave tonight, Noel."

"Now what the fuck does that mean?" Noel said, leaving the kitchen.

• • •

Don Zacharia

Welcome home, Meyer. It's so nice to have you back where you belong.

There were at least one hundred people there. They spilled over the ground level of the Moser home, the den, the living room, the dining room; and even the kitchen at times was crowded. As the evening went on, the party moved outdoors through the kitchen and the den. The Moser home was a modest one, not equipped for the size of the crowd that was there Saturday evening. Not that anyone seemed to care. Meyer was home.

Steve Moser and his wife, Marilyn, with the help of some friends, had photocopied every newspaper story, every headline, every magazine article about Meyer's heroics as an athlete. Meyer, who was a hero for a long time in a town that idolized sports stars, particularly white ones, was damn good news copy. When you entered the Moser home that evening, you were visually assaulted with hundreds of news stories, plastered against the walls, hanging from the ceiling, covering the windows, in the kitchen on the refrigerator and the cabinets, outside tacked on the trees. They were placed in no special order, and you moved from Meyer Meyerson cracking a home run pushing his Little League team into the state finals, to Meyer Meyerson scoring forty points for the fifth time in the season, to Mt. Vernon defeats Stamford twenty to seven as Meyerson scores two touchdowns. It was, in its entirety, an extraordinary display, perhaps three hundred different news stories. As Noel looked about he felt a shudder of anticipation go through his body. He held tightly to Susan's arm.

"It's like a Meyer Meyerson museum," Phoebe whispered.

There was a lot of drinking going on. Phoebe was right about what they were drinking—mostly beer. There was also a lot of shouting back and forth and hand-shaking and back-pounding as people spotted old friends they hadn't seen in over a decade. But the real feature was the sports stories about Meyer and the teams he played on. They were occupying everyone's attention.

"Where is he?" Phoebe, for the first time in her life, seemed intimidated.

"Jesus," Phil said, "I've heard you talk, but I don't believe this."

"I suppose," Noel said, reading an old basketball story (Roth—0 for 2), "that he was big in this town far beyond reality."

"Where is he?" Phoebe asked again.

"He's over there," George said, pointing.

In the middle of the den a bunch of middle-aged men in a three-point football stance were posing for a Polaroid shot. They were the undefeated Mt. Vernon football team of 1954. And there was Meyer, looking exactly the way Noel thought he would look, hunched over in the T-quarterback position, hands apart, palms facing each other, ready to take the snap from his all-county center and host, Steve Moser, who was stripped down to his undershirt and looked very red in the face. Meyer looked over the defenses; he looked left, he looked right. Noel closed his eyes. Meyer's voice rang out, "READY, SET, HUP ONE—HUP TWO—HUP THREE—"

"One thousand one, two thousand two, three thousand three," the person who snapped the picture was counting. "That should do it." He pulled the film from the camera and everyone crowded about him. "For chrissakes gimme some room, will yuh?" He waved the picture about in the air, drying it, and passed it around. There was a great deal of howling and laughter as the picture made the rounds. The crowd broke up and Meyer spotted them and came over and shook hands warmly with them all. First George: "George, how are you?" Then Susan: "How are you?" She leaned over and kissed his cheek. For just a second their eyes made contact. "I'm fine," Susan said. He shook Noel's hand. "Long time," Noel said.

"You look terrific," Meyer said to him.

Noel patted his stomach. "A little heavier—"

"Not compared to some of those guys. You see Hogjaw? He must have put on a hundred pounds."

Noel introduced Phil and Phoebe and Lois.

"I'd like to speak to you later, Noel," Meyer said.

"Sure thing," Noel said, pleased.

Hogjaw came over, still in his undershirt. "Stop hogging the guest of honor."

"See you later," Meyer said.

Don Zacharia

"He looks incredible," Noel said after Meyer left. "He looks like he could do it all over again if he wanted to."

Susan nodded.

Later that evening but before the match trick.

Noel and Meyer were drinking beer. They were sitting on folding chairs in a corner of the yard. The party swirled before them. Noel felt awkward. They were remembering old times.

"Whatever happened to Charlie A?" Meyer asked, referring to a favorite history teacher.

"He died three years ago."

"Ahh, too bad."

"Do you remember Ted Ramsey?"

"Of course."

"He was killed in Vietnam."

"I heard that. In Dayton I heard that. I heard most things out there about a year after it happened. I heard about you and Susan getting married the same time I heard about your daughter being born."

"Well, we didn't hear *anything* about you other than the fact that you were there to stay."

"You didn't hear that I got married?"

"Vaguely. I don't remember the circumstances. It didn't last too long, did it?"

"Four months. She was a bitch on wheels. She was screwing around a week after we got married."

"That's tough. Marriage is tough enough but that is tough. Everybody seems to be getting divorced these days."

"Not you and Susan."

"No. We've had our moments. Boy, have we had our moments, but we're hanging in there."

"I'm glad to hear that. I'm really glad to hear that."

"Thanks."

"I heard you hit it big."

"How? What do you mean?"

"Making the big bucks."

"Ahh—rumors of my success are greatly exaggerated. I've done OK."

"Twelve stores—"

"Twelve stores! Are you kidding? That's what I mean by rumors. I only have four and that's enough headaches. Where the hell did you hear twelve?"

"I don't know. Somebody told me that in Dayton. I guess four is plenty. It's like you're big but small enough to still watch out over it."

"That happens to be a very interesting concept."

"You certainly have done well, Noel."

Noel, pleased but embarrassed, nodded.

"Which brings me to a favor," Meyer said.

"Shoot."

"It's a real favor."

"Shoot. Anything."

"I'm moving back home. That's what this trip is all about. There is very little left in Dayton to keep me there other than my business, and I've arranged for the sale of that to a couple of guys who are in maintenance. It's a steal. For seven thousand they're getting all my equipment, my sixty-eight station wagon, and my entire route. I have one account, a medical building that is good for six hundred a month. In my business, that's a damn good account. Those guys really got a bargain. I've held on to my folks' house, and I thought for the time being I would move back in. The neighborhood is totally black now but that's OK. And I'll see how many of my father's old accounts I can pick up. My father didn't have any big stuff like the medical building, but I guess I can't be choosy. Anyhow, here's the favor. I thought you had twelve stores, but four, as you say, is plenty. What would the chances be of getting your account? If I could get one major account like yours, it would help my situation. I'd be on my way. I don't know what kind of arrangements you have now, and this might sound conceited to you, but I'm probably the best damn floor waxer in America."

"The account is yours," Noel shot out.

Don Zacharia

"All four stores?"

"Of course."

"I'll be competitive. I'll figure the price by Dayton standards, which I'm sure are a hell of a lot less than you are paying now."

"Yes," Noel said, "I'm sure they are." What Noel didn't say was that he had wall-to-wall carpeting in all of his stores.

Phoebe, after her initial shock of finally meeting Meyer Meyerson, had moved into the swing of the party as if these had been her closest friends all of her life, and now in the center of the yard was leading a group of people in a game called Simon Sez. Phoebe was very animated in her movements and was attracting a lot of attention and more and more players. "OK, OK," Phoebe shouted, "a new game starts now. Is everybody ready?" "Yes," came back the chorus. "Phoebe sez—do this." She spread her legs and suggestively began rotating her hips. Half the players imitated her. "Dummies," Phoebe shouted, "dummies, dummies, dummies." She pointed to each player who had imitated her. "You're out—you're out—out—out. It's not what *Phoebe sez*, dummies, it's what *Simon sez*." There was a murmur of protests, but Phoebe, waving them off, would have none of it. "Simon sez," Phoebe said, speaking very slowly, "for those intellectuals left, *Do This!*" She placed her hand on her stomach and began rubbing it.

"Meyer," Noel said, "remember that game against Mamaroneck when I made fifteen baskets in a row?"

Meyer looked at him puzzled. "No, I don't right off."

Noel had looked all over the house. He had looked at every single clipping and every single story about Meyer, trying to find some reference to the game in his senior year when he had scored fifteen baskets in a row and thirty-one points in the game. It didn't seem possible, but he wasn't able to find either the story itself or any reference to it. He was sure he had overlooked it. There was a terrific amount of drinking going on, and with the exception of Noel no one was paying too much attention to the clippings anymore. Some of them had been torn off the wall and were either left lying on the floor where they had fallen or were hastily pinned or tacked back up, sometimes covering another story. Noel was sure he had overlooked it. He decided to start looking again, at the beginning, in the foyer, and look through each story until he found it. It had to be there. He wanted to find it.

Later that evening but before the match trick.

Susan was holding court. "I am working in a total environment." They were just about to play George Fruned's version of a game called Truth. Susan was surrounded by Noel, Phil, Phoebe, George, Lois, the hosts, Marilyn and Steve Moser, the guest of honor, Meyer Meyerson, and a handful of men who for one reason or other didn't want to let Phoebe Radcliff out of their sight. "A labyrinth can be made out of a number of things, but once you make it out of something as significant as barbed wire, then you have added another dimension. It becomes something more, since it is not so easy to choose a path and follow it or change your path when you want to. What I am saying is that your choice really becomes a cage, and it is very difficult to get out of that cage or that confinement, and I believe getting out of a marriage is very similar to that."

Phoebe nodded her approval. Phil looked at Noel. Noel made a motion with his hand and rolled his eyes as if to say to his friend, so what else is new? George was watching Meyer, who in turn was saying very little but in turn was watching and listening to Susan very intently. Everyone else looked bewildered.

George explained the game Truth for the newcomers and gave the signal for the game to start. Susan was the first to play, and she was asked what the most important thing in her life was.

"My work," she answered immediately.

The judges held up their scores. Susan got a 7.2, 7.4, 7.7, 8 and

Don Zacharia

1. Eight was a perfect score and rarely given. There was a scattering of applause. Phoebe handed a folded note to the judge who had given Susan a one. The judge read the note and shrugged. "It's the way I see it," he mumbled. "Male chauvinist-pig," Phoebe said in a loud clear voice.

The same question was asked of Noel. "My work," he answered with a grin. His scores were 3.3, 3.4, 3.5, 4.4 and 8.

It was Lois Fruned's turn. "What is the most deviant sexual fantasy you have ever had?" It took Lois a few minutes to answer, which of course, affected her scores. "Bestiality," she finally said, looking at the carpet. Lois got three 8's, which was unheard of and a 7.5 and a 7.3.

It was Meyer's turn. Susan was watching his face, remembering a time years back when, after a victorious football game, she had necked with Meyer. Meyer was a hero, and Susan treated him like a hero, taking off her blouse and bra and letting Meyer suck on her nipples while she rubbed her leg into his groin until he came. "Did you?" she asked him, confused. He nodded yes. "You were so quiet. As if you didn't want me to know."

There was some confusion as to who should ask Meyer the question. Lois, as the last player, was supposed to, but she reneged, saying privately to George that, if she did, there would be the implication that it was her question, when in reality all the questions were his. There was a compromise. Four people would ask the question at the same time: Lois, Phoebe, Phil and Noel. Phoebe was in charge. She stood up. "All in unison, now—on the count of three—one, two, three—Meyer, have you ever had a homosexual relationship that was consummated?"

Meyer, who had been living in Dayton, Ohio, for fifteen years, didn't answer the question.

Later that evening but before the match trick.

Meyer was sitting in a folding chair, Susan on the ground, her back propped by a tree, a half bottle of scotch tucked into her lap.

The Match Trick

Susan was dreamy. In the bathroom she had shared half a joint with Phoebe.

"Do you know what you are?" Susan was talking to Meyer. "You are MacArthur returning to the Philippines; you are an MIA returning to his family. Do you have any idea of how often your name is mentioned? Do you have any idea of how often stories are told and retold about all those games you played in? You are mostly—" feeling the need to further explain it to Meyer—"a hero returning home."

"I am mostly," Meyer said, drinking a Budweiser from the bottle, "none of those things. I am a floor waxer from Dayton trying to relocate. I am a white man in a black man's job. I am divorced once, and yet to have a meaningful relationship with a woman."

"It doesn't matter what you really are, it only matters what people *think* you are. Look around you. This party, these people. Do you think they are doing this for a floor waxer? They did this for what you were. For how they remember you. For how they would like to remember you. Enjoy it. A year from now very few of them will talk to you, least of all have a party for you."

"And you?"

"That's unfair. I am not like them. You were my first lover."

"I was? I must have been sleepwalking. You and Noel are going to make me crazy. He keeps talking to me about a basketball game where he says he made fifteen baskets in a row. I know I have blocked out an awful lot of my high-school years, but I can't conceive of having forgotten an incident like that, and now you tell me that I was your first lover. Well, I *know* I wouldn't have forgotten that."

"In my mind. In my mind you were always my first lover."

"Oh. How was I?"

Ignoring the crack, "In reality I was a virgin when I married Noel. Looking back, I cannot believe that. Are you surprised?"

"Yes. Everyone always thought you were screwing everyone."

"No, no. I was screwing no one. I dry-humped a million men— all that scummy underwear." Susan made a face. "It's not the way

75

Don Zacharia

I like to think of myself. It's not the image I have, and you know something, I'm not so wild about my image today. I don't think I have changed a bit. How ridiculous; how absurd, how could I possibly have allowed that to happen? Do you know how angry it makes me just to talk about it? I wish I had fucked the garbage man. Me, Susan Golden, a virgin! What a joke our wedding night was. Poor Noel, he tried so hard to screw me for two years and I wouldn't let him, that when he really could, he got drunk and it was a farce. Oh, believe me, we did everything else. I used to go down on him and suck him and make him come in his handkerchief. But Susan Golden wasn't going to let him put his dickie inside Susu's twat, not on your *life*. That night I wasn't even aware of it. He says he came, but I *certainly* wasn't aware of it. He fell asleep in a drunk and I took a bath, and if I had any place to go, I would have left him then. If you were around, I would have gone to you, but you were in Dayton. The only other place I could have gone was home and that was ridiculous. So I stayed in the tub all night. I kept refilling it with hot water. In the morning Noel asked me what was wrong with my skin. It was all blue and puckerish. He apologized for what had happened. It really was as much my fault as his. In the afternoon we took a plane to Puerto Rico. Things got better. They couldn't have gotten worse. Noel became so successful so quick—it helped, his success. It helped Noel and it helped me. If you're going to be sensitive, it's just as nice to be rich sensitive."

"Do you remember Sandy Sussman?" Not waiting for an answer, Susan went on, "She did what we all did. High school, college, marriage, two children, then one day she took a walk and didn't come home. She told her husband to go fuck himself, a stockbroker type, took the two children and moved to Manhattan and now lives with a black professor in Greenwich Village. We keep in touch. We have lunch together. I wanted to have them up to the house but her professor is very arrogant and I think he and Noel would kill each other. I asked Sandy if she was happy, and she said no, she wasn't necessarily happy but she was *surviving*. She says her lover sometimes beats her, but that's OK because that's more than her husband used to do. She says she can breathe now. I've thought of doing that. I've thought of doing what Sandy did. Sometimes I leave with the children and sometimes I leave without them. In the end I always leave Noel. I cannot stand what I am: a suburban housewife who in her spare time attempts to create art. I am much better than that, Meyer. Do you want to make money? Forget about floor waxing. Open up an art-supply store in the suburbs. You'll make a million dollars. Every woman around here who ever held a crayon in her hand and is bored becomes a painter or a sculptor. She paints and sculpts and has that stuff framed and sells that *shit*. I mean they really sell that *shit*. Do you know how that infuriates me? Why don't they become writers? Do you know why? Because people would laugh at them. I know someone who after she had finished with a painting lets her cat walk over the canvas while it is still wet. And then she frames it and sells it for *money*. The PTA has an art show and all those women display their work and people *buy* their paintings off the wall for chrissakes. They wanted me to display some of my work, not my barbed-wire sculptures because they couldn't get insurance for that. Very professionally I told them to fuck off. I didn't, really, but I wish I had." Susan took a long drink of scotch.

"We are all straight lines. We all do exactly what we are meant to do—predestined to do. Every now and then there is an exception. Sandy is an exception. You, you were an exception, Meyer. Maybe you still are. I don't know. I don't know why you went to Dayton and I don't know why you are coming back. I want to be an exception too, but it is impossible. Something is stopping me. I couldn't even bring myself to screw a man before I got married and I've never had an affair. If I die never having slept with another man, I'll kill myself!"

Meyer laughed.

"Will you have an affair with me?"

Meyer didn't answer her at first. "In your mind or a real one?"

"No, no, a real affair." Susan giggled. "I will be a fabulous lover."

Don Zacharia

"Yes, of course."

"Monday?"

"Monday what?"

"Will you meet me in Manhattan Monday morning? We can accidentally meet at the train station and ride in together. I will spend all weekend anticipating. I will spend all weekend preparing. Will you?"

"Yes."

Coach Warren arrived quite late, after ten. He was greeted warmly by many of his old players, who hadn't seen him in over a decade. Noel couldn't get over how old he looked. He appeared to have lost fifty pounds, his face yellow, his body emaciated and tired. Noel approached him after everyone else. The coach was drinking rye and ginger.

"Coach." Noel held his hand out. "Coach Warren, how are you?"

Warren shook his head, stared at Noel and then shifted his eyes. "I'm sorry," Warren said, "I don't remember you."

"Roth. I'm Noel Roth."

Warren looked at him blankly. He shook his head. "Were you on the track team?"

Noel walked away.

The match trick.

Noel was half drunk. He was standing on a picnic table that was pushed up against the side of the house. Phil, with a big grin, was sitting on the table, his legs dangling over the side. Noel was shouting, trying to get everyone's attention.

"Gather around—everybody—it's show time in Hogjaw's backyard." He clapped his hands repeatedly. *"Come on—come on—I'm going to show you a miracle. Hey—you—sit down over there. You want to see a miracle? Let's go—let's go—it's show time."* He yelled at some people in the corner of the yard who seemed hesitant about

joining the group that was forming in front of him. *"Come on—join the party."*

"What's up, Roth?" someone shouted. "You gonna make a speech?"

"I'm going to make history," Noel shouted back. "That's what I'm going to make. Make room over there for Coach Warren. He doesn't want to miss this."

Meyer was sitting next to Susan. "What's going on?" he asked her.

"Don't ask me." She turned to Phoebe, who stared at her and nodded. "Meyer," Susan said, "I'm sorry about this evening. I'm sorry for what is about to happen."

The entire party was now in front of Noel; half of them were sitting, and half were standing. It was after midnight. A lot of drinking had been going on all evening and there was an abundance of back pounding and arm punching. Noel began: "To those of you who don't know me, I'm Noel Roth." There was scattered applause and he grinned. "The only man to ever make fifteen baskets in a row."

"Wake me up when it's over," someone yelled.

"Quiet," Noel said. "Quiet." He waited, rocking back and forth on his heels. When everyone was still, he started again, speaking in a low staccato voice: "You are about to see the match trick. The match trick has only been performed three times before this, and always by me. I am not a magician, and the match trick is not magic. It is not sleight of hand or deception. It is a physical demonstration of absolute control of my body for a fleeting moment, two or three seconds. How long does it take for a major-league fastball to reach the batter's box? That's how long the match trick takes. I have never seen or heard of anyone doing it but me. It is the ultimate dunk shot; the home run out of Yankee Stadium; the seventy-yard pass for a touchdown. It is making fifteen jump shots in a row. It–is–the–climax–of–athletic–achievement. Pay attention, for you will never see it again. Never. Before I start, there is one thing you should all be aware of, and if anyone wants to leave after what I'm going to tell you, please, I understand. Every time I have

Don Zacharia

done the match trick, someone in the audience—within a week—"
Noel hesitated, letting the sentence hang. He stared at George
Fruned, and then at Coach Warren. "Within a week—someone—
death." He shook his head and waited. No one got up to leave.
Perhaps it was a combination of the evening's events: the homecoming of Meyer, the drinking, the late hour, Noel's hypnotic speech,
but whatever it was, there was an eerie quality to what was beginning to take place. The earlier horseplay had ceased, and everyone
sat quietly, staring at Noel.

"All right," Noel said, "I will begin now. THE MATCH TRICK."
He clenched his hands in front of him, closed his eyes and began to
breathe rapidly; inhaling and exhaling in quick audible gasps. As
quickly as he started, he stopped and stared out at the audience,
his glance darting from person to person. Everyone avoided his
eyes. He touched his face with both hands, running his fingers over
the outline of his lips, his eyes, his nose. He ran his hand through
his hair repeatedly. He stretched his arms out and closing his eyes
let his arms hang in midair. He turned his head from side to side
and then up and down. He started the breathing exercise again,
only this time shook his wrists at the same time. He suddenly
stopped and nodded to Phil. "I'm ready," Noel whispered. "Ready."

Noel got down on his hands and knees, his back facing the audience, his head facing the house. He arched his back and tightened
his leg muscles. Phil knelt next to him, half-facing the crowd, half-
facing Noel's back. He lit a wooden match and cupping the flame
with his hand let it burn for a moment. Holding the end of the
match he placed the flame directly in back of Noel's arched ass.

"Closer," Noel grunted.

Phil moved it closer until it was one inch from Noel's backside.

"Closer," Noel grunted again.

Phil moved it even closer.

"Yes," Noel said, "perfect."

Noel farted; the force of the fart blowing out the match. He stood
up and bowed.

"What's the trick?" someone said.

"That," Noel said, "is the match trick."

80

NOEL'S NIGHTMARE

It was two in the morning. Susan was not home yet. Noel looked about his living room. Everyone was still there. He rubbed his eyes. Everything—the furniture, the people—seemed distorted, out of place, the wrong size, like looking through a telescope the wrong way. Lois had made bacon and eggs, and Rudd and George were wolfing down their food. Phil was drinking black coffee; Phoebe, disheveled, was sipping tea.

Noel told Phil to close up the house, excused himself and went to his room. He knew he had to lie down, to close his eyes. His body was exhausted, numb. He closed the door to his room, took his shoes, shirt and pants off and lay down on the bed. There was a tightness in his chest.

Downstairs, Rudd made a phone call in the privacy of the library. He called headquarters and asked to speak to the chief.

"What's going on?" the chief asked him. "You go to movies or something?"

Don Zacharia

"No. I'm still here at the Roths'."

"Did she turn up?"

"I'm not sure. Something fishy is going on here, Chief. Something that doesn't meet the eye. Do you know what I mean?"

"Not exactly. What the hell do you mean you're not sure? Did the missing party come home?"

"They say she didn't, but something is funny. It doesn't square up. I'm going to poke around a little bit more."

"Jesus Christ, Rudd, it's two-thirty in the morning!"

"OK, OK, just a little longer."

"Stop off at the garage on your way in and pick me up the early-bird *News*."

"Right. So long, Chief." Rudd hung up. There was a mirror on the wall and he stared at his reflection. He closed his right eye, then opened it, and then closed his left eye. He did it again. Everything appeared different, Walter thought. Walter liked looking people directly in the eye. He practiced it. He felt it told him a lot about people, about situations. Roth never once looked him in the eye. Something was going on, Walter thought, under the surface something was going on. Something wasn't square in his eye. Rudd nodded at himself. He was going to find out.

Noel was dreaming. Noel had a recurring dream. He had dreamed it, or variations of it, a thousand times. Sometimes he thought he understood his dream; most of the time he didn't. He spoke to Susan about it, and she even spoke to her psychiatrist, who just shrugged. Noel was dreaming that he was a single-engine airplane and he was flying down the Hudson River. When he came to the George Washington Bridge, he had a choice that he was very aware of—to fly over the bridge or to fly under the bridge. He flew under the bridge. Then he was no longer the plane, but a passenger in the plane, and a woman was the pilot. Noel was frightened. They were high on a mountain, and he couldn't remember how they were going to take off. Noel was really frightened.

The phone woke Noel up. He looked at his watch. It was ten after six. "Hello."

"Mr. Roth?"

"Yes."

"This is Sergeant Rudd. You haven't seen the *Daily News* yet? Of course you haven't. I got a question from outta left field for you. Does the name Meyer Meyerson mean anything to you?"

"Yes."

"Could the Mrs. have been with him yesterday?"

"Yes."

"Mr. Roth, I think I got some terrible news to tell you. This morning—I mean yesterday morning—how should I phrase this?—Meyer Meyerson and a woman who has yet to be identified—who we have reason to believe was the Mrs.—were killed by a Westinghouse air conditioner."

THE FUNERAL

Identification was a problem. There was little doubt that the woman with Meyer Meyerson was Susan Roth, but the coroner's office would not release the body until there was medical corroboration. Events moved quickly that Tuesday. After Sergeant Rudd's call, Noel called Phil, who came over immediately with a copy of the *Daily News*. Phil was ashen, his eyes bloodshot, his face creased with pain. He started to say something to Noel, but the words choked in his mouth. He handed Noel the newspaper.

The *Daily News* had made a front-page story out of Susan and Meyer's death. Noel read the headline: FALLING AIR CONDITIONER KILLS COUPLE IN LOVERS' EMBRACE. He studied the meaningless picture on the front page of a cop named Max Johnson standing with his hands on his hips and in the background a tarpaulin covering the couple who had been killed. Noel smiled at Phil and turned the page and started to read the story about a man identified as Meyer Meyerson and an unidentified woman who were, according to Max Johnson, "kissing when the air conditioner conked them." Noel felt lightheaded; detached. His head was swimming with a thousand thoughts and he had to push himself to read on. He was finding it difficult to focus. He asked Phil how he was, and if he would mind putting up some coffee. "Meyerson," the story went on, "had been living in Dayton, Ohio, but two decades ago was a local phenom in high-school athletics, owning dozens of existing records in football, basketball and baseball." Noel threw the paper aside. He picked it up again and started rereading in the middle of the story a quote from the cop. "I didn't see the air conditioner crash into them—I heard it. I was ticketing a white Vega when it happened. I noticed them for the first time a minute before the accident. They were across the street standing exactly where they are lying now. They were kissing when the air conditioner conked them. What got my attention was that she, the deceased, was standing on her tiptoes, and still could barely reach him, the deceased." Noel threw the paper down again. The look on his son's face as he was leaving for camp flashed into Noel's mind. He liked his son. He told Phil to take it easy. "You look like death warmed over," he said. He picked up the paper again and studied the picture on the front page. It was out of context. It didn't register. He opened the paper to the sports pages. "Seaver pitched a four-hitter and lost. It figures," he told Phil.

At seven-thirty, Noel called the camp and made arrangements with the camp owner for his two children to be driven home immediately. He didn't go into details with him. At eight the New York police called. Phil spoke to them. They understood that it was likely that the unidentified woman in yesterday's East Side accident was Susan Roth, but they needed medical evidence before they could release the body. Could someone from the family or a friend get Susan Roth's dental charts and medical records and X-rays and bring them down to the coroner's office? Phil said that he would.

Phil talked to Noel. He said things to him that morning that were difficult for a man like Phil Radcliff to say. He struggled at times to fight back the tears. Most of what he said was disjointed, but it didn't matter because for the most part Noel wasn't capable of listening. Noel was bewildered. He kept thinking how angry Susan was going to be when she read the story, but he knew there was something wrong with that.

At noontime the children arrived home. Noel, as best as he could, told them what happened to their mother. He showed them the newspaper. At first they both stared at him blankly, then his daughter began to cry, and David, following his sister's lead, began to sob. Noel held them. "You two want sodas?" he finally asked them. They both said yes and the three of them shared two bottles of Coke.

Phil went to the coroner's office with Susan's dental and medical records. He handed them to a man his age dressed in dungarees and a doctor's jacket.

"Are you the husband?" the man asked.

"No. A friend."

He looked at Phil's face. "I'm sorry. We'll let you know one way or the other in a couple of hours."

At three-thirty P.M., August 24, 1973, the coroner's office, using some old X-rays of a broken ankle, identified the body they were holding as that of Susan Roth.

That evening Noel and Phil went to the funeral parlor to make the arrangements. Susan was being buried in the morning. Phil had volunteered to do it by himself, but Noel, who seemed to be handling himself better than anyone could believe, insisted upon going.

"Watch Noel," Phoebe said to Phil before he left.

"What do you mean?"

"I don't know. He's acting as if nothing has happened."

Phil nodded. He knew that Phoebe was right.

"A terrible day, Mr. Roth." The funeral director grasped his hand. Noel followed him into an elevator. An elevator! It gave the appearance of being a one-story building. Noel looked at his shoes. They went down one flight, or maybe they didn't. Noel wasn't sure. He had no sensation of movement. Maybe it's a trick. The door opened and they went into a large cold room filled with coffins.

"It's very cold down here," Noel said.

"It's very cold down here," the walls echoed.

"Hello, hello, hello," Noel said.

"Hello, hello, hello," the echo came back.

"Two—four—six—eight—who—do—we—appreciate—"

"Two—four—six—eight—who—do—we—appreciate—"

"The price you see on each casket—"

"The price you see on each casket—"

"The price you see on each casket represents the entire cost of the funeral. The only extras are limousines. They are fifty dollars, including the driver."

There must have been two hundred coffins down there, and Noel was amazed at the price variance. They had one as high as fourteen thousand dollars, all the way down to a plain wooden job for four hundred dollars that looked like it was made in the high-school shop. Noel ran his fingers over the fourteen-thousand-dollar casket. Phil watched him carefully, nervously. Susan, Noel thought, would laugh her head off at this one. "I'll take this," Noel said, touching the ornate silver design at one end of the coffin.

"Noel!" Phil cried out.

The funeral director clicked his heels. Noel walked away. The elevator door opened. "Are there stairs?" Noel asked.

"Right over there, sir. I would like you to sign some papers in my office." The director, who worked on a 10 percent commission, felt his face sweating. It wasn't every day he made a killing like this one.

"Upstairs," Noel said.

"Noel—" Phil was following Noel up the stairs. He cornered him at the top before he could open the door. "Noel, for chrissakes, give yourself five minutes—"

Don Zacharia

"Phil, I want that coffin. Don't argue with me. I want it."

"Five minutes, Noel. That's not Susan." It was the wrong thing to say and he knew it. Noel pushed him aside and opened the door. The director was waiting for him, patting his lips and face with a handkerchief.

Noel, the decision made, suddenly felt just fine. I'll make out, he thought. I'll survive. I'm all right. "Are you all right?" he asked the director. "You look kinda white to me." Turning to Phil, "I know it's not Susan," he hissed, "but Susan isn't here, is she? I'm here. Do you want to help me or do you want to wait outside for me?"

Phil stayed. They all went into the director's office, and he presented the contract. "I insist that I read it," Phil said. Noel waited. He felt pretty good, kind of tired, but pretty good. He looked at the director. "You should get some sun. You look white."

"You made a beautiful selection, Mr. Roth, an excellent casket. I am sure you will be pleased. The wood is twelve inches thick and comes from the Córdoba region of Argentina."

"Argentina is a fascist regime," Noel said.

Phil winced. The director felt he needed a drink. "It seems to be in order," Phil said, handing it to Noel. "Three thousand down and ninety days to pay off the balance with no interest charges." Noel signed every place the director indicated and, with Phil watching carefully, made out a check and then left.

Phoebe wept, Lois didn't. Phil felt tears and wiped them away with his hand. Noel felt fine. His daughter cried and he squeezed her hand. His son, taking his father's lead, fought back the tears. The rabbi droned on. Susan's mother, Mrs. Golden, was hysterical. Noel was in anguish over her wailing. The loss of a grown child is the greatest loss there is. Who told him that? At one point her crying became so loud that the rabbi hesitated with the service. Oh, please, continue, Noel thought. If anything, Mrs. Golden's sonorous howling was distracting everyone from the reality of what was taking place. More people were looking at her and whispering

The Match Trick

about her than were listening to the young rabbi. The rabbi was eloquent—as eloquent as he could be with Mrs. Golden screeching, and considering that he didn't know Susan or Noel from a hole in the wall. It pays to be friends with a rabbi and be an active member of the temple, Noel thought, so when you die he can say he knew you personally and people will know that the words he is saying are sincere. Those are fake words and fake feelings and a fake service. Oh, to know a rabbi.

Noel came from a nonreligious home and was totally indifferent toward religion—not true—he wasn't really indifferent. Most of the time he didn't like it, suspected it of providing false ideals and false hopes, and was suspicious of people who became involved with it. Susan had come from a somewhat traditional religious home, but had become an atheist. Noel found her attitude, although he often disagreed with her, easier to handle than many of their friends. Susan, going overboard by her own admission, refused to attend Passover dinner at the beginning of her "awareness."

"What does she believe in?" Mrs. Golden implored Noel, no longer capable of talking to her own daughter.

"She believes in lead pipes," Noel replied. It upset Noel too.

"You're a phony," Susan told him. "You either are or you aren't. You can't be two things. I know what I am. What the fuck are you?"

Noel, confused, wanting to be two things, had no answer. They missed two Passovers during Susan's renaissance, and Noel used to dream about taking a piece of Mrs. Golden's gefilte fish into his mouth. Susan, instead, bought a wok and on Passover would cook the most outrageous meals: steamed pig knuckles with mysterious-looking vegetables.

The third year, Susan relented. "I'm going," she told Noel, "because you and my mother have worn me down. Believe me, that's the only reason." She went. Mrs. Golden was beside herself with happiness at Susan's return to the fold. But Susan straightened her out in no time when she sat down to dinner in her dungarees, boots, and hands and face and hair smeared with clay from her day's work. She refused to wash before dinner. Beth and David looked on with wonderment. They always had to wash before dinner. "You don't understand," Susan told them, "it's not the same thing." "Listen to your mother," Noel said. "Right," Susan said. Mrs. Golden, if she had a sharp knife, would have killed first Susan and then herself. So they had Passover dinner. David asked the four questions in English, running the sentences together. Mr. Golden hid the matzos; nobody could find them. "If they went to temple, they would know where to look," Mr. Golden sniped. The evening was a disaster.

"You're right," Noel told Susan on the way home. "I'm sorry. All I ever missed was the food."

"Hurry up and get home," Susan said. "I'm filthy. I want to take a hot bath."

That night in bed while they were making love, Noel told Susan that he loved her more than ever; that she was right and he apologized for all the grief he had caused her and all he missed at Passover was the food. Susan, tightening her pelvis the way they had taught her in natural childbirth classes, knowing how much Noel loved that, and also knowing that it made him come in seconds when she put that kind of pressure on his prick, whispered in his ear that she would make him gefilte fish three times a week.

The rabbi droned on. Mrs. Golden was quieter, encouraged by Mr. Golden to hold a handkerchief to her mouth. She now would give a muffled sob every few moments. Noel studied the casket, pleased by his purchase. It was beyond him what was inside that box.

Fifteen in a row. Really. Noel's mind was wandering into the damnedest things. In January of 1954, against Mamaroneck, Noel's team had two black guards who couldn't play, one had the flu and the other was temporarily suspended because he flunked everything. That left Coach Warren with only three guards: Noel, Billy Shutz, a tall, talented, awkward sophomore, and Jim Armbuster, who played even less than Noel, and was on the team only because his father and Coach Warren were friends. Before the game Coach Warren spoke to Noel: "I'm letting you play as long as you can. Signal me when you're pooped and I'll have Armbuster spell you. I don't have to tell you to work the ball into Meyer—" The coach smiled at Noel and patted him on the ass. "Give me what you can." The other team wasn't stupid. When they saw that Mount Vernon's two starting guards weren't even suited up, they sluffed as many as three men on Meyer. With five minutes to go in the half, Mt. Vernon was losing by nine, Noel hadn't taken a shot, and Meyer had only six points. Meyer called time out. "Whadda you want to do?" Coach Warren asked him. He did that often with Meyer. "Lemme play guard with Noel, and let Billy play forward. I'll bring the ball up. If they double on me, I'll get it to Noel and you go for the basket or give it to Billy." "Okay," Warren said, "we'll do it." As they were walking away from Warren, Meyer spoke to Noel. "Shoot whenever you can," he told him. Meyer brought the ball up. He was a hell of a guard for a high-school team, six feet four and an excellent ball handler. Every time they tried to double or triple Meyer coming up the floor, he would zip the ball to Noel, who would go for the basket. Noel took four shots for the balance of the half and made all four. At half time they were losing by five. In the second half they did the same thing. "Let's not f—— around with success," Coach Warren said. For Noel, it was like magic. He couldn't miss. Meyer kept feeding him the ball, Noel would go for the hoop, pull up short, swish, from every place, once from thirty-five feet. Noel couldn't miss. Noel thought he might never miss again. He made eleven more in a row in the second half, fifteen in a row in all. Everybody was sure it was a record. He missed his last two, but by that time it didn't matter. Noel's team won by twelve. The final stats showed Noel fifteen for seventeen and one for five from the foul line for thirty-one points. He outscored Meyer by four. In the locker room Noel was pounded black and blue. "Hey, cut it out. You guys are killin' me—hey—" He became an instant hero. It was all right. The next game was five days later. The two black guards had returned and Noel wondered what Warren was

Don Zacharia

going to do. A man who shoots fifteen in a row you don't sit on the bench. Noel started and played a minute and a half, during which time he never touched the ball. Warren pulled him out and Noel didn't play again. It was a close game. Noel, sitting on the bench, couldn't concentrate. To this day, sitting in that chapel, listening to a rabbi whose name he didn't know talk about his wife whose name the rabbi didn't know, that moment clawed at Noel. Why couldn't it be Warren whose funeral he was going to?

Oh, was it hard to concentrate. The rabbi—no. He breathed a sigh of relief. Even the rabbi was uncomfortable with this one: so much terrible publicity. Aaron Blum had asked to say a few words and was talking not about Susan but about himself. Nice. He looked old—ninety—a hundred and ninety. "I am not a minister, a rabbi, at best—" his voice faltered, and someone in the back whispered louder—"at best I am a worn-out artist, living in the past, dusting off old awards, dreaming of things that never were, waiting to die, spending the last few days of my life teaching artless people about art, and into my life—long since spent—six years ago—came Susan Roth."

Noel fingered a card in his jacket pocket. Cupping it in his hand, he studied it. WALTER RUDD. Second baseman? No. Sometimes it is difficult to remember. Noel wished Blum would finish. He would like to breathe fresh air, take his jacket off, stretch. Blum missed his calling. He should have been a rabbi. Everybody was crying. —"Wearing a pair a work boots that looked too big for her and a dress that swept the dirt on my studio floor as she walked about—" *"Arggh—Susan—my Susan—"* Mrs. Golden was beside herself. Aaron Blum's tale of Susan's appearance was too much for her. She had quieted down before to just a few intermittent sobs, but now she was hysterical again. Blum went on. " 'I am a serious artist,' was the first thing Susan said to me. She was so intense in those days. How old are you, I asked her? 'Thirty,' she replied. 'I am eighty-four. I am almost three times your age—' "

How Now Brown Cow. Blum and Rudd are two of a kind. They should pal around together. It's Blum and Rudd who are the scatological twins. *Susan.* College was an awkward time, lonely, fumbling to score. Eating hero sandwiches in the park by myself. Everybody in America seemed to know everybody. Lonely, so, I was really lonely then, really by myself. There must be five hundred people here.

"Susan and I discussed death many times—" Letting Blum speak was a mistake. Who needs this? "Death was very much a part of her work, her thoughts. She had a friend in college—a man who committed suicide. How vividly she recalled that. What a mark it left on her life, her work. She told me that she went to his funeral and there were ten people there. That bothered her. To be that young, to die, and to have only a handful of people care. 'When I die,' Susan said, 'there will be five hundred people at my funeral. They will be fighting to get in.' When I die, I told Susan, there will be less than ten people at my funeral. 'When Picasso died,' she countered, 'there were five thousand people at his funeral.' We both laughed at our absurdities, and went back to work. So—"

"My mother gave me a nickel/to buy a pickle/I didn't buy a pickle/ I bought some chewin' gum/chew-chew-chew-chewin' gum/oh, how I love chewin' gum—"

Noel in the first limousine was singing a tune he remembered from his childhood. How strange that those words are so clear to me now, he thought. I haven't thought of that song in twenty-five years. His daughter stared at him. His son was looking out the window at some people he knew. Mrs. Golden was in the second limousine with Mr. Golden and friends of theirs. Mrs. Golden seemed somewhat more composed. She rested her head against a cushion the director had provided for her, and, eyes tightly shut, was shaking her head from side to side, as if the very act of what she was doing could erase the events of the last few days.

"How are you feeling, Mama?" Mr. Golden asked her. She continued to shake her head from side to side. "Mama-Mama," he pleaded. "Mama, Mama, please stop—" Mr. Golden tried to hold her face in his hands but she pushed him away. She sobbed, "It is my fault— my fault—"

Don Zacharia

The Fruneds and the Radcliffs were in the third limousine. Lois, for the first time had started to cry, but now was trying to compose herself.

"I can't believe," Phoebe said to Phil, "what we were doing just two nights ago while we were waiting for Susan to come home." She sobbed into her handkerchief, "Oh, Phil, I feel so awful. Will I ever be able to forgive myself?"

Phil shook his head. "It seems like it was a lifetime ago that we were at Noel's waiting for Susan to come home." He reached for Phoebe's hand. "It doesn't seem like two days ago."

"I feel awful," Phoebe cried. Her eyes bloodshot, there was no hiding the despair that showed on her face.

"Noel seems to be taking it well," George said.

"I don't think so," Lois said quietly. "I think something has happened to him. I think he is acting very strangely."

Phil nodded. He looked out of the window at some kids throwing a ball against a wall. "I have a feeling you're right."

For a time, Noel thought he would faint. It was blazing hot. Two black men, a Puerto Rican, and a white man with skeleton-like fingers lowered the coffin into the ground. The way they were straining, you had a feeling it was heavier than most. There were hundreds of people standing still. The women dabbed at their faces with handkerchiefs. Dr. Hersey, an old friend of the Goldens, insisted that Mrs. Golden stay in the air-conditioned limousine. It was so quiet—the rabbi chanting the prayer of the dead—that some boys off in the distance, rushing the season, were playing a game of touch football and occasionally a shout could be heard. Lois held a handkerchief to her mouth, feeling she was going to be sick. Phoebe studied the hole in the ground where the coffin had just been lowered, comprehending, but not really; sometimes her mind slipped and she thought she would call Susan that night. Phil was watching Noel, concerned, waiting. The rabbi was chanting. A slight wind came up, giving some relief. Noel looked around to the left and to the right. Something was missing. Something always seemed to be missing. He ran a finger over his lips, enjoying the sensation. What was it? He looked about again. His son, unable to watch, tired of acting like his father, had turned his back on the burial and was studying the people. The rabbi picked up some dirt and dropped it into the hole. It was a movement without sound. He nodded to the man with the skeleton-like fingers, who pushed his spade into a mound of freshly moved earth and then using his foot pushed it farther in. Noel remembered. Noel remembered what it was. In three quick steps he moved to the side of the grave. He looked at the coffin—"Oh—Susan," he cried out. "Oh, my God." The gravediggers were confused. They looked to the rabbi for help. Noel looked up and saw the enemy, the man with his shovel at hip level filled with earth. "Get out of here," Noel hissed. Without warning Noel hit him in the face. The rabbi took a step toward Noel, but Noel's glare stopped him short. "SUSAN—" Noel fell to his knees—"SUSAN, SUSAN, SUSAN, SUSAN—" The name poured from his soul.

What Noel Roth uttered on his knees in front of his wife's opened grave was an anguished diatribe of words and half-words. An inner howl from a part of his mind never touched before. A string of sounds and actions that are forever repressed in most people. Only in the inner wards of psychiatric hospitals could you hear such unintelligible screeching. He pawed at the ground, clutching dirt and throwing it in back of him as if he were attempting to break down the walls of that neatly dug grave. "SUSAN—SUSAN—SUSAN—SUSAN—SUSAN—" It was babble. Pushed together it became an ugly sound that cracked the stillness like the frantic scream of a starving infant. Phoebe instinctively moved toward Beth and David. She reached out for Beth's hand and at the same time tried to cup David's face into her body. She wanted to shield them from what was taking place, but it was impossible. Everyone watched in terror, not moving, this man rocking back and forth, now on his hands and knees, eyes shut, mouth open, tongue darting in and out, alternately mumbling and screeching unintelligible words. This man with just the beginning of a bald spot. He began to sob—not cry—not droplets of tears that he could wipe away with a finger—but gasping sobs that seemed to emanate from his chest, intermingled with one word that he kept screaming. "SUSAN—SUSAN—SUSAN—SUSAN—" A lifetime of stored water washed his face, ran down his chin, his neck, which seemed strained to the bursting point. Some men shook their heads, grateful that it was not them, ashamed for themselves at Noel's weakness. His face was caked with dirt. Noel was gasping. He began to choke. He tried to scream but no sound came forth. He pushed his fingers into his mouth, shoving a nail into his throat. He coughed violently and felt a rush of air enter his lungs. He coughed blood into his hands. "Susan, Susan," he sobbed.

Phil came forward. He picked Noel up and held him. Noel collapsed into his arms, sobbing softly into his shoulder. Phil just stood there, his arms around Noel. Two men. In the distance you could still hear sounds from the football game. That and Noel's sobbing were the only sounds. Finally Phil said, "Come on, Noel, let's go home." He led Noel down a grassy hill. Noel, blinded by his tears, his mind stripped, allowed himself to be led. Phil opened the car door and took him home.

The crowd left quickly, silently, anxious to get home. The rabbi spoke to the gravedigger Noel had hit, and as best as he could, apologized for Noel's actions. The cars, which had driven up in such neat formation, lights on, scattered. Some men went back to work. It was still early enough in the day to get in a round of golf, and some men did that. When everybody had left, the gravediggers began filling in the hole. It took no time at all. There was one person left who stood watching them. Sergeant Walter Rudd.

In a camera store on Forty-Second Street, for $29.95, Walter had bought a miniature camera disguised as a cigarette lighter. Every time he pressed the lighter in the middle, a flame came out of the top, but it also took a picture from the side. With an unlit pipe in his mouth, Walter spent the entire morning taking pictures of everybody and everything he could. As Walter had told the chief, something wasn't meeting his eye.

SHIVA

It was Thursday, the day after Susan was buried. The deli man said in his day he had seen some orders, but this was the number two of all time, topped only when H.D. the movie mogul died, and how could you compare H.D. the movie mogul to poor Susan Golden Roth?

Phoebe and Lois did the ordering. Noel wasn't doing anything but trying to understand how his wife could be dead and the whole world be alive. Phoebe and Lois ordered fifty pounds nova, twenty pounds sturgeon, four turkeys, four roast beefs, one hundred rye breads, eighty dozen mixed bagels, some with seeds and some without, two meat loaves with garlic and two meat loaves without garlic. Besides that, a lot of people brought over a lot of fruit, and a lot of people brought over a lot of cakes and pastries, and a lot of other people brought food that they themselves had cooked. It was all laid out on the dining-room table, and everyone was standing around eating roast-beef sandwiches and lox and bagels and drinking. Some other people were sitting wherever chairs were available, with paper plates balanced delicately on their knees. The local police were directing traffic. Everyone was there.

Noel got off the toilet, buttoned his pants and washed his hands. Downstairs there were five hundred people in his home. He walked into his son's room. David was watching TV, an old "Star Trek."

"I've seen this one six times," David said to his father.

"You must know the ending."

"Yes. I've never seen so many people in the house."

"It's a tradition, an old one."

David flicked the TV stations around and settled back with "Star Trek." "Do you want to sit up here with me and watch?"

"I'd like that very much but I can't. I have to go downstairs. Can I bring you a sandwich?"

"No. There's nothing there I like."

"God."

Downstairs his home was filled to capacity with people eating and drinking and laughing and talking. Everyone was very solicitous of Noel. As he moved from room to room people would press back clearing a path for him. Noel felt like the Pope. There were an awful lot of people there whose faces looked familiar, but names he didn't know. Every room was packed. Noel wondered why they came. Someone asked him if he had eaten and he said no, and they said he should eat because now he had to fill two roles. Noel moved on, confused by that. People smiled at him, saying things with their eyes that he couldn't understand. He was confused by that also. Lots of people asked him if they could get him a sandwich.

"Do you want a chicken liver and onion, Noel?"

"No, thank you."

"It's important that you should eat."

He moved on.

"Can I fix you something?" a friend asked.

"Keep your health up," someone else said, whose name he didn't know. "There's only you now. You have to be both a mother and a father now."

Noel blinked. "How long does this last?" Noel asked Phil.

"Seven days. It's a tradition."

"God." He moved on.

"Did you eat something?" someone asked Noel.

"Fuck off."

Noel went into the kitchen. It was a beehive of activity.

"We're out of CCL," someone shouted.

"Above the phone, two down from the vet's number and one up from frig repairs is the deli. Call him and ask him to deliver—oh, shit—how much?—at least—oh, shit—at least one hundred pounds CCL and more rye bread."

"If he doesn't use it," someone else said, "he can always freeze it."

Someone spotted Noel. "Hi yuh, Noelie, how you doin'?"

"What's CCL?"

"I think, Noel, people should start leaving so the people who are waiting outside could start coming in. I think there should be a time limit on how long certain people stay. I think that people that really knew you and Susan should be allowed to stay, but the others should only stay for five minutes so other people could come in."

"There is no flow," a tall, rangy girl whom Noel had never seen in his life said.

"What's CCL?" Noel asked. They looked at him unfamiliarly. Could it be that he was in the wrong house? "What's CCL?"

"Chopped chicken liver."

"Oh." Noel went into the dining room. Someone was doing a magic trick making a quarter disappear.

"Noel, did you eat something?"

"Yes. I had a sturgeon and lox and CCL triple decker with onion and lettuce and tomato and a glass of milk."

"Do you want something else?"

"No, thank you."

"Watch the quarter. Watch the quarter, watch very, very carefully."

"How are you, Noel?"

Don Zacharia

"Watch it closely."

"I miss Susan."

Someone shut the radio off. The toilet flushed. A dog barked and wouldn't stop.

"There. Where's the quarter now?"

It went on that way, all day and all night. Everyone showed. It was even more hectic and crowded in the evening. "I can't stand it any more." Noel was talking to Lois.

"George and I rented a house on Fire Island. After this is over, why don't you take the children and go out there for a few days. It's very quiet and it might help you get everything in perspective."

"I can't stand it anymore."

"Did you eat?"

"I can't stand it anymore."

There were so many people in his home that evening that Noel felt its very seams giving way.

The young rabbi was there and he was talking to a group of people about the one time in his life Moses found it necessary to use physical force.

Noel was pressed into a corner of his den.

"You got a match?" someone asked him.

"I can't stand it anymore."

"Are you Noel Roth? You are Noel Roth. I want to tell you I'm really sorry for what happened."

A man and a woman Noel didn't recognize were talking. Perhaps they were neighbors. He listened in on their conversation.

"It's the worst thing I've ever heard of in my life," the woman said.

"Better him than me," the man said.

"I wonder how he feels? Inside, I wonder how he feels?"

"Pretty awful, I guess."

"What shame," the woman said. "What disgrace. How will he ever be able to hold his head up again? What a poor man."

"Like I said, better him than me. I'm going for another drink. You want something?"

"No. Yes. I suppose. See if someone will make me a martini."

Noel looked for the door. He couldn't breathe. An elbow hit him in the chest. A woman brushed his leg. Noel couldn't stand it anymore.

It was a disaster. Everyone panicked except Noel's son. He knew exactly what to do because Noel and Susan had rehearsed it with him many times. As soon as the alarm went off, David, cool as a cucumber, opened his bedroom window, climbed out on the garage roof, gracefully leaped to the tree growing nicely alongside the garage and shimmied to the ground. Standing there with gleaming eyes and a slightly bloodied knee, he kept urging people not to panic and to move away from the house in case there was an explosion.

When everyone was out of the house, Noel, feeling better, locked the doors, shut the alarm off, poured himself a scotch and waited for the firemen. He let them in when they came, relocked the door, and invited them all into the den: ten firemen, two patrolmen and Sergeant Rudd.

"Hello," Noel said, smiling at Sergeant Rudd. "It's nice to see you again."

"Mr. Roth, your alarm system went off." He was staring at Noel. He pulled a small notebook and pencil out and waited. Everyone seemed terribly bewildered.

"Would you gentlemen like something to eat? A sturgeon sandwich, turkey, CCL, anything—?"

"Mr. Roth, your alarm system went off. There are five hundred people on your front lawn—"

"How about some beers?" Noel stood up, remembering.

"No," Sergeant Rudd said. He sounded like he meant business. "I don't mean to belabor a point—" he tapped his notebook with his pencil—"but a series of events seems to be taking place here that I intend to get to the bottom of. When your alarm went off in headquarters, two fire trucks and two police cars came here at speed r–e–d."

Don Zacharia

"Speed red?"

"That's a police term; Speed red, speed blue, speed pink, it describes the approximate speed the vehicle should use in getting to the destination." He paused here as if lost in thought over what he had just said. "Speed red is a fast speed endangering the lives of the officers who are driving the vehicles and endangering the lives of pedestrians."

There was some shuffling about and some of the other officers nodded solemnly. There was one who was kind of grinning, though. "I set the alarm off, Sergeant, because I wanted to get all those people out of my house. I'm sorry. I didn't think you would all come." Noel swept his hand around the room. "I thought you only dealt in missing persons."

"Mr. Roth," Sergeant Rudd said in a sharp voice, hitting his notebook with a pencil, "if I put that in this notebook, it would set off a series of events that might lead to your indictment."

"God." Noel was immediately sorry for his choice of a word. "What I meant to say, Sergeant, was that I thought I smelled gas." Noel nodded toward the basement. "You know my wife—" he lowered his voice and looked at his shoes—"my wife was a sculptor and stored gas tanks in the basement that she used in her work. I worry about those gas tanks a lot. Soon as I get a chance I'm going to have them taken out before they blow the house up. I thought I smelled gas and because I feared an explosion with all those people in my home, I turned the alarm system on."

"I'm sorry, Mr. Roth." The six patrolmen nodded almost in unison. Two of the men disappeared toward the basement. The sergeant kept writing in his notebook for what seemed to be an awfully long time, although he never did turn the page. Noel watched him closely.

When they finally left, satisfied with Noel's story, Noel insisted that they all go with bags filled with rye breads, turkeys, roast beefs and everything until the kitchen was nearly bare of food. Noel let them out, even more bewildered than when they came in. Loaded down with tons of groceries, it would have been a hell of a number if they had to draw their guns. Most of the people had gone home, but there were still about a hundred of them milling about the front lawn killing his grass. Noel motioned to Phoebe to come in.

"Noel, what the fuck is going on?" Phoebe said wildly. "What were those policemen carrying?"

"I'm taking the children to Fire Island tomorrow morning. Lois has offered me her house—"

"There will be people coming here. You have to sit shiva six more days."

Noel leaned over and kissed her forehead. "Phoebe, I can't help that. I can't stand this anymore. I can't handle it. It is not what I am. It is not what Susan was. Make up a story. Tell them I had a nervous collapse. Tell them whatever you want. Tell them to go to the Roxy instead."

The next morning as the ferry slipped into its slip, Noel saw Nevers for the first time. Standing so casually, waiting for someone, Noel wished for the moment that it was him. Every turn of her head, every gust of wind, caused her bright red hair to become even more disarrayed. Noel tried to catch her eye, but no luck. What a beauty. She was wearing an old fashioned man's T-shirt cut out at the armpits, with thin shoulder straps, and the skimpiest bikini bottom. Watching her breasts slip about, more exposed than not, Noel had the feeling that at any moment she was going to take her T-shirt off and casually start fondling her nipples. She was causing quite a commotion on the ferry. How nice, Noel thought, if she was waiting for me. "Welcome to Fire Island," someone in back of Noel said.

Noel and the children were the last people off the ferry and Noel walked over to her. She was still intently peering at the ferry and Noel had the feeling that a thousand men had walked over to her like Noel, looking for that one really smart line, letting her know that they were different. "Hi," Noel said. She didn't even turn her head to see who was talking to her. Noel thought it might be a practiced response. "There is no one left on the ferry. We are the last people off, so if you are waiting for someone, they are not on this ferry."

"Thanks," she said, still not looking at Noel.

"My mother died the day before yesterday," David said.

"Jesus." Beth smacked David in the head. "You don't have to tell the world."

David looked hurt. "Let's go," Noel said. They started to walk. She caught up with them at the grocery store.

"Hey, kid," she spoke to David. "You want to pull my wagon?"

Walter Rudd was on the ferry also. Rudd had two weeks' vacation coming, not that Fire Island was the kind of place that he would normally go to, but Walter Rudd had made a decision. He was going to tail Noel Roth and see what came of it. Wearing a sweatshirt he had bought on Fourteenth Street with the words LOVE and PEACE printed across the front, a cap that made him look like Lenin, and a fake beard and mustache, he had gotten off the ferry before Noel and the children and was frantically trying to reload his cigarette lighter. He had taken only two pictures of Noel talking to the girl before his film ran out. "Damn," Rudd mumbled, angry at himself for not having checked his camera before the ferry landed. "There's certainly something going on here that doesn't meet my eye."

SEXUAL ABERRATIONS

Nevers. I met Nevers in Fire Island, two days after Susan was buried. Nice. That night I s'd her c. on the beach. Nice. I told my kids I was taking a walk. My son wanted to join me. His mother forty-eight hours dead, and my son wants to join me for a walk on the beach, and I told him no. Nice. I told him I felt like being alone and tomorrow I would take a walk with him. Nice. I met Nevers by arrangement at the end of the boardwalk. We walked for no more than five minutes on the beach. She was barefoot and I was wearing loafers that I took off and carried. Nevers was wearing the same top that had caused all the commotion when the ferry docked and a silky wraparound skirt that flashed open when she walked. Once my hand touched the silkiness of her skirt, sending a shiver through me. We walked to the dune and I sat down. I trickled some sand through my fingers. Had I done this before? There was a quarter moon hanging behind some clouds.

Don Zacharia

Nevers was standing above me. I don't think we said ten words to each other. "This will make you feel better," she said. She lifted her skirt up, and with nothing else on, legs apart, pushed her c. into my mouth. Nice. I mean, really, nice. I should be sitting shiva but instead this is what I was doing. Nice. I hadn't even held her hand. I looked up. Nevers had pulled her T-shirt above her breasts and was pulling on each nipple. She pushed my head back down and with one hand holding the back of my head was rotating her hips and rubbing her c. over my lips. She told me after that my mouth was shut tight. I don't remember. I don't know what I was feeling at that moment. I have thought about it a million times since, but I don't know. I know only one thing. I wasn't pushing her away. I wasn't leaving.

"Open your mouth," Nevers told me, "and put your tongue out." I did. "Don't you feel better already?" She dropped her skirt over my head. "Stop moving your head," she ordered. She held my head in its place, buried in her groin, pushing her c. all over my face, so hard that I had difficulty breathing. The amount of stuff flowing from her c. was unbelievable. My mouth and face and nose and eyes were filled with it.

"Keep your tongue as stiff as you can. I'll do the rest," she moaned. She did. Running her soppy clitoris over my rigid tongue, she came. There was nothing quiet or subdued about it. Anyone walking on the beach would have been aware of what was going on and Nevers couldn't have cared less. The entire time she was coming she was talking to me, telling me exactly what she was feeling, "I feel so good, baby, so fucking good; you are making my c. feel so good. Yes, right there with your tongue—hold it stiff—let me move on it—don't move your head—I'm beginning to come—right now—I feel it beginning— my nipples are as hard as diamonds—oh, Jesus—oh, sweet Jesus, I love being sucked like this. I love a man like you to suck me like this."

Her movements slowed. I was in another world, imprisoned by her legs, her dress over my head creating a memory I couldn't grasp; aware for the first time that my hands were touching the sides of her thighs; I didn't want it to end. Yes, she was right, I was feeling better.

106

Nevers moved away from me, running a hand through her hair. "You're ready for more, aren't you?"

I couldn't answer, trying to collect myself. She reached out and pulled me up and began kissing my lips, cleaning my face and mouth with her tongue and lips. It was the first time that I kissed Nevers on the lips. Nice. If I could tell Phil about it I know what he would say. A stiff cock (tongue) has no conscience.

I reached for Nevers, thinking that she would at least do for me what I had done for her.

"Forget it," she said, reading my mind and pushing me away. She kissed me once more, taking my tongue into her mouth and sucking on it in soft round movements, creating sensations in my throat and chest. "You have had all I could possibly give you. I have to go now. Why don't you go home to your children? Goodbye."

She left over the dune. I stumbled after her, holding my shoes in one hand, slipping to one knee as I fell in the sand. She was gone. That's how I met Nevers. Nice, isn't it?

I didn't see Nevers until two nights later, and then it was only because I went looking for her. It was late, after midnight, and I went to one of the two bars by the dock, and there she was with a bunch of gays. I watched her for a while. She was the center of everything, dancing wildly and beautifully, gracefully, with five or six men at a time. Everyone was looking at her. I don't think I have ever seen anyone who appeared to be having such a good time as Nevers was that evening. She came over to talk to me.

"When are you going back?"

"Tomorrow."

"Goodbye."

She started to leave but I grabbed her arm. "What's your last name?"

"Forget it. Let go of my arm."

I did. "I'd like to see you again, very much."

"How much?"

"Very much."

"Did you like what happened the other night?"

Don Zacharia

"Yes . . . very much."

"What's your phone number?"

"I'll write it down."

"Don't write it down. Just tell me."

I did.

"I'll call you in a month, perhaps."

She rejoined her friends. I watched her for a while and then I left. The last week of September Nevers called. I had been thinking of her and what took place a thousand times. She was very brief and to the point on the phone. She didn't ask how I was or anything but asked if I wanted to see her and when I told her yes she gave me her address in Greenwich Village. "Monday at eight. Don't be late." She hung up.

IN THE WOODS

Just a week after Susan died, Phoebe, who always knew what the right thing to do was, spoke to Noel about the Psychiatry Center in Culver. It was after Noel came back from Fire Island, and instead of going to work each morning, the way he was supposed to, he took a chair deep into the woods behind his house and spent the days there.

It was early September, 1973, a rich, lush autumn: sun-drenched days with cool brisk evenings, a welcome relief from the tedious August humidity. The nation was ablaze with the trapping of Richard Milhous Nixon. Not a day could slip by without a new revelation, a new disclosure, a new scandal, a new charge, a new defense. Noel, to the bewilderment of everyone who saw him in those days immediately after Susan's death, became a Nixonite, a defender of the President. Out of deference to what he had just been through, no one, mostly Phil and Phoebe because that's about the only people who saw him, debated or challenged him, but listened in con-

Don Zacharia

fusion to this lifelong liberal, defender of the underprivileged, suddenly spring to the aid of the liberals' enemy of all time. Phil took it harder than Phoebe. "It's like Golda Meir defending Hitler," he said, confused by his friend's abrupt philosophical change. Phoebe just shook her head. Susan had abhorred Nixon, felt that he represented everything evil about America, and Phoebe thought that Noel's retreat into the woods and sudden passion for Nixon wasn't such a big deal. "It's his way of showing anger at Susan," she told Phil. "Buying that absurd coffin was the same thing. And besides," she went on, "he's first sitting shiva, for himself and, in some strange way, for Nixon." On the surface, Phoebe, as always, appeared to be in control. Certainly, compared to Phil, it seemed that way. Phil was brooding so darkly, you would have thought it was *his* wife who was killed, not his best friend's.

It wasn't as if Noel sat in the woods each day with his chin in his chest, nonverbal, with eyes that wouldn't focus. If anything, Noel was fairly lively back there. He read newspapers and weekly magazines, threw rocks at the trees, pawed at the ground with his feet, digging shallow holes that he always covered up and smoothed over with his hands. He read Nixon's *Six Crises*, making voluminous notes as he went along. He had a little portable radio with fading batteries and he would listen to the news all day. It was not unusual to find Noel with Nixon's book open upon his lap, radio pressed to his ear with his left hand, and with the right hand making notes about some obscure passage. He talked to Phoebe and Phil whenever they came over, which was often; and his children, Beth and David, would individually come back to spend time with him after school. Beth, who was thirteen and pretty sophisticated, thought her father's spending every day like that was weird. That's what she told her friend Anne-Jane. Since her mother died, Beth was receiving a lot of attention from a lot of different people who felt compelled to *say* or *do* something but didn't quite know how to do either. So they just fussed over her, brought her things, mostly underwear, and offered to drive her to the library.

"I have enough underwear," she told Noel in the woods, "to last me three lifetimes, especially pastel ones with little flowers. It's almost, Noel—" she started to call him Noel right after Susan was killed—"that every pair of panties has a message connected to it. Do all those people think that Mom left me with empty drawers?"

Noel felt awkward with his daughter in those days and weeks after Susan's death. He listened carefully to what she was saying, more aware of her torment than he was of his own, but having no idea how to deal with either.

"Everybody keeps telling me," Beth said that afternoon, "that I have to grow up in a hurry."

"What the hell does that mean?"

"I don't know. I was going to ask you. You're the parent. First they tell me that I have to grow up in a hurry, then they ask me if I want to go to the library, then they give me a pair of underpants, then they leave."

"In that order?"

"Yup."

Noel smiled. He looked at Beth. First children. What enormous pleasure she had given him. Firstborns should always be daughters. It works better that way. Memories of tucking Beth into bed wearing a nightshirt three times too big flooded his mind. "I have given you a classic daughter," Susan once told him. It occurred to Noel, looking at his beautiful daughter that lovely fall afternoon, three weeks to the day that his wife and her mother were killed under circumstances *so bizarre* that he had difficulty even *thinking* about it, that all was not lost.

David, his eleven-year-old son, didn't think there was anything weird about his father's spending all day in the woods by himself. He confided to him, that *years ago*, he said, he used to do the same thing. As sophisticated and playful as Beth appeared to be, David was serious. It unnerved Noel that an eleven-year-old, whose basic concern should be dribbling a basketball, should be so damn serious. It had nothing to do with Susan's death. David was always serious. When David was three he was serious. He complained to Susan about it more than once.

Don Zacharia

"Do you know what we should do?" David said to his father after school. "We should live here."

"We do live here, Dave." David had plopped himself down on the ground in front of Noel. Noel was glad to see him.

"I mean we should sleep here, right here, in the woods, tonight, with sleeping bags. You and me."

"Oh, David. I think we would get eaten alive. In the morning when they found us we would be two big mosquito bites."

"Beth wouldn't like that, would she?"

"Christ, no."

"Or maybe she would."

He was, everyone said, the image of Noel, and when Noel looked at pictures of himself as a young boy, he was pleased by the resemblance. If only he wasn't always so serious. "I'll tell you what we'll do; later on we'll go camping, real camping."

"When later on?"

"In a couple of months."

"In a couple of months it will be winter, and if you won't camp out now because of mosquitoes, what will you do in the cold winter when it snows?"

"We'll go someplace where it isn't winter. We'll go to California or to Florida. You, Beth and me."

"You promise?"

"I promise."

"You won't break your promise?"

"Have I ever?"

"You double promise."

"I double promise. I double-double promise. We'll pitch a tent by some river and go for long walks and hikes in the woods. We'll find a place where no person has ever been before and carve our names in the trunk of an oak tree. That will be our space. Each day we will have to be careful so that we don't get lost. That will be your job, Daverino. At nighttime we'll all sleep in one big tent. We'll catch fish, big fish, big delicious trout that we'll broil over charcoal—shit, David, the trouble is you hate fish—I *mean* hate, double hate, double-double hate fish—"

112

"I'll eat fish," David said, his eyes gleaming. "Like that I'll eat fish. I bet Beth won't. I bet Beth won't even come."

"Sure she will. What is she going to do? Stay over at Aunt Phoebe's? That's a laugh."

David made a face. He thought Phoebe, Aunt Phoebe as both he and Beth called her, was much too strict. Whenever Susan used to get mad at David or Beth, she would threaten them with sending them over to Aunt Phoebe's to live for a week. "She'll straighten you out." It was a standard line.

"How's school?" Noel asked, changing the topic.

"It's OK. It's different than what it was before mom died."

"How?"

"I don't know. Just different. Ask Beth. She thinks so too."

"You know, I'm glad you come to visit me like this."

David shook his head, not understanding. "What do you mean?"

"I mean, I look forward to you visiting me. I look at my watch around two o'clock and I say to myself in another hour or so old Daverino is going to be here, and that pleases me."

David smiled and stood up. "I gotta be going." He leaned over and kissed his father. "I'll be back at five or so. Will you be here?"

"Sure."

David gone from the woods, Noel wiped a tear away. Noel Roth took stock. I am left with a classic daughter, a too-serious son, a couple of damn fine friends in Phoebe and Phil, a dog, no, not a dog, we gave him away, and—

So it happened that Phoebe came into the woods to talk to Noel about the psychiatry center that she wanted him and the children to go to. Since the funeral Phoebe had been a good friend, supportive of Noel, but not interfering. She saw to it that the Roth household continued to run on a daily basis, hired and fired a housekeeper (too young), checked the expiration dates on the cottage cheese and yogurt, and did a thousand other things that make up the everyday scheme of a suburban household.

Her days since Susan's death were filled with Susan's family. She told herself more than once that *her* family unit was intact. Was that not the core? Was that not what counts? Losing your best friend—who even thinks of something like that? She knew that in her lifetime she would never have another friendship like she had with Susan, and now, mysteriously, stupidly, without form or reason or direction, it was over. Susan's death was so inappropriate; so without the hint of any redeeming qualities that it was impossible for Phoebe to deal with it. And to Phoebe's credit, she realized that if she felt that way, what about Noel, Beth, David? Why, logically, Phoebe thought, should it matter how one dies? They're dead, aren't they? Dead is dead. There're no shadings. Better Susan should have been murdered, a car accident, suicide, God, yes, suicide. Suicide seemed glorious in comparison to how Susan died.

It's crazy, Phoebe thought, really crazy, but in the long run it's going to be me who suffers the most. In years yet to come, when Noel, Beth and David will be leading normal lives, it will be me who still longs for Susan; me who still yearns for her company. The nicest moments of my life were not spent with my husband or sons, but with my girlfriend. Ugh. What a piece of shit that word is. Girlfriend! Friend! Pal? Confidante? The English language is sometimes lacking. Lover? Yes, lover. I loved her. Yes. What's wrong with that?

Last spring Phoebe and Susan were having lunch in a Soho café before going to a museum to see an art exhibit, and Phoebe, flushed by the spring day, the California wine they had just finished, the keen looks of admiration they were both getting, told Susan in the middle of a conversation about primitive art that she loved her. That's just the way she said it, just out of the blue, "I love you, Susan Roth. I love you."

Susan said nothing.

"Am I blushing?" Phoebe said, picking up the conversation after a long pause. "My face feels warm, as if I have had too much wine and sun."

Later, in the museum, Susan reached out for Phoebe's hand and they walked through the exhibit holding hands the entire time, getting more than one misinterpreting stare.

Susan and Phoebe had two totally different relationships with each other. One in conjunction with Noel and Phil: they were suburban wives and mothers, playful, cunning, sensitive, involved, sexy, sophisticated. They shopped at the local grocery store, carpooled, wore the right clothing, got mildly involved in the PTA, scouting, town politics and gossip. They did the things society expected of them. The other relationship, that very special bond the two women had with each other, wasn't so easy to define; wasn't so boxlike in definition. By local contemporary standards, they were much *too* close to be *just* friends. Phoebe smiled, thinking about it. How they used to laugh at all those absurd rumors. More than anything, they had a friendship that to the two of them (especially Phoebe) was the mainstay of their lives.

Susan worked in her studio each morning. Up at seven, she made a quick breakfast for the children (Noel fended for himself), and by seven forty-five was downstairs working. Noel, grumbling, would come down before he went to work, drinking a cup of coffee he wasn't pleased with. Noel never said it, but looking at his wife at eight in the morning wearing a welder's mask and blasting away at some distorted piece of metal with an acetylene torch wasn't exactly the way he had planned his life. He never stayed too long. Susan was aware of his hostility, and never made it easy for him. She worked all morning, and at one o'clock on the button Phoebe came sweeping into Susan's studio. It was always a grand entrance—her arms filled with lunch, glassware and dishes, a bottle of wine, a book they were both reading. Phoebe had a way with food. Given some basic ingredients, the results were always astonishing. They kissed, both cheeks, and Susan, her eyes dancing with pleasure at the sight of her friend, started cleaning up. Lunch was always elegant: cloth napkins, a tablecloth spread over Susan's workbench, the best dishes, expensive goblets, good wines, Meursaults or Pulignys. Occasionally, for no reason, champagne. It was an incongruous scene. Susan's studio looked like a World War Two battlefield: bales of barbed wire and lead pipes scattered about,

Don Zacharia

the floor covered with remnants of past work, blobs of cement, pieces of metal kicked into the corner, old newspapers, used acetylene tanks, and into this disarray Phoebe came feeling like Mother Mercy. Afternoon in Susan's studio was the highlight of each day. Phoebe remembered leaving with a feeling of intoxication, not from the wine, but just the stimulation of spending those two hours with Susan. Oh, could those two women, so dissimilar yet with similar husbands, talk, exchange ideas and thoughts and dreams; some realized, some never.

And now? Susan is dead. Killed by a Westinghouse air conditioner. I can't measure it, Phoebe thought. It is beyond absurdity. A practical joke being played by—by whom? By those who still live? Where is my salvation? My relief? How do I mourn? By seeing to it that Noel's refrigerator is defrosting properly? Does Noel realize that Susan spent more time with me than with him? Does Noel know that Susan spoke to me more than him? What makes him special? Because he slept with her? Hah, what a laugh that is. Does Noel know that Susan loved me more than— Should I tell him? Don't upset his apple cart. One mustn't fuck around with Noelie swinging from the trees in the woods. Oh, Susan, how did such a thing happen to *us*? An air conditioner? Meyer Meyerson? I could cry. What kind of gross miscalculation is that? What a bummer.

Noel was wearing what he wore every day: dungarees, sneakers and a tan V-neck cashmere sweater with no shirt under it. He looked, Phoebe thought, better than ever; better than anyone. It's a joke, a joke. Everything reversed, fucked around. He was holding the portable radio to his ear and shaking his head, obviously unhappy with what he was hearing. Putting the radio on his lap, he clicked it off.

"I need new batteries."

"How are you, Noelie?" Phoebe forced a smile.

"Personally, I'm pretty good, pretty good. Do you know what

just happened, Phoebe? Senator Weicker, that liberal bitch from
Connecticut, just said that for the good of the country Nixon should
resign. He said that it will save the nation. The only thing that's
going to save this fucking nation is if everyone will forget Water-
gate and leave Nixon alone and go about their business. There's
going to be a bandwagon, Phoebe, a regular bandwagon, and
they're going to railroad that poor slob right out of office."

Temporary insanity, Phoebe thought. Susan, who had despised
Nixon from his early California days, would croak if she could hear
Noel today. Phoebe knew she was going to have a tough time
convincing Noel about the Center she wanted him and the children
to attend, and she wasn't wrong. She explained to Noel what the
Center was all about; that they were specialists in dealing with
survivors, preferring to work with the family unit. She told Noel
how important it was that the children, now, not six months from
now, but right now, receive professional help; that the kind of
trauma they had been through needed immediate attention, and
the Center, she emphasized, had remarkable success in the field of
bereavement therapy.

Noel didn't appear to be impressed. "It sounds to me," he said,
"that people with a problem should go there."

Phoebe stared at him, not sure if he was kidding or not. "A lot of
people think you should go there, Noelie."

"Yeah, like who?"

"Lois, me, Phil, the rabbi—"

"The rabbi," snorted Noel. "The rabbi doesn't know me from a
pisshole in the snow. What the hell he's got to say or do about
anything?"

Phoebe changed tactics. She knew that normally Noel, unlike
Phil, didn't object to therapy or analysis. Susan had gone for years,
and Noel was receptive to it. It was just that at this time of his life,
the thought of leaving these woods for *any* reason was more than
he could deal with. By the time Phoebe left him that afternoon,
they compromised. Phoebe was going to go ahead and make ap-
pointments for the children at the Center and take care of the

driving. If at some later date Noel decided to go on his own, fine. Noel agreed. It was all Phoebe was expecting. As soon as Phoebe was gone, Noel put the radio on and pressed it to his ear.

Nothing changed. Noel stayed in the woods. If Noel missed anything in those days it was the springer they had given away in June. In the stillness of the woods, touching last year's leaves, sensing but not seeing the way the sun's shadows played with the foliage, sometimes Noel imagined that the dog was still with him, next to him, sleeping on his side with his eyes half open and his legs tucked in. Noel, reaching down, could almost pet him. Almost.

Phil saw Noel every day. He tried to get Noel to come over to their house for dinner, or go to a movie, or play golf, or go for a walk, or *anything*, but Noel just kept putting him off, smiling strangely and saying maybe later, maybe later. After a while Phil stopped asking. He would come by and lean up against a tree while Noel sat in his beach chair, and the two of them would remain like that for as long as thirty minutes without a word being said. To Phil, it was dreadful.

One day, breaking a long silence, Noel told Phil in a rambling voice that at times became incoherent and close to tears and other times was like a machine gun, spewing words out in such rapid fashion that they spilled over each other, "Do you know the thing that I think about the most, Phil? That basketball game in high school where I scored thirty-one points. I think about it constantly. I remember the game in detail: every shot I took; where I took it from; every point I scored. I lie awake at night and think about that game and I get goose flesh. *It's like that one singular adolescent event was the zenith of my life.* And here I am, a grown man with two children and stuck in these woods. Do you know why I am stuck in these woods? I'll tell you why, old pal, old buddy. Because I need Susan to tell me how to get out. My values are fucked up, Phil. I need an audience to achieve satisfaction. I have the best men's clothing stores in the state; why does that not please me?

Why was I more excited by Susan's minor successes as an artist than my major successes as a businessman? Can I tell you something weird, Phil, really weird? I have watched a lot of professional basketball games. I have never seen anybody with the exception of the centers, guys like Chamberlain and Jabbar don't count, I have never seen anybody make fifteen in a row. Even Jerry West, Phil. I saw Bradley make eleven in a row but then he missed from the corner and lemme tell you when he got to ten in a row I put the whammy on him. Now how can that be? How can I have done it and not them? I'm so afraid, Phil. I'm afraid, Phil, that when I come out of these woods I won't know how to react; I won't know what to do. My life was so patterned. I did the same thing every day and every night. What do I do now? It's hard for me to even think of Susan and how she died. I think of everything but I don't think of that. Why couldn't she have died normally? Why that way? Why suddenly is the world aware of Noel and Susan Roth? It's like the grand joke of all time: Susan Roth cuckolds her husband on prime time TV. Do you know why I can't get out of these woods? Because I am humiliated. *Because I am screwed to pieces with what Susan did to me.* The few times I walk on the street, when people see me they cross the street or hide behind trees to avoid me. I swear to God, Phil. How do you think that makes me feel? Me. How can this have happened to me?

"Can I tell you something terrible? The worst fucking thing you have ever heard in your life, Phil." Noel's voice took on a harsh piercing sound. "I didn't do it, but I've thought about it a thousand times, a million times. I wanted to call the coroner and ask him if he could determine if Susan had intercourse before she was killed. I thought of all kinds of fancy reasons for asking the question. I even dialed his number twice but hung up. That's what I think of, Phil. Every day, that's all I think about. I think of having Susan's body brought up and having a coroner check her cunt for sperm samples. Now are you happy? Are you pleased? Are you better off that I've told you? Are you going to tell Phoebe? Will it please her?

"Do you know what I did forty-eight hours after Susan's funeral?

Don Zacharia

I sucked a woman's cunt. Can you believe that, Phil?" Noel sobbed. "Can you believe anything as scummy as that? I think about that and I think about Susan, and I can't believe what I did, but Jesus Christ, Phil, I did. I met a woman the first day on Fire Island and that night I sucked her *cunt*. That's how I mourned, by taking a cunt into my mouth. Isn't that nice? What a piece of garbage I am. A pile of *crap*. What do I do now, Phil? What do I do when I come out of these woods? How do I do it? I am out of control. Can you understand that? What do I do? How do I survive? Why is this happening to me?"

Phil winced with each sentence. Phil, who by his own admission was not an introspective person and liked dealing with life on black-and-white levels, found Noel's monologue more difficult to handle than his silence.

Nothing changed. Noel stayed in the woods. Not true. One thing did change. David bought him four new batteries for his portable radio, and using a dime, they unscrewed the back, and with David telling him how to do it, he inserted the four batteries, plus to plus, minus to minus, put the radio back together and put it on.

"Jesus, David," Noel said, confused by the loud music exploding from the radio, "it works."

David smiled, was pleased. "Mr. Pearson," referring to the owner of the local stationery store, "said they will last two thousand hours. I think he was kidding. He also asked about you."

"Thanks, pal." He shut the radio off. "When you see him again, tell him I'm doing fine and ask how's he doing."

"He was busy. The place was packed with kids and mothers buying school supplies. But soon as I walked in he noticed me, which I thought was kinda nice, and asked how I was and how you are."

"Well, that was nice of him, noticing you that way. That's because you're a retailer's son."

David thought about that. "You think so?"

"I think so."

"How much money do you think Mr. Pearson makes in September?"

"Jeez, Dave, I don't know."

"More than you?"

"Well, I don't think so. But then he doesn't have thirty-five people working for him."

David nodded, agreeing. "Do you think September is his best month? Bigger than December?"

"It's kind of hard to say. I wouldn't think so. What do you think?"

"I wouldn't think so either. In September it's just one item, school stuff, and it's all at once. In December it's the whole month and it's a lot of different stuff."

Noel shook his head vigorously. What a kid. Christ, he's more serious than ever. "You wanna shoot some baskets with me later? I'll spot you H–O–R."

"Nah. That's not much fun for me. Mrs. Bloom wants to know when you are coming up to the Center?" Mrs. Bloom was the therapist who was working with Beth and David.

"In time. In time. What's she like?"

"She's nice."

"I bet." David, unlike Beth, had no reluctance in talking about his therapy sessions with his father. "Is she bugging you about your dreams yet?"

"I don't dream anymore. I told her that but she says I dream but don't want to remember them for my own reasons."

"Shit," Noel mumbled under his breath. He put the radio on and a recent popular song blared out. "This is going to take some getting used to."

David was lying down and was throwing a rock straight up into the air and catching it. "It plays good, doesn't it, Dad?"

"It plays well."

Beth walked over and kissed her father. "Hiya, Noelie. It plays well," she said again to David. "You bought new batteries?"

"Yup. David got them."

Don Zacharia

"It plays good, doesn't it, Beth?" David said.

Beth looked at him angrily. "Smart ass."

"Come on," Noel said. "What's up, sweetie?"

"Today in American History we had a class vote on Nixon resigning. It was eighteen to six for resignation."

"How'd you vote?" David asked her.

"Resignation."

"I wouldn't have," David said, aware of his father's new political feelings. "I don't think he should resign. I think he should stick it out."

"Terrific, David," Beth said. "That's why they don't have straw ballots in the fifth grade."

"Straw—straw what?"

"Straw ballots," Noel explained to his son. "It's an expression meaning an unofficial vote. It seems to me that the two of you are at each other an awful lot these days."

"You mean since Mother died," Beth snapped.

"Well, yes, I suppose I mean that, Beth."

"Look, I didn't come back here to pick a fight," Beth said, her voice cracking.

"Beth," Noel said gently, "nobody's picking a fight. David, are you picking a fight?"

"Well, maybe it's not David I'm angry at," she sobbed. "It seems to me," there was no hiding the tears now, "that the two of you are getting along just *fine*." With that she fled with one parting cry at David, "Aunt Phoebe is picking us up in ten minutes."

David was still throwing the rock up and catching it. "She's like that all the time these days, Dad. It's like she got a thorn up her ass."

Noel winced at his son's crack. Beth's outburst had totally unsettled him. When David left, he put the radio on, but the volume once again jolted him. I could make it lower, he thought, but he shut it off.

THE CONCORD

It was Phil—not Phoebe, not the Center, not the children—but good old dependable Phil who finally did something about getting Noel out of the woods. Phil Radcliff, Mr. Hard Hat himself, after Noel had spent a month in the woods, went to a psychiatrist.

He saw him Mondays, Tuesdays, Wednesdays and Thursdays at 9 A.M. For Phil, who had spent his life ridiculing psychiatrists and mocking people who went to them, it was a monumental decision. He wasted no time in laying the groundwork. "My best friend's wife was killed under very awkward circumstances a month ago. In my opinion he has stopped functioning and I need help in dealing with him. There is something else."

Phil talked. Oh, did Phil talk. For forty-five minutes a session he talked nonstop telling the doctor everything about his relationship with Noel up to the time of Susan's death; how Noel had reacted at the cemetery; and how since he had come back from Fire Island, he spent each day in the woods in the back of his home, taking no phone calls, not going to work, seeing no one but Phil, Phoebe and the children. "There's something else—" and he continued. Once when the doctor tried to interrupt, Phil held his hand up and said, "I'm not finished yet. I have more to tell you." At the end of each session it was Phil who broke off when the time was up, never the doctor. After six sessions the doctor had yet to say one word, and he got a headache that stayed with him for two weeks. Phil paid him cash, sixty dollars after each visit, pulling out a fifty and a ten and passing it to the doctor, holding the money in his hand until the doctor took it. "That's not necessary," the doctor said after the first visit, but Phil insisted upon it. "I don't often get cash," he said, staring at the bills.

"Neither do I," Phil said.

He offered Phil a receipt each time, but Phil always refused. On the sixth visit, Phil went into Noel's sudden affiliation and affection for Nixon. The doctor really raised his eyebrows at that, but still didn't say anything. On the eighth visit, with ten minutes left, Phil asked him a question.

"Doctor," he said, "you never talk to me. What should I do with Noel?"

The doctor, who had not said a word in eight sessions, rubbed his temples.

Phil repeated the question. "Doctor, I asked you a question. Didn't you hear? What should I do *with Noel?*"

The doctor was caught off guard. He coughed twice and thought about taking a sip of water but didn't. Finally he spoke. "Mr. Radcliff, what do you *feel* like doing?"

Phil waited, sure there was more coming. Finally he said, "What do you mean?"

"I mean, what do you *feel* like doing with him?"

"I feel like taking him away."

"Where to?"

"Someplace crazy. Someplace so different that it will be like a splash of cold water, a slap in the face."

The Match Trick

"Like where?"

"I don't know like where. Someplace really, really different, like—like—like the Concord Hotel."

"The Concord!"

"Yes, the Concord."

"Well," the doctor said, rubbing his temple, "if you feel like doing that, you should."

Phil looked at him with disbelief, stood up, paid him with a fifty and a ten, waited for the doctor to take the money from his hand, and left. If there ever was any doubt in his mind, there certainly wasn't now. Shrinks, Phil thought, were bananas.

After Phil left the psychiatrist's office Friday morning he went home and told Phoebe his plans. "And if he doesn't go?" Phoebe asked him. "I'll go back to work," Phil said.

Phil found him in the woods, slouched down in his chair. Noel had cleared away all the leaves around him and was digging into the earth with his fingers. The radio was on his lap. "Let's go," Phil said. He had decided on the way over to be aggressive.

Noel looked at him without answering.

"Let's go. You've been here a month."

"I know how long I've been here. I'm aware of what I'm doing."

"Come on. Let's go." Phil started to walk toward him.

"I don't want to go anyplace, Phil. I want to stay here. I'm not ready."

"That's bullshit. You've been doing this to yourself long enough. I'm tired of you feeling sorry for yourself. You and I are going away for the weekend. Just the two of us. We're going to have bacon and eggs every morning, play thirty-six holes of golf a day, have a couple of beers, a steak dinner and to bed by nine—"

"It sounds like a shitty commercial to me."

"Let's go."

"I'm not going. I'm really not."

"You're going if I have to drag you."

Don Zacharia

"Are you gonna sock me?"

"Noel, it's been weeks—"

"I'm aware of that. I'm aware of each day. There's a tree back there and each day I stay here I make a notch in that tree."

"You're coming with me."

"Knock me out."

"Come on—"

"Forget it, Phil. I'm just not ready for that."

Phil grabbed his arm.

"Hey, let go. You're kinda skinny to be fucking around."

"Noel, I hate to do this—"

"Oh, God, he's really gonna sock me."

"We've known each other a long time and I've been closer to you than I ever thought I could be to a man. I've never asked a favor, not one. Have I? I've done a lot of things for you and never once have asked or expected anything in return. Now I'm asking that you come with me. If you say no, OK, I'll leave. But if you say yes, it's a favor that you are doing for *me*, and someday, Noel, I'll repay that favor."

Noel looked at him. It wasn't what he expected. He shook his head. "That is a shitty thing to do to me, buddy. Real, real shitty."

"Are you going?"

Noel hesitated. "OK, where to?" He shook his head.

Phil smiled. "What's the diff? It's a quiet place. Just us. Pack some stuff and let's go. I've got your clubs."

"I don't feel like partying. I don't want to meet *anybody*. I don't want to play golf with *anybody*. I don't want to eat with *anybody*. I'm just not up to that."

"You don't even have to *look* at anybody."

"Bacon and eggs in the morning, thirty-six holes of golf, two beers and a medium-rare steak."

"I promise," Phil said. They walked out of the woods with Phil humming.

· · ·

The Match Trick

That evening they sat down for dinner in the main dining room of the Concord Hotel.

"Phil," Noel said, alarmed, "this table is set for fourteen people!"

"It's the smallest table I could get, really. Would you relax?"

"I'll eat in the room." Noel stood up.

"Sit down. This place is half empty. You don't talk to anybody and I won't talk to anybody. Just relax."

Noel sat down. Across the dining room in six-foot letters the sign read: THE MANAGEMENT OF THE CONCORD WELCOMES YOU TO THE LARGEST DINING ROOM IN THE WORLD. "Very intimate," Noel snarled.

The maitre d' came over trailed by three men, all of whom had blue blazers on with emblems over the left breast pocket. He held a chair out for one of the men. They looked amazingly similar. Noel felt queasy. "The fairer sex," the maitre d' said, winking at Phil, "are changing and fashionably late."

"I'm going to the room," Noel whispered.

"Sit down," Phil grabbed his arm and pushed him down. "I'm Philip Radcliff." Phil offered his hand around.

"Rocky, Rico and Joe Petrocelli."

"I'm pleased to meet you."

"The pleasure is mine and my brudders."

"This is my friend, Noel Roth." Noel smiled weakly, keeping his hands tucked between his legs. "You're brothers," Phil said. "Coming over to the table, I said to my friend Noel I'll bet you a ten spot they're brothers."

"You win your bet," the one next to Phil said.

"Now wait a minute—you're who?"

"Rocky. I'm Rocky. Rico is next to me and the good-lookin' one is Joe."

"Christ, it's hot in here," Joe said. "The air conditioner must be fritzed."

"What line of work are you in?" Phil asked.

"Vulcanizing tires."

"All of you?"

Don Zacharia

"Yup. How 'bout yourself?"

"A lawyer."

"A legal beagle. He's a legal beagle," Rocky repeated to his two brothers. They both shook their heads apprehensively. "How 'bout yuh?" he directed the question to Noel. Noel didn't answer. "How 'bout yuh?" he repeated the question. Phil punched Noel in the leg.

"I'm in manufacturing," Noel mumbled.

"That's a good line to be in," Joe the younger said, breaking off a huge piece of bread.

"What you manufacture?" Rocky asked.

"Magnets. I manufacture magnets."

"Where did you say you were from?" Phil broke in.

"Detroit."

"Detroit! *You come all the way from Detroit to the Concord?*"

"Betcha ass. This is our eighth year in a row. Right, boys?" They both nodded. "Greatest place in the world."

"This is our first time."

"Kiddin'."

"No. No kiddin'. This is our first time."

"Well, lemme tell yuh, the two of yuh are in for a treat. The food is like nothin' you ever had. You forget it's kosher after a couple a meals. They got a substitute for everythin'. You want bacon and eggs in the morning, they give you something looks like bacon, tastes like bacon, but I'll be a mother-fucker if I know what it is. The activities are outta sight. You're busy from morning to night. There's nothin' like it in the whole Middle West—I'll tell yuh that. And at nighttime—well, pal—that's what this place is all about." He gave Phil an exaggerated wink.

"We're up here just for the golf."

"Yuk, yuk. Listen, counsel, lemme give you a tip. Bein' it's yuh, I'm gonna let you in on my speriences. I've been comin' here eight years and I've scored each year. I'm battin' a thousand. 'Less I'm stupid yuh can't bat more then a thousand." He turned to his brothers for confirmation and they both nodded.

"I'm really sweatin'," Joe the younger said wiping his face with a napkin.

128

The Match Trick

"Shut up," Rocky said. "The first thing to do is take care of that creep maitre d'. Each man puts up two bucks and you bein' the legal beagle slip it to him. Believe me it's a sawbuck well spent. He's the guy who decides which tables the cunts sit at. He's like God for chrissakes. Agreed?" His brothers each put up two dollars. "If you give him a ten spot instead of singles it makes a better impression," Rocky said, handing the money to Phil.

"I'll put a deuce up for you," Phil said to Noel getting up.

"What kinda markup you make in magnets?" Rocky asked Noel.

"We double up."

"Jesus. I wish I could say the same for vulcanized tires."

"That air conditioner gotta be fritzed," Joe the younger said.

"Take a guess what we work on?"

"Thirty percent?"

"Ha—if we worked on thirty percent we'd own this joint. Last year we grossed forty million."

Noel blinked. "That's a lot of money."

"It's a lot of fuckin' tires, that's what it is. We work on peanuts. What's your gross?"

"A million two."

"A million two in magnets! Holy Christ!"

"Every house has them," Noel said.

"Can I take my jacket off? I'm sweatin' my ass off," Joe said.

Rocky looked around. "You can take it off now but you gotta put it on when they serve dinner."

Joe took his blazer off. He had on a short-sleeved white shirt and the biggest muscles Noel had ever seen in his life. Noel couldn't take his eyes from Joe's arms.

"He lifts weights," Rocky said. "Show him." Joe flexed his muscles. Noel thought the fabric of the shirt was going to split.

Phil came back. "Here's the scoop. I negotiated. Tonight he has only three ladies—"

"Cunts," Rocky interrupted. "They ain't ladies, they're cunts. The ladies we left at home."

"Right. Cunts, boy are you right—Jesus, are you right. Tonight he has only three cunts because it's Friday but tomorrow night he

129

said he will have five cunts and no other men. Just us."

"Terrific."

"Can't we get some more bread?" Joe asked.

"Money well spent," Rocky said.

"You gotta believe."

"Bein' it's yuh I'm gonna give you some more of Rocky's speri-ence how come I never missed scorin' in eight years. The biggest mistake you make as a hunter is goin' for the good-lookin' cunts. If I'd went for the good-lookin' cunts I'd be battin' a hundred 'stead of a thousand. That's the mistake you Easterners makes. I go for the *ugly* ones. The *ugly* ones need it. The *ugly* ones are achin' for it. The uglier they are the better they need it. What I do is line up the ten ugliest cunts in the hotel, make a mental note and number them down in my head and then just like this—" Rocky knocked over the salt and pepper shakers with his fingers— "I knock them off. Oh boy, look what's comin'. Put your jacket on, Joe."

The maitre d' was approaching, trailed by three women, two of whom were of medium height and dark-haired. The third was taller, blond and good-looking. The three of them looked as if they had spent the last week getting ready for their entrance.

"Gentlemen," the maitre d' pulled himself up, and with a sweep of his hand said, "may I present the women." He helped each one into a chair and marched away.

Silence.

Finally, Joe the younger spoke. "The air conditioner is on the fritz."

"I'm quite cool," the blond girl said.

Phil stood up. "Ladies, let me do the intros. I'm Philip Radcliff, this is my friend, Noel Roth, and on my left are Rocky, Rico, and Joe Petrocelli."

"You're brothers," one of the dark-haired girls said. "You sure don't look alike."

"I've heard that before," Rocky said. "Where do you girls call home?"

"I'm going home," Noel whispered to Phil getting out of his chair.

130

"Shut up, will you, Noel? Relax." He pulled Noel down again.

"I'm going to mary-lou," the blond girl sang out. "Company?" The three women pranced away.

"Don't like 'em. Too good-lookin'." Rocky stared at Phil as if it was his fault.

"They look kinda doggy to me," Phil replied defensively.

"Counsel, you might know about makin' wills, but when it comes to cunts I tink you should bow to me." His two brothers nodded their heads, agreeing.

Phil stood up.

"Where you goin'?"

"I'm going to ask the maitre d' to change the women."

"Sit down. For chrissakes," slapping his forehead, "you don't do tings like that."

The three women came back. "We're from Queens," the blond one said.

"Queens," Rocky said. "Queens? Don't we have a customer in Queens?" he asked Rico.

"The brothers Mustacchio."

"Rico got a photographic memory. We got two thousand customers and Rico remembers each one of 'em."

"I'm like a filing cabinet," Rico said.

"I believe the word is photogenic," the blond girl said.

Rocky glared at her. "You know the brothers Mustacchio?"

The girls shook their heads. "Where are you from?" the blond girl asked.

"Detroit."

To Phil: "And you?"

"Crownhill."

"Rat-de-tat-de-tat."

"Did I miss your name?"

"The crowd here really looks bad," one of the dark-haired girls said.

"A bad weekend," the other dark-haired girl concurred.

The waiter came over. Hands folded in front of him, he circled the table twice. "Table Eighty-six, my name is Ramon, R–A–M–O–N.

Don Zacharia

Welcome to the Concord. I will be your waiter for your stay. I was born in Puerto Rico so if you want to hear 'Your Yiddish Mama,' you got the wrong boychick, but if you want to hear 'Latins Are Lousy Lovers' "—Ramon went into a snappy rendition of the song, half in Spanish and half in English, moving his body and feet gracefully and snapping his fingers. The girls giggled and the brothers applauded. *"Table Eighty-six,"* Ramon said, *"Attention."* He clapped his hands. "If you want menus I can give you menus, but let me save you the trouble: reading's for the goyim. We have six appetizers tonight! We have chopped chicken liver, herring in sour cream sauce, fruit cocktail, shmaltz herring, fresh melon and homemade gefilte fish. There are eight people here, so for starters supposing I bring over thirty-two appetizers, and if you want doubles or triples, holler for *Ramon.*" He made a motion with his hand and two busboys came over, piling the table high with food.

"We have three soups—"

"Is this," Rocky Petrocelli eating his fourth gefilte fish said to Noel Roth spooning an overripe melon, "the most fantastic place in the world?"

After dinner Phil and Noel went into the bar for a drink. The sign over the bar said WELCOME TO THE LONGEST BAR IN THE WORLD—and it was.

"You know something," Noel said, "I'm not unhappy you dragged me here."

Phil smiled and said nothing.

"Tomorrow," Noel said, "golf until our hands fall off."

"I'll leave a seven o'clock call."

"I'm going back to the room. One question: How did you ever pick the Concord?"

"If I told you, you wouldn't believe me."

Noel got up and knocked over the salt shaker with his fingers. "Good hunting."

"I never did get to know your name." Noel had stopped on the way out of the bar to talk with the blond girl who was at dinner with him. She did not fit Rocky's idea of what to look for at the Concord; not a beauty, but with long blond hair, pleasing features, a little on the plump side, but as far as Noel could see, not bad.

"I'm Ellen," she said. Her two dark-haired friends eyed him suspiciously.

"Would you like to go for a walk?" Noel asked her.

"Sam," she called to the bartender and snapped her fingers. He reached underneath the bar and handed her her pocketbook. She slung it over her shoulder. "See you later, girls."

"Don't do anything I wouldn't do," one of the dark-haired girls said.

"Rat-de-tat-de-tat."

They sat down in the lobby.

"You're a very sensitive man."

"Thank you. What makes you say that?"

"You're so quiet. I find a relationship between quiet men and sensitivity."

"Yes," Noel said.

"Would you like to go downstairs? There's a very intimate bar downstairs that's very quiet. I'm sure you will like it."

"All right."

The name of the bar was "Intimacy," and the sign above the door read THE MOST INTIMATE BAR IN THE WORLD. They sat down in a love seat facing each other and ordered drinks. It was so dark Noel could barely see her. "You've been to the Concord before?" Noel asked.

"It's my second home."

"I guess you like it."

"It's all right. You meet some interesting people. Not sensitive people like you but interesting people."

"Oh."

The waiter came over with the drinks, a candle, and a long-stemmed rose in a vase.

"I just love this room," Ellen said.

"Yes."

"You're married, aren't you?"

"No, I'm not."

"Baloney. You don't have to kid me. I understand. I sleep with a lot of married men."

"I'm really not married."

"Really?"

"Really."

"Wow! The world is full of shocks. You're not kiddin'?"

"Truth."

"Divorced or a bachelor?"

"Neither. I'm a widower."

Silence.

"I'm sorry—oh—I'm really sorry—"

"It's OK."

"I'm sorry. There I go puttin' my foot in my mouth. That was a very unsensitive thing for me to have said."

"It's OK, Ellen. My wife died a long, long time ago. Years and years and years ago."

"You sure I didn't offend you?"

"I'm positive."

"Well, anyway, I'm sorry. No wonder you're sensitive."

"Thank you again."

"What did she die of?"

"She died—she died of a disease."

"A *disease!*" Ellen backed her chair away from the table. "What kind of a disease?" Her voice suddenly seemed filled with fear.

"What the hell difference does it make? A disease is a disease. She had a disease. A general disease—"

Ellen stood up. It was so dark in the Intimate Lounge that Noel could barely see her in the flickering candlelight. "I wish you had told me that before you had brought me down here. I come into a room with somebody who has a cold and the next day I have a cold. I go to an internist in Manhattan who says I'm the most susceptible person to disease he's ever seen. Excuse me, but I feel very uncomfortable, like I want to scratch all over. I'm going back to my friends."

With that she left, or at least Noel thought she left. It was so dark he couldn't tell. Noel didn't know whether to laugh or cry. He laughed. This place, Noel thought, ordering another scotch for himself, is without a doubt the most fantastic place in the world.

The next morning Noel and Phil played golf after a breakfast of fake bacon and eggs. "You want triple in eggs?" Ramon asked them.

"I want some real bacon with my eggs and I want some real milk with my coffee," Noel snapped.

"It's kosher," Ramon said, rolling his eyes upward, "no milchidika with fleischidika."

The brothers Petrocelli and the girls were nowhere to be seen. At seven in the morning in the Concord dining room only the golfers seemed to be about.

The sign over the golf club house read WELCOME TO THE MONSTER—THE WORLD'S MOST DIFFICULT GOLF COURSE. (And it was.) Both Noel and Phil were competent golfers. Phil was an eight handicap and Noel an eleven. As their caddy had predicted, a short wiry black man named Leon who was always chewing on an unlit cigar, "This course gonna lick your ass," and it did. Phil shot a ninety-five and Noel a ninety-seven. Leon was a kibitzer and a hustler and had made a ten-dollar bet with Noel that he wouldn't break ninety. "It's a sucker's bet," Phil had told him when he made it. After the first few holes Noel agreed with him.

At lunchtime they discussed their game. "It's either the worst round of golf I've ever played or the hardest course in the world," Phil said.

"I wonder what the shmuck would shoot here?" Noel laughed. "I'd bet him a thousand dollars that he couldn't break two hundred," Noel answered his own question.

"I think it used to be an ocean," Phil said, "and they filled part of it in and built a golf course. I've heard of people losing thirty golf balls in the water."

"I'd love to make that Leon eat his cigar."

"Don't press it, I've heard that the pros refuse to have a tournament here because most of them couldn't break eighty. Do you want to play again today?"

"I sure do."

They took a cart and played eighteen more holes after lunch. Phil shot a ninety-six and Noel one hundred and two. Noel couldn't believe it. "Jesus! One hundred and two—don't tell a soul. Tomorrow I'm gonna bring this course to its knees."

"Come on," Phil said, "I'll buy you a beer." He put his arm around Noel and the two of them walked toward the clubhouse.

When Phil and Noel went to dinner that evening the brothers Petrocelli were already there. The maitre d' appeared immediately.

"Gentlemen, we have a problem. Women," he said shaking his head and looking up at the ceiling, "are a mystery. The three ladies who were with you last evening are no longer with us—"

"It's no loss," Rocky interrupted.

"I have," the maitre d' said, paying no attention to Rocky's remark, "two lovely ladies from Pennsylvania who will be joining you in a minute." With that he turned on his heels and left.

"Nazi fuck," Rocky said after him.

In a moment the maitre d' returned with two of the ugliest women Noel had ever seen in his life. A field day for Rocky, Noel thought. The girls immediately introduced themselves: Brenda McGill and Mary Howard, shook hands all around and sat down. Secretaries, as it turned out, from Hershey, Pennsylvania. Ramon came over and did his number, and Rocky was pitching really hard at Brenda, who was sitting to the left of Noel. If she goes to bed with Rocky, Noel thought, she will be in the hospital by tomorrow. Rocky looked like he weighed at least two hundred thirty, and if Brenda, who was bone-skinny, weighed over ninety pounds, Noel would be surprised. She was wearing what looked like somebody else's Sunday church dress, a silky maroon dress that hung on Brenda like she was a wire hanger. She had a high forehead, short, unpleasant hair that looked brittle, as if it were set ten minutes ago, a bony nose that dominated her face, nondescript eyes with eyebrows that she had penciled in badly, a small mouth and a chin with a trace of a cleft. On the left side of her neck was a large brown mole that Noel was trying hard not to look at. She had, wonder of wonders, what appeared to be small but pleasant breasts. Altogether, Noel thought, a dream for Rocky.

"I love the way you done your hair," Rocky said.

"Will somebody pass me the shmaltz herring," Joe the younger said.

"Is Rocky your Christian name?" Brenda asked.

"Whadda yuh mean, Christian?" Rocky was defensive.

He will kill her, Noel thought. Rocky's organ must weigh as much as this frail girl sitting on his left.

"I adore the name Rocky. It's so—manly. Anybody with a name like Rocky certainly *isn't* gay." Brenda smiled.

"What did you say?" Rocky came halfway out of his chair, his neck muscles bulging.

"I said, somebody with a name like Rocky certainly isn't gay."

"Oh. I thought you said somethin' else."

Noel wasn't sure. Of course he was sure, some things in life you can't fake. Without so much as a turn of her head, a nod, a smile, a whisper, Brenda had taken her frail right hand, which Noel was sure Rocky could snap with two of his stubby fingers, and was rubbing Noel's crotch, tugging unsuccessfully at his fly. Noel coughed and covered his lap with his napkin. Be cool, he thought, what a marvelous hotel. He coughed again and looked around. Brenda, unable to unzip his fly, was gently massaging his groin, occasionally tightening her grip.

"I think," Joe said, "they're cuttin' down on their food."

"Brenda is a nice name too," Rocky said. "It has a nice ring to it."

"Brenda—Brenda—Brenda—Brenda—" Joe sang.

Don Zacharia

"Shut up."

"Rocky, would you pass me some bread?" Brenda asked.

"It's stale. This place ain't what it used to be," Rocky said.

"I think it's a terrific place," Noel jumped in.

"He speaks. Hey, Counsel, your friend speaks. I thought all along you were a ventriloquist and he was your dummy." Rocky broke out in laughter, followed by Joe and Rico.

Brenda turned her head to Noel and, cupping her mouth with her left hand, spoke to him in a whisper. "Why don't you slide down in the chair a bit, unzip your fly and pull your cock out of your pants. Rocky," turning back to him, "you are a funny man."

They were having soup. Rocky had mentioned to Ramon that he thought he was cutting down on the food, and Ramon, acting as if his mother had been insulted, brought out triples in matzoh-ball soup. Noel was in ecstasy. He had done what Brenda had suggested and Brenda was sometimes pulling and sometimes tickling his penis, and if that wasn't enough, the way the fabric of the napkin was touching the head of his organ created such a delicious warmth through his body that Noel at times was losing touch with what was taking place at the table.

"Could you get off this way?" Brenda whispered to him.

"Yes—damn soon," Noel whispered back.

"Marvelous. Please do."

"Whadda yuh tink of the matzoh-ball soup?" Rocky asked.

"They're a little heavy," Brenda said.

"Someone once told me that making matzoh-ball soup is an art form," Joe the younger said.

"I love em," Rocky said, spooning a whole ball into his mouth.

"They could be a little lighter," Phil added.

"They have Chinese cooks here—that's why. Hey! What's wrong with your friend, Counsel? Are you OK?" Rocky asked Noel.

"I'm OK," Noel panted. "I just got a little dizzy." He was having the longest orgasm of his life.

"You got white and shut your eyes and began bitin' your lip like you were havin' a convulsion."

138

"Don't worry about me," Noel said breathing heavily. "Your soup is getting cold."

Brenda, using just two fingers now, was still pulling on the head of his penis, squeezing out the last drops of sperm. Noel felt himself shudder. Brenda cleaned him up with the napkin and brought it to the table and put it in front of her. "Excuse me," she said. "I have to go to the ladies room." She stopped next to Rocky. "Make sure you're here when I come back," she said coyly.

"I'll be here," Rocky said hoarsely.

She touched Rocky's face with her right hand and smiled at him. "I can't wait to see you after dinner," she said.

Rocky, remembering some distant movie, kissed the palm of her right hand and then her fingers.

Brenda gracefully withdrew her hand. "I love the way you kiss my hand," she said and walked away.

"Ge-fil-to fish," Rocky said. "Her hands smell and taste like ge-fil-to fish."

In a minute the maitre d' came over to the table and told Noel there was a phone call for him. Noel hunched over and went into the lobby and picked up the house phone. It was Brenda. "Hi, I'm in my room. Room four eighty. Why don't you finish dessert and come up here? I have two bottles of Haitian rum." Noel said yes, went back to the table, had two more bites of sherbet and excused himself, saying he was tired and wanted to get a good night's sleep before his golf game.

When Noel got to Brenda's room, she was nude. She began kissing his face and neck and tugging at his clothes. "Hey, hold on a sec." Noel pulled away.

"Hold on, bullshit. I prance around that chocolate town eleven and a half months waiting and dreaming about these two weeks. I want to spend the next twelve hours fucking."

"Hey," Noel said weakly as she undid his pants and tugged them down his legs, "I just had an orgasm. I'm almost thirty-seven years old—I need a couple of hours—"

"Five minutes," Brenda said, sinking to her knees and slipping

Don Zacharia

Noel's organ into her mouth and doing some wonderful thing that gave Noel gooseflesh. "Five minutes," she mumbled.

Noel left Brenda's room at seven the next morning and after he had showered and changed his clothes found Phil in the dining room.

"Good morning." Noel winked at Phil.

"There's a man looking for you."

"Who?"

"Rocky. He says he wants to kill you. He says you stole his woman."

"Ah, come on."

"How'd it go?"

"Truth?"

"Truth."

"Okay. What I'm gonna tell you is gonna be the truth."

"You swear?"

"I swear. First off, I have to give you a preamble. This has nothing to do with my age—I'm thirty-six—and when I was nineteen I was the same way. Once I've shot my load I can't get it up again for at least six hours, sometimes longer. It's a physical defect. Maybe I should rephrase that—"

"I think you should lower your voice," as two men from the next table were looking at them and laughing.

"Let me put it to you this way—"

"You look terrible. Did you sleep?"

"Not a fucking second, but I feel strong. Where was I?"

"Keeping your voice down."

"After I ejaculate," Noel whispered, "I am incapable of ejaculating again for long periods of time. Sometimes when I ejaculate in the morning, I can't even ejaculate again that evening. Does that surprise you?"

"Noel," Phil was staring at him wide-eyed, "I don't think I'm interested."

140

The Match Trick

"That's the preamble, now the truth. Phil, I had *seven* orgasms. Seven, Phil."

"I don't think I want to hear this—"

"I don't think you understand." Noel leaned over the table and punched a finger into Phil's chest. "In a period of nine hours I came seven times, finished off two bottles of Haitian rum, didn't sleep a second, and you know something, Phil, I feel very strong." Noel sat back and ran a hand through his hair. "Now let me tell it to you in detail—"

"My favorite country club duo gettin' ready for the second slaughter," Leon, their caddy was kibitzing them again.

Phil was swinging two woods and Noel, holding his driver horizontally, was doing stretching exercises. It was a beautiful September day, clear, crisp, sunny, with little breeze. From the first tee almost the entire golf course was visible. "I think this course tends to psych you," Phil said, touching his toes.

"You country-club folk really into exercise."

"Pay no attention to him," Phil asked.

"What's the action, Leon?" Noel asked, doing back turns.

"I'm 'fraid time you finish doing your cal-a-sen-tics you'll be too tired to swing—"

"Did I hear you say you're not interested in a bet?"

"Sheeet—Leon's the name—bettin' my game." Leon, chumping on his cigar, pulled out a thick roll of money held together by a rubber band. "Don't take no checks—don't take no credit—and we play summer rules."

"What a place," Noel said.

"He's hustling you, Noel. That guy makes a fortune on this golf course with guys like us. The assistant pro told me he makes five hundred to a thousand bucks some weeks."

"I feel strong," Noel said. "I feel *very* strong." He walked over to Leon. "I'll make four separate bets with you. One hundred bucks a bet, on breaking eighty-five, ninety, ninety-five and a hundred."

Don Zacharia

Leon with a smile peeled off four hundred dollars. "You been lyin' up nights thinking about these bets." He pointed down the first fairway. "Let's go."

The first hole at the Concord is a par four sharp dog-leg left. The key shot is the drive. There is water on the left, right and straight ahead. The ideal place for the drive was close to the water on the left. Noel pushed his drive to the right, making his second shot a difficult one: one hundred and eighty yards over water to a green trapped on three sides. Feeling confident, he hit a four-wood, which he knew was not the safe club, and caught a trap on the side of the green. He came out very short, and three-putted for a double-bogey six. "Some start," he said to Phil. Leon, once the bets had been made, had stopped kibitzing and had become an excellent caddy, giving advice only if asked, always being in the right position and describing each hole before they teed off.

The second hole at the Concord was a par three. Depending on where the tees are located, it can be anywhere from one hundred and thirty to two hundred and ten yards. The markers were halfway, making it a one-hundred-and-sixty-yard hole. The green itself was an island surrounded by water on all sides and two bunkers. The last two times Noel played the hole he had plopped the ball into water both times. This time, still somewhat unnerved by his trap shot on the first hole, he hit a four iron a little fat to the front edge of the green, leaving himself a seventy-footer. He three-putted again for a bogey four. After two holes Noel was three over par. The third hole was the most difficult hole on the course: a long par five that called for two perfect woods and then a medium iron over one hundred and twenty yards of water to a tiny green. Noel, feeling more confident, with a certain amount of rhythm returning to his swing, did just what he was supposed to do with his driver and a three wood and knocked a five iron to twenty feet of the pin. He two-putted for a par. He parred four, bogied five and six, parred seven, knocked in a fifteen-footer on the par three eighth for a birdie and ruined what could have been an exceptional front nine by hitting the ball into the water on nine and taking a double-bogey six. He shot a very respectable forty-two. The back nine was a miracle. Noel, playing the best golf of his life, coming out of traps twice within five feet of the cup, chipping and putting with such confidence that he knew he couldn't miss, hitting every iron to the green, and twice hitting three woods to greens, shot a thirty-seven. "I can't miss," he told Phil. "I just can't miss. I feel that I can make any shot I have to make. How strange." He shot a seventy-nine for the day. It was the first time Noel had ever broken eighty, and to have done it on a course like the Concord was almost beyond belief. Leon was a gentleman about paying Noel. "You couldn't do it again in a million years."

Noel was floating. "It's my day," he told Leon. "In everyone's life they get one day, and I'm having mine." He asked Leon to verify his scorecard.

They were having their third round of beers in the clubhouse, with Noel telling for the sixth time anyone who would listen about his great round. Like all golfers—even though it was the greatest round of his life—Noel was trying to explain how his seventy-nine could have been a seventy-four with a little bit of luck. Noel ordered another round of beers for everyone about him. "What a fantastic place," Noel said. "I love this place."

"Uh huh," Phil said, "look who's here."

Joe the younger, spotting them, hurried toward their table. "I been lookin' all over for you guys. You gotta get outta here. My brother Rocky been lookin'—" pointing a finger at Noel—"for yuh all mornin' and if he finds yuh he's gonna kill yuh."

"Let's go," Phil said, standing up.

Noel didn't move. "Are you crazy, Phil? I've got a date with Brenda tonight and I want to play golf again tomorrow. I want to do the whole thing all over."

"You don't understand," Joe interrupted. "Make him understand," he pleaded with Phil. "You don't know my brother. You hurt him in a very vulnerable spot. For the first time since he's been coming to the Concord he hasn't scored and he's blaming you. If he finds you he's gonna kill you. I've seen some people my

Don Zacharia

brother has worked over. They're not the same when he's finished with them! They look like used tires."

Phil grabbed Noel. "We're getting out of here."

Noel pushed him away. "I'm not running from any vulcanized tire moron. What the hell is he so mad at me for?"

Rocky burst through the door with Rico holding on to him. He looked like a wild man. Joe made a grab for him and got him in a bear hug.

"*I'm gonna kill him,*" Rocky screamed, pulling Rico and Joe toward Noel.

"Get him outta here," Joe pleaded.

Phil tried to grab Noel but Noel pulled away. "Fuck you, Rocky." Noel gave him the finger.

"*I'm gonna kill him.*"

"Get him outta here," Joe screamed. "I can't hold him forever," Joe's face was beet-red with the effort of hanging on to Rocky.

"YOU NAZI," Rocky screamed.

"*Fag fuck,*" Noel screamed back. "*When you get home put the American flag over your wife's face when you fuck her because if she doesn't have to look at your fag fucking face when you're fucking her it will be the biggest favor you can do for her.*"

"*Arrghh. I'll kill him—lemme go—I'll take him apart.*"

"*I don't fight with fags,*" Noel screamed back.

"Let's go," Noel said. They ran for the car. "I'll kill 'em. If he wants to fight me, arrange it. You be my second and I'll kill 'em. FAG," Noel shouted at some people as they were driving out of the golf course. "FAG—NAZI—CUNT—FUCKS."

144

THE CENTER

When Noel came back from the Concord Sunday night, September 27th, three things happened. He went back to work the next day, which pleased everyone (especially his accountant). He called Phoebe and told her to make an appointment for him at the Psychiatry Center, and Phoebe, never one to fool around, made an appointment for Tuesday. And Nevers called him up and he made plans to see her the following Monday night. Beth was pleased by the first two decisions, but David wasn't so sure. His father going to the Center was OK, but he missed his visits to Noel in the woods. The first couple of days when Noel went back to work David went into the woods and would sit and just hang around by himself, talking to the trees, throwing rocks at nothing. He thought he would build a clubhouse back there some day. A place to go to even if it rained.

• • •

Don Zacharia

Noel was uncomfortable. It was his first visit to the Center and he was having some second thoughts. He was sitting in a large airy therapy room (whatever a therapy room was supposed to look like) filled with children's toys, dollhouses, play stoves, children's desks and chairs, games, blackboards, hundreds of crayons scattered about, children's paintings, and all in total disarray. To Noel, who loved order, it looked like a hurricane hit it. He was sitting in a child's chair, low to the floor, with a short hard back.

"All the money in the world we don't have," Frieda Bloom said, sensing Noel's discomfort. "I would like very much to do this in something more traditional, a small room, darker, with *normal* chairs and *normal* couches and a desk with drawers, but I'm afraid this has to do. In the mornings it is a nursery for children, mostly under four, who have suffered a loss. It is very difficult for young children; they don't know how to verbalize their grief so they take it out on destroying this poor room. We've long since stopped trying to keep it in order on a daily basis. I apologize if it is making you uncomfortable."

"No," Noel said, wondering how the hell in chaos like this *anyone* could possibly be cured of *anything*. Noel had come fully prepared to dislike this woman whom he had heard so much about from his children. He had built up a stereotype of what she would be like: a mousy suburban stringbean of a lady wearing a pants suit; having gone back to college in the middle of her life discovering that meddling in other people's lives was more fun than doing the dishes. He couldn't have been more wrong. Frieda Bloom was a slight woman, easily, Noel thought, in her middle sixties, born and trained in Vienna; she seemed at every point to be one step ahead of Noel. She had a small, tired face, as if thirty years of dealing with other people's tragedies had taken its toll. She spoke slowly, picking her words that seemed to come out sometimes in awkward sentences. Both Beth and David liked her very much, and Noel, having just met her, at least didn't *dislike* her.

"Equally, Mr. Roth, I would have liked to have had you here the day after your wife was killed. But," she held her hands up, "we take what we can get, and in your case we got your children and not you. Welcome, at any rate, to the Center. Some parents we never get. They think we perform voodoo here. My name is Frieda Bloom. Your children call me Mrs. Bloom and I would like it if you would call me that. I am not a doctor, to clear the air. It disappoints your son. He is already impressed by such things. Such a serious boy. I explained to him that for me to become a doctor I would have to go back to college, then four years of medical school and then three years of internship and *then* I would be eighty, and that doesn't make much sense. He agrees with me about that. But his disappointment lingers. So, I am Mrs. Bloom. I graduated from the Vienna School of Psychotherapy in 1936, spent the war years in England, and immediately after the war returned to Germany and started to work with survivors. Tragedy, like all things, comes in many shapes and different quantities. In those days, we had plenty of work. We would deal with two thousand people at a time. We had, as one of my colleagues said, a surplus of tragedy. I doubt that we did any good. I would stand up in a large outdoor auditorium in front of a thousand people staring at me with unseeing eyes, listening to me with ears that couldn't hear, attempting to comprehend something that is still, thirty years later, incomprehensible, and I would try to tell them that in time, in time, everything would be better. More than once people in the audience would slump over and die just as I was telling them they would be all right.

"In 1952, I came to America, to Bloomington, Indiana. Can you imagine? Bloomington is far from Vienna. I started a program there working with children who had suffered parental loss, and that's all I have ever done since. Let me give you some facts; we do wonders with children, wonders. With adults it is not so easy. The results are not so recognizable. Besides me, we have four *real* doctors on the staff, and at least two dozen or four dozen social workers. Social workers these days outnumber the patients."

Noel laughed. He was warming up to this lady.

"How are you getting on? The way your friend Phoebe described you, I expected to see a scarecrow."

"I've lost a few pounds. I could well afford it."

Don Zacharia

"You were unprepared for Susan's death?"

Noel flinched at the bluntness of the question. "Yes, I was unprepared. How can one prepare for that?"

"Impossible. One can't. Let me tell you something curious, and when you leave here, think about it, and next time we will discuss it. If Susan had a long terminal illness, one in which you both knew that the eventual result would be her death, having a year to think about it, a year to plan for it, you would still be unprepared. Perhaps just as unprepared. Unbelievable, no? This man Meyerson," changing the topic so quickly that Noel felt jarred, "is a source of conflict with your children, as I am sure with you?"

"What kind of conflict?" Noel interrupted.

Mrs. Bloom eyed him suspiciously. "Have your children not mentioned it to you?"

"No. Why should they?"

"They have mentioned it to me. More than once. Have you not mentioned it to them?"

"No."

"Are you comfortable with it? Assuming that malfeasance of journalism was nothing more than the worst kind of exploitation, are you comfortable with it?"

Noel didn't answer.

"Do you understand my question? We are very blunt here. I should have warned you. Are you comfortable with the *way* in which Susan was killed?"

"No," Noel finally said, "I suppose I'm not. But then," he said, qualifying his answer, "there are a great many things I am uncomfortable with since it happened."

"It."

Once again Noel didn't answer. He looked out of the window feeling closed in.

"Noel Roth, what I am going to say will seem cruel and much too fast. I have been accused of moving much too fast, but I always feel that I don't have enough time. It, as you say, didn't happen. What happened is that your wife, Susan Roth, and a friend of hers,

The Match Trick

under awkward and suspicious circumstances, were killed by a falling air conditioner. Now, nothing we can do can change that. But perhaps by talking about what took place, perhaps by bringing it to the surface, it won't someday appear quite so disturbing.

"Your children, particularly Beth, are very concerned with the *way* in which their mother died. Of course they are concerned, as any child would be at having a parent die, but in their case, the presence of Meyerson, the allusion to what might have taken place in the past or in the future between Meyerson and their mother is causing conflicts that we can't afford to ignore. And it is not helped, Mr. Roth, by your ignoring it as if it never happened. Beth is building up a concept that her mother was *killed* because of her relationship with Meyerson."

"That's ridiculous," Noel shot out, sorry that he had let Phoebe talk him into coming here.

"Is it? Please Mr. Roth, I *slapped* you and you flinched. That your daughter should act that way is not ridiculous; on the contrary, it's, considering the circumstances, normal. After all, she read the papers. She read how her mother was kissing Meyerson just before she was killed. How do you think she should feel about that? How do *you* feel about that? Her imagination and being thirteen years old does the rest. Our problem with Beth is to make sure she can intellectually and with a degree of normalcy work some of those conflicts out. It would compound the tragedy if Beth grew up subconsciously thinking that her mother was killed because of some sexual act she had committed and/or was about to commit."

"Beth has never said a word about it to me," Noel said defensively.

"It's hardly the kind of thing a thirteen-year-old girl will bring up to her widowed father. But it is the kind of thing I hope we can talk about here." Mrs. Bloom held her hands up. "I have, for beginnings, bopped you enough, no? Tell me, to leave on an easier note, when you were driving up here today to visit the notorious Mrs. Bloom, what were your thoughts?"

Don Zacharia

"My thoughts?"

"Yes."

"I was thinking about the Administration."

"The administration! What administration?"

"The Nixon Administration."

Mrs. Bloom eyed him suspiciously. "Are you making a joke? Your children tell me you make a surplus of jokes."

"No. No. I'm serious. What do you think of Nixon?"

"What do I think of Nixon?" she repeated the question. "OK. I think the sooner he resigns or is impeached, whichever comes first, the better off the country will be."

"I'm not so sure you're right. I used to think pretty much like you about the Administration but recently I have been changing some of my feelings. I think Nixon has done many wrong things, but I also think that the media are persecuting him."

"Persecuting Nixon?"

"Yes, persecuting."

"Well, I don't know what to say. You certainly are entitled to your opinion. Perhaps we will talk about it some other time."

"Yes."

"It is enough for one day, no?" She stood up and extended her hand. "It was nice finally meeting you and I'll see you when the children come Thursday."

As Noel Roth left, Frieda Bloom shook her head. Now what the hell is all that about? she thought.

MISS NEVERS

Nevers. Nevers lived in a duplex apartment on Waverly Place in Greenwich Village, and when Noel got there promptly at eight-thirty she wasn't there, but a young black girl named Melonie was. She let Noel in. The apartment was sparsely furnished, with a nice contemporary mixture of dark woods, lacquered tables, plants that seemed as if they had been there forever, wicker chairs and a very comfortable-looking couch. The lighting was indirect and subdued, giving the room, the only room Noel saw that evening, an elegant feeling. Noel sat down on one of the wicker chairs. The black girl was watching him and he smiled at her.

Melonie was wearing the most bizarre collection of clothes, or lack of clothes, that Noel had ever seen. Black high-heeled calf-length boots, short shorts so skimpily cut that the cheeks of her ass were half exposed, and a halter top that did nothing more than just cover her nipples. She was fairly tall, not particularly pretty

in the face, with a pronounced Afro, and a body so perfectly tapered, so perfectly proportioned, that Noel didn't know quite what
to do with his eyes. He glanced at the wall in back of her, the
ceiling, the floor, but it was difficult not to look at Melonie. It was
hard to figure her age—eighteen or nineteen, maybe a little older.
But whoever she was, Noel thought, she didn't fit in with the look
of the apartment, and besides, who in the hell was she?

"You Rothman?"

"Roth, Roth, Noel Roth."

"Miss Nevers said you might be by."

"Was she unexpectedly called away?"

"She ain't here."

"Well, I didn't think I had the wrong night," he said smiling,
trying hard to be casual.

"You always so fuckin' fidgety, Rothman?"

"What?"

"I sez my eyeballs never seen nobody so fidgety. You gonna wear
through that fucking chair you keep jumpin' bout."

Noel crossed his legs and clasped his hands together.

"I think I'm gonna change your name from Rothman to Fidget.
You Mr. Fidget. Jesus, man, look at you. You need to relax. You
need a Lude. Don't look at me cause I don't deal in no Ludes but
you sure could use one."

Noel, not knowing what she was talking about, continued to
smile.

"Mr. Fidget, you want a toad?" Melonie offered him a tray with
at least two dozen perfectly rolled joints.

"Ah—no thanks." Trying to be nonchalant. "If you could point
me toward the scotch.

Melonie nodded toward a wall cabinet and Noel poured himself a
double and sat back down. Melonie had lit a joint and was inhaling
deeply.

"Miss Nevers has the best shit."

"That's nice."

"You ain't much company. I don't mind tellin' yuh sittin' here
with yuh is bor–*ring*. You sure you don't want some of this shit?"

"No, thank you. Are you—are you—are you the housekeeper?" Noel blurted out.

"*Am I the housekeeper?*" Melonie exploded. Standing up with her hands on her hips her voice went up two octaves. "AM I THE HOUSEKEEPER?" She had a gold tooth that dazzled Noel. "Shit, Rothman, do I look like any housekeeper you'se ever seen?" She pulled aside her halter exposing firm melon size breasts. "Do you know any housekeepers with tits like dese? You so fuckin' fidgety it reached your brain cells." She sat back down, not bothering to put her halter back on. "You got children?"

"Yes, two," Noel said looking at the wall.

"Dey as fidgety as you? If dey is I feels for 'em."

"Look, I'm sorry for what I said before. I think I need another scotch." Noel poured himself a second drink and sat back down. Melonie hadn't moved. She might just as well be nude, Noel thought.

"How old your children?"

"Thirteen and eleven. The girl is thirteen and the boy eleven."

"The girl look like me?"

Beth, who was into layers of clothing, a shirt, a sweater, another shirt, baggy dungarees, looked as much like Melonie as the George Washington Bridge looked like a snowplow. But Noel, being careful not to offend her again, said, "She doesn't look exactly like you."

"Has Miss Nevers met her?"

Miss Nevers? Why does she call her Miss Nevers? What the hell is going on here? "She met her briefly for a few minutes."

"I'z fifteen."

"WHAT?"

"You know how many times you say 'What' tonight? You say 'What' so many times I'z sick of it. Between what and fidgeting you makin' me fidgetywhat."

"You can't be fifteen."

"Okay, I'm a hundred and fifteen."

Noel sipped his scotch. Wait until I tell Phil about this one, he thought. "Melonie, Melonie, you ever hear the expression 'Curiosity got the cat'?"

Don Zacharia

"That somethin' to do with fuckin'?"

"No. No. Never mind that. Would you mind if I asked you just what it is you do here in relationship with Nevers?"

"I ain't the housekeeper."

"That's for sure. Are you her friend?"

"I ain't her friend. I guess you could say you'll find out." Melonie flashed that gold tooth at Noel. "Was the coffin closed at your wife's funeral?"

Noel flinched as if someone had just tried to throw a punch at him. "Why—yes."

"Miss Nevers told me dat story. Dat some fuckin' crazy story. Fer a week after dat I walkin' down the street bumpin' into shit cause I'z lookin' up all the time. Did you see her?"

"See her?"

"After she got her head knocked off?"

Noel groaned. "No."

"Gruesome. I like gruesome things. I mean, I like 'em, and I don't like 'em. A lot of things people don't like, I like. I don't mind lookin' at gruesome things, but I do mind. A lot of people don't like dat but I'z different dat way. I like gruesome movies and gruesome magazines where there's lots of blood and guts hangin' out and I would have liked to seen how your wife looked in the coffin all smashed to shit."

The phone saved Noel, whose head was beginning to swim and eyes misfocus.

"Yes, he's here." She nodded at Noel. "He's not doin' nothin'. He just sittin' and fidgetin'. What? She wants to know how you feel? He looks white—I know he's white—I mean he looks whiter than most white people—OK." Melonie hung up. "Miss Nevers says she'll be home soon. You play five hundred rummy?"

"Five hundred rummy? Are you kidding? I'm the world champ."

"I'll play you for twenty-five cents a point." Melonie slithered onto the floor across from Noel and began shuffling a deck of cards. She adjusted the halter, covering her breasts. "I don't want nothin' distractin' you. Come on, Rothman, put your white-fidgety-mother-fuckin'-what-what-what-ass down here and let's play some five hundred."

They played until eleven-thirty, when the buzzer rang. "That's Miss Nevers." Melonie was ahead eight hundred and sixty-five to four hundred and forty, one hundred bucks, as she quickly pointed out.

Noel stood up. Nevers came into the room. She was so hypnotically beautiful that Noel felt weak, unsure of himself. She said hello to him and asked him how he was. Noel could barely answer. His mouth was dry, his throat constricted, his lips numb. What happened next to Noel Roth was so out of context with every learning experience he had ever had, so out of touch with the summation of Noel's previous life, such a *total trespass* on everything that he had ever been conditioned to do, that he couldn't talk about it for years to come, and couldn't even *think* about it for days.

With Melonie shuffling the cards and watching with limited interest, with Noel nervously shifting from one foot to the other, mouth agape, heart beating wildly, Nevers lifted her dress up above her hips, opened her legs, smiled at Noel, and told him to get on his hands and knees and crawl over to her and suck her just the way he did on Fire Island.

Noel, without a second's hesitation, did as he was told.

SIXTH GRADE SOCCER

Noel was suddenly very busy. Besides working and catching up on all that missed time in his business, he went to the Center Mondays by himself and Thursdays with the children. He spent Friday nights with just Phoebe and Phil, and all day Sunday the Roth and Radcliff families got together. He saw Nevers three nights a week, Monday, Wednesday and Saturday, often coming home as late as five or six in the morning. He would sneak into his house, unmake his bed, and wait for morning. He didn't want Beth or David to know that he was staying out until daybreak, and when occasionally asked by Beth what time he came home, he would lie and say around midnight or so. What he didn't know was that Beth was checking up on him, and would set her clock radio for four A.M., wait until Noel came home, write down what time it was and then go back to sleep. The only person she told about her father's deceit was Mrs. Bloom.

The Match Trick

If all this wasn't enough, Noel talked David into going out for the sixth-grade soccer team—no mean feat considering how David felt about athletics. The concession that he had to make and the argument that convinced David to do it was that he would coach the team. Noel didn't know all that much about soccer, having grown up mostly on basketball and baseball, but he learned. He read some books, watched the high-school team practice, befriended the high-school coach and pestered him with questions, and Phil, good old Phil, no matter what the situation, he was always there, helped him, and Noel gave him the unofficial title of Assistant Coach. Phil brought some notoriety to the team, having himself been a champion soccer goalie, something Noel quickly pointed out, and Phil in return, told the disbelieving sixth-graders that their coach, their very own coach, father of David, Coach Noel, as he wanted them to call him, held, did you hear me, I said *held*, the all-time record for making consecutive baskets in the *history of the world*. Nobody said anything, and seeing that some of the sixth-graders were already as tall as Noel, there was an undercurrent of skepticism that reached David's ears, but never Coach Noel's.

David was a fullback, but wanted to be a goalie. Having grown up on Phil's stories upon stories upon stories of his glorious goalie days, that was, in David's mind, the only position to play. But there were some problems. After all, the sixth-grade soccer team just didn't spring out of the air. Before they were a sixth-grade team, they were a fifth-grade team, and the only real difference between the sixth-grade team and the fifth-grade team was fullback Roth, Coach Noel and Assistant Coach Phil. They had a goalie, and a good one at that; a tall scrappy boy named Monte Wolff who would make catlike saves and then proceed to kick the ball three-quarters of the way down the field. Noel discussed with Phil making David the goalie.

"Outright murder," Phil said. "The other parents, all of whom come to the Saturday games, would lynch you from the goalposts. Total parental disregard for doing what is good for the team and good for the youngsters and such action would result in immediate

Don Zacharia

dismissal, bringing nothing but additional shame and humiliation to David."

"Jesus."

"Besides, that kid Wolff is good."

"I gotta find a way."

"Forget it."

So David continued to play fullback and daydreamed about playing goalie. Playing fullback in sixth-grade soccer, according to David, wasn't such a deal. The forwards and halfbacks, and particularly the goalie, was where the action and glory was.

"You're the coach," he told his father. "I don't see how it's any different from owning your own business. You tell your employees what to do, what departments you want them to work in, so why can't you tell Wolff that he's the fullback and I'm the goalie? Besides, he's an asshole."

The season went on. They practiced Wednesdays after school and played Saturday mornings. They were five and 0 by the end of October, obviously the cream of the sixth-grade soccer league.

"I gotta get Daverino into goalie," Noel told Phil again. "I gotta figure out a way to do it."

"Forget it, buddy. Have you met Wolff's father? He looks like a fire hydrant except he's six foot six and in *shipbuilding* with *Greeks*. Forget it."

One Saturday morning Noel met Monte Wolff's parents. His mother, a young attractive suburban-looking type with at least eight bracelets on one wrist and his father, exactly the way Phil described him.

"Pleased to meet you," Noel said, shaking hands.

"Coach, you're doing a fine job," Mr. Wolff said. It was a statement. Mrs. Wolff nodded approval.

"You have a fine boy," Noel said. "Fine boy. Top athlete."

"I'll let you in on a secret," Wolff said. "The high-school coach is salivating, s–a–l–i–v–a–t–i–n–g, waiting for Monte to get to high school. He has a calendar on the wall and each day in his office crosses off yesterday. That means nine hundred days until the *Wolff* is in high school."

158

"No kidding." Noel thought about the remark. He had gotten to know the high-school coach pretty well, and it didn't seem like the kind of a thing he would do. "I'm not a bit surprised," Noel said. "A kid like that can turn a team around. He is as tall as I am already." (And I used to play basketball.)

"How are you getting on, Mr. Roth?" Mrs. Wolff asked.

"Oh, I'm OK." Noel pawed at the ground. "Please call me Noel."

"I'm Doris—and this is Hank."

Everyone shook hands again.

"We all were pleased that you decided to coach the sixth-graders. It was kind of a brave thing for you to do."

Noel shrugged. "Do you know my kid David? He plays fullback."

"Damn fine," Hank Wolff said. "Damn fine."

Noel waited, sure he was going to say something more, but he didn't.

"How are you getting on?" Mrs. Wolff asked again.

"Well," Noel looked at the sky, "you know, it's not easy. Since Susan died." He heard Doris Wolff catch her breath, "It hasn't been easy. We're just trying to do the best we can."

"Well, everyone knows what hell you have been through, and everyone thinks you are doing a wonderful job. When you look at your son, and then at you, you wouldn't think—" Mrs. Wolff just couldn't finish the sentence and was sorry she started it.

"David is in therapy three days a week," Noel exaggerated.

"Therapy!"

"Yes. It seems to be helping him with his loss."

Mrs. Wolff shook her head. Noel felt he'd better get on with it before she burst into tears. "Did you know—Susan?"

Mrs. Wolff nodded. "Not well," she whispered. "She seemed— I'm really sorry I didn't know her better. She seemed like an exceptional person. Not at all—stereotyped."

Noel nodded. He put both of his hands in his pants pockets. "I have to ask the two of you something. It's awkward, so if I stumble, please excuse me. Daverino, Davie, my son, I call him Daverino, has this crazy ambition to play goalie. Naturally it's out of the question. I mean, I told him right off the bat—forget it. Do you

159

Don Zacharia

think maybe you could speak to your son, if we get a real one-sider, I mean a laugher when we're winning seven or eight to nothing, do you think you could speak to Monte and ask if he would mind if I let David be a goalie for a couple of minutes?"

Mrs. Wolff, with tears in her eyes, leaned over and kissed Noel on the cheek, and they walked away, neither of them saying a word.

That Wednesday at practice Monte approached Noel. "Coach, this Saturday why don't you let Dave start at goalie?"

"Start!" Noel playfully punched him. "Get outta here, Wolff. You wanna get me killed? You're my goalie."

"Coach, it's OK."

"Wolff, the parents would run me outta here if I did that. Parental favoritism, no thanks."

"It's OK, Coach. My mother has spoken to all the other parents, and I've spoken to all the other players, and we all agree. Everyone knows about it except you and Dave."

That Saturday, with David wearing Wolff's goalie shirt, which was about a foot too long for him, and with Coach Noel and Assistant Coach Phil screaming directions from the sidelines until both of them lost their voices, with Assistant Coach Phil's wife biting her fingernails until there was nothing left, with even Beth Roth, the goalie's older sister joining the tumult, Coach Noel's sixth graders, with Daverino Roth in the goal the whole game, won three to nothing.

NOEL'S SECRET

On the surface, Noel's life seemed to be returning to normal. At least, a lot of people thought that, including Phoebe, who was generally pleased with the way Noel was behaving. Phil wasn't so sure about Noel's recovery as his wife was. His support of Nixon seemed more fanatical than ever, and if that wasn't enough, Phil knew that Noel was starting to go out two and three nights a week, *just like that*, without once telling Phil where he was going or what he was doing.

Noel and Phil had always told each other *everything*. They had trusted each other with the secrets and indiscretions of their lives, never once holding back. They had the kind of relationship few men have, and what made it work all those years was total mutual trust. Now, for the first time, Noel was altering that trust, changing its makeup, by not leveling with Phil. He asked Noel a couple of times what he had going for him, and Noel with a wink put him off. Phil

Don Zacharia

was sure it was a woman. As that dumb cop said on the night they were all waiting for Susan to come home—it seemed like an eternity ago—there are no mathematical alternatives. But if Noel was seeing a woman, why so undercover? Why with such regularity? Why every Monday night, every Wednesday night and every Saturday night? And more important, why was he so secretive about it? Noel was many things, but when it came to fucking, shyness wasn't one of them. Phil thought about that scene in the Concord dining room after Noel had spent the night with Brenda from Pennsylvania; how could a man who recounted that, not be able to tell his best friend a month later, the name of the woman he was seeing? It bothered the hell out of Phil. He never discussed this with Phoebe, who wasn't aware of Noel's mysterious nighttime behavior.

Noel's therapist, Mrs. Bloom, didn't know anything about it either until Beth brought it up to her in a private session, and later, in front of Mrs. Bloom and David, confronted her father with what she knew. Mrs. Bloom did know that Noel was terribly troubled by some recent occurrence in his life—something he found impossible to talk about. Once he blurted out to her that he was doing something so despicable that he couldn't bear to even think about it. She had no idea what he was talking about and gently prodded him to open up, but every time she brought it up, Noel shook his head so violently and such a look of pain crossed his face that she dropped it. She was very troubled by this and spoke to her supervisor about it—a real doctor, as David Roth called him, Dr. Reed, who was the head psychiatrist at the Center. The doctor was familiar with the Roth family, and his conclusion (and he was very firm about it, almost dogmatic, Mrs. Bloom thought) was that Noel was having a homosexual relationship.

"It's almost a classic case," Dr. Reed told Mrs. Bloom in a conference they were having about the Roth family. "I don't think he's having an affair as such, that would be too threatening to his masculine image of himself, but I'm willing to bet he's hanging out in gay bars and picking up one-nighters."

Mrs. Bloom wasn't convinced. For her, it was all too pat. The whole trouble with psychiatrists, she thought, is that they think people act like textbook cases. And by textbook standards she could understand why Dr. Reed came to his conclusion. But, she, plain Mrs. Bloom, as she liked to refer to herself, wasn't convinced. What troubled her was that she was afraid that whatever Noel was doing until five in the morning three nights a week was *worse* than a casual homosexual relationship. But what? Now, she thought, if I were Noel Roth, a frustrated athlete, unhappy forever with my self-image, fantasizing always about success in another field, and my wife was *publicly* killed while obviously about to engage in some kind of affair with a *real* athlete, a real honest-to-god old-fashioned athlete named Meyer Meyerson, not a fake one like me, what would I do??? Suck some boy's cock? Let myself get fucked in the ass? It all fit so nicely, but Frieda Bloom wasn't buying it.

"He wants to," Dr. Reed told her, "so deprecate himself, so flagellate himself, so debase himself, so fustigate himself before he can turn the corner and come back, and what better way for a man involved in a macho image like Roth is than to have a homosexual relationship?"

"You mean, Doctor, he wants to give himself a slap in the face?" Mrs. Bloom asked.

Dr. Reed smiled. "Yes. That's more or less what I mean."

But she still wasn't convinced. She was afraid that somehow in reality it might even be worse. But what? Voodoo? Bloodletting? What? Wouldn't it be a joke on everyone, she thought, if Roth was doing some kind of secret work for Nixon on all those missing nights. *Gevalt. That would be worse.*

It was Mrs. Bloom, realizing Noel's pain, realizing his inability to verbalize what suddenly was controlling his life, realizing that the further you let something like that go, the more difficult it becomes, who suggested to him that he start a diary. "Sometimes you look like you're going to burst," she told him. "Why don't you try writing about it? It can be very personal, very private. You don't have to show it to anybody."

Don Zacharia

But other than Mrs. Bloom, and of course Dr. Reed, everyone thought he was doing just terrifically, and, in a way, he was. He made a deal with Beth and David that the three of them should start to do things together as a unit. They all liked doing such dissimilar things that once every two weeks the family would do whatever one member wanted. And no bitching about it, Noel added.

They went to a Knick game, which was Noel's choice, and saw the Knicks clobber Boston. They went to City Center to see Alvin Ailey, which was Beth's choice, and watched Judith Jameson do a wonderful Duke Ellington jazz routine, and they went to a Star Trek convention, of all things, which was David's choice. The Star Trek convention was amazing. Noel was sure he was going to be the only adult there, but the place (the Hilton Ballroom) was packed with men and women from all over America. Noel met a doctor from Iowa who gave him the Trekkie handshake. Noel didn't know what to do until David clued him in.

Mrs. Bloom had convinced Noel that Beth was having a very hard time of it, and Noel, aware of Beth's hostility toward him, tried spending some private time just with her. Once the two of them went out for dinner, once to the movies, but most of the time they went for long walks. David wasn't crazy about it and at first sulked until Noel spoke to him. "It's just," he said to David, "that Beth needs me right now in a way that you don't, and if it is going to make you jealous about the time I am spending with Beth, I want you to know that I understand that. Okay, Daverino?" He punched him in the arm. It was OK and it wasn't OK.

"For Beth," Mrs. Bloom told him, "a thirteen-year-old girl whose mother was just killed, you are doing a difficult thing to her."

"To her?"

"Yes. To her. She knows you go out at nighttime two and three times a week. You refuse to tell her whom you are seeing or what you are doing, and although you say it's your private business, she doesn't see it that way. She assumes you are seeing a woman, and that's a difficult thing for her to cope with. What I'm going to say is hard, Mr. Roth, but Beth wants Beth to be your date. Can you understand that? Among the many emotions she is feeling about you in relationship to another woman is fear, what we call the wicked grandmother syndrome, and mostly just plain old-fashioned jealousy. And to make matters worse, she can't even focus on what to be jealous of. You *must* speak to her. I don't expect you to go into detail; you can't even do that *here*. I am not suggesting you are seeing a woman. It's what Beth *thinks* you are doing, and that is what counts."

Noel brought it up one night while walking with Beth. "I am sure you must wonder where I go and who I see when I leave home a couple nights a week?" Beth didn't answer. It was dark and he couldn't see her face. "I know," Noel went on, "how difficult it must be for you, and I wish I could tell you tonight what's happening to me, but I can't. I'm asking you to trust me, and I promise it will work out. You have to know that I would never intentionally do anything to hurt you, although I'm sure the very thing I am doing is hurting you. You have to know that I would never lie to you, because if I did that it would destroy the kind of trust we need to survive. It's just, how can I explain this? I'm going through a very difficult time in my life—that's a laugh—I mean just speaking about myself, selfishly, forgetting my love and the responsibility that I feel for you and Dave, forgetting all that, I, personally am having a very hard time with my life. I guess you could say I have a problem, and all I can say is for you to hang in there with me because it just can't always be this way. And I love you."

Noel put his arm around his daughter's shoulder and touched her face, wet with tears. With his fingers he tried to wipe away the tears, but it was impossible, like dropping a sponge in the ocean.

There was a kosher delicatessen directly across from the Center, and each Thursday, which was the Roth family consultation day, before they went into that nursery that Noel hated, they bought three fat kosher franks with the works, mustard and plenty of sauerkraut, three Cokes to wash them down with, and went to visit Mrs. Bloom. At first they bought one for her but she pleaded with them not to.

"If I eat one of those I will be in the coronary-care unit by nightfall, and then what, David? What then?"

"I'd visit you," he said, munching his hot dog, "if they'd let me in. Hospitals have age requirements on who can visit patients."

Noel was stretched out on one of those little chairs, uncomfortable as ever. Mrs. Bloom had offered more than once to get him a regular chair, but Noel refused. "I feel I gotta suffer in here," he cracked. "These hot dogs are the best hot dogs in the whole world."

"Superlatives. I have never met a family with so many superlatives."

"Did you hear about Daverino playing goalie last week?" Noel asked.

"Yes. You told me and David told me and Beth told me, and even your friend Phoebe told me when she dropped your children off. He pitched a shutout."

"Jesus, Mrs. Bloom, he didn't pitch a shutout. In soccer you don't pitch, you goal-tend."

"Sports, in America there is such a plethora of them, I get confused. Excuse me," she said to David, "I'm sure that whatever you did it was splendid. Well, what shall we talk about today? Who has a complaint?"

"Here we go. It's Get Noelie time."

"I have a complaint," David said. "Beth is supposed to make her bed each morning and she never, never, does. She hasn't made her bed in a month."

"What business is it of yours?" Beth shot back. "You shouldn't even be in my room."

"I make my bed—"

"Big deal, Dave. When you grow up we'll give you a star for bed-making."

"Well, I don't think it's fair."

"Life sucks, kid brother."

"What do you think, Mr. Roth?" Mrs. Bloom asked.

"Ah, shit, what the hell do I think about that? I don't know—"

"Daddy—" Dave was angry— "she hasn't made her bed in a month. Every night she gets into a messy bed and I think that stinks."

"I don't believe this," Beth said, tapping her foot. "I don't believe this conversation is happening."

"Mr. Roth?"

"Well, I don't know—"

"Well, I know," David interrupted. "When Mother died—"

"Was killed," Mrs. Bloom interjected.

"Why is that important?" Noel shot out. "Why every goddamn time when one of us says 'died' you jump out of your skin and say 'killed'?"

"It's important."

"That's a wonderful answer."

"If you give me a minute, I'll tell you why. I've told you before that you three should not delude yourself as to what happened to your wife and their mother. The truth is critical and once you begin to play with it, distort it for your own comfort, it will lead to more distortions, and eventually you will lose sight of what happened."

"OK, OK, let's get on with David," Noel said, his face strained with anger. "You were saying that when your mother was killed by a falling Westinghouse air conditioner while kissing Meyerson, HOW'S THAT, MRS. BLOOM? WASN'T THAT TERRIFIC? DO THE ROTHS GET AN 'A' IN FAMILY THERAPY TODAY?"

"Please, Mr. Roth, you seem very angry today."

"Shit, angry, you make me uncomfortable." Noel lowered his voice. "Both mentally and physically. This chair is the only thing that makes me angry."

"Well, considering what all of you have been through, it's not so terrible to be angry."

"Wonderful, that's just wonderful. When you go to a dentist, he gives you Novocain. I get a feeling that you're saying that's wrong. If you were a dentist, you wouldn't give Novocain because pain is good because how else do you know what non-pain is."

"It's hardly the same thing."

Don Zacharia

"Oh, sure. Of course not. Maybe the Roth family would like a little Novocain during their mourning. But you make Novocain sound like heroin."

"Mr. Roth—" Mrs. Bloom seemed exasperated— "comparing what a dentist does to alleviate the pain when he is filling a tooth to how you and your family should react to your wife's death, is *no comparison. No one* could possibly make an argument about that. No one but you, that is."

"I agree with Mrs. Bloom," Beth said, "it's a *stupid* premise, Noel."

"Naturally, I wouldn't expect you to agree with me." There was a cut in Noel's voice. Beth always agreed with Mrs. Bloom, and David, more often than not, would agree with his father.

"How about beds?" David said.

"What beds?"

"Beth. Is she gonna start making her bed like we all agreed to when Mother was killed?"

"Oh, shit. Are we back to that?"

"David, if you ever so much as stick your nose in my bedroom, I'll smash your face in."

"Oh, yeah—"

"My bedroom is my private property."

"Well, it's in the house isn't it?"

"I want a lock on my door," directing her request to Noel. "I want a lock."

"A lock! Beth, for chrissakes, I'm thirty-six and I don't have a lock on my bedroom. We've never locked up anything in the house."

"Well, I want a lock on my door. I want to keep that creep out."

"A lock isn't the answer. Once we start doing that, you'll get a lock, David will get a lock, I don't think that's the answer. I don't think that's the kind of house we want to live in."

"Then I want a guarantee from you that your son stays out of my bedroom."

"Beth, please, David, I think if Beth makes a request that you don't go into her room unless she invites you, you should agree to that."

"How about making her bed?"

"He spies on me, Noel. He actually spies on me."

"How about making her bed?" David wasn't letting up.

"Why don't you let me work that out with Beth?"

"That's not fair."

"I agree with David," Mrs. Bloom interjected. "That's not fair to David."

"OK, OK, Beth, we agreed—will you start making your bed?"

"No."

"Oh, boy." Noel looked around the room. The room was in its usual condition: total havoc. "Why are we talking about Beth making her bed when no one has straightened up this place in a decade?"

Mrs. Bloom smiled. "Mr. Roth, I'm not going to take a position on this. This room is this way because we have made a decision that it is easier for everyone, particularly the children, to leave it this way."

"Beth, just saying no isn't a satisfactory answer. We agreed after Mother was killed that you and David will start making your own beds. Now don't ask me the significance of this, or why we agreed to that, but we did. Your brother feels justifiably, what? put upon, taken advantage of, in that he is living up to his end of the agreement and you are not. And besides, baby, why does this particular issue have to be such a deal?"

"You don't make your bed," Beth shot at him.

"What? Ah, shit, Beth." Noel looked at Mrs. Bloom pleadingly. "Beth, I'm thirty-six years old, and that entitles me to certain, not many, but certain, privileges. True, I don't make my own bed, I hire a housekeeper and one of her duties is to make my bed, and interestingly enough, not yours or David's. I also drive a car and you don't. I drink scotch and you don't and also go to sleep later than you."

"I'm aware of that," she cut in, "very aware."

"What the hell does that mean?"

"Why nothing, *Noel*, nothing at all. I'm also aware that three nights a week you unmake your bed when you don't have to. Isn't

Don Zacharia

that amazing, Mrs. Bloom? Isn't that positively amazing? I bet you didn't know that." Beth seemed to be losing her composure. "I bet you didn't know that three nights a week *Mr. Roth* comes home at SIX in the morning, RIPS his bed apart, never gets into it, and then lies to me about what time he gets in. Oh," trying to mimic Noel but more of a sob than a mimic, "he tells me in the morning, 'I was home at twelve-thirty last night, sweetie.' "

Mrs. Bloom bit her lip. For the first time it was out in the open.

Beth was sobbing, and Noel felt no compassion.

"I don't feel," Noel said, trying very hard to control himself, "that you have any right to be spying on me."

"Spying on you," Beth sobbed. "You mean when I woke up not feeling well and vomiting and when I went in to tell you that I was sick at four in the morning and you're not there, *that's spying, Daddy?*"

"Oh, God," Noel groaned.

Beth wasn't finished. "You lied," she sobbed. Close to hysteria, she was almost unintelligible. "You lied," she screamed at Noel. "You gave David and me this big father lecture about never lying and then you lied. Why—are—you—doing—this—to—me, Daddy?" She dashed out of the room, holding her face, crying uncontrollably.

Noel, anguished, turned to Mrs. Bloom. "What do I do now?" he whispered.

"Go after your daughter," she said.

Noel found Beth in the back seat of the car struggling to gain her composure. He sat down next to her. For a long time no one spoke.

"Wouldn't it be nice," Beth said, breaking the silence, "if a chauffeur with one of those caps on and a spiffy uniform got in the front seat and drove the two of us away?"

"Where to?"

"I don't know. Just away from everything. I've never driven with a chauffeur. There's a girl in my grade who gets chauffeured to school each morning. Can you imagine? Everyone gives her the fisheye. I think it's pretentious."

170

"The only time I ever used a chauffeur is when your mother and I got married."

"I didn't know that."

"I was a big spender before I had money, which is a neat trick. I had this monster navy-blue Cadillac with a very proper black chauffeur pick your mother and her parents up and drive them to the temple before we got married. It wowed the shit out of her parents."

"Daddy," Beth said, smiling, "that was a nice thing to do."

"Your mother didn't think so. I suppose she did and didn't. Susan was going through her revolutionary stage in those days. Castro had just swept through Cuba and he looked a lot different than he does now. A lot of people, your mother included, thought he was some kind of a hero. A Robin Hood with a beard and a tommygun— and riding to a synagogue to marry *me*, with her *parents* in a *limousine* with a *black chauffeur*, wasn't exactly in your mother's image. She got over it."

"Anyhow, that's a nice story."

"Would you like to go away?"

"I think it would be nice. I think we all could use it."

"Maybe for Thanksgiving we'll go away with the Radcliffs. We'll find some inn in Vermont where they serve blueberry pancakes and sausages for breakfast."

"That's a nice picture, Daddy."

"Your mother always used to say I was pretty good at painting verbal pictures."

"I think we all could go away. Instead of everybody trying to help each other, we all seem to be fighting each other. I'm fighting with David all the time, and I don't want to do that. I never fought with him before."

"And then there's you and me," Noel said.

"Yes," expectantly, "yes?"

"I need some time, Beth. I instinctively know what my responsibilities are. I don't need Phoebe or Mrs. Bloom to tell me that. I understand what my role should be—the remaining parent, Christ, I've heard that from so many people I choke on it—I know instinctively what the *right* thing to do is, but right now I'm not capable of being Mr. Tower of Strength that everyone wants me to be. So what am I supposed to do about it? Jump off a bridge? What would that prove? Everyone has everything all figured out, but there's a hitch and that hitch is me. I'm having problems, Beth, problems in coping, problems in handling my life. I am out of control. Don't you think I know how important it is for me to be with you? I know that, but I am not capable of it." Noel's voice broke off. "Look, it's really hard for me to talk more about it right now. I think I've had all I can handle. We better go back inside. Mrs. Bloom will think we are killing each other."

With Noel's arm around Beth, they went back inside. Mrs. Bloom was talking to David. She waited for Noel and Beth to seat themselves. "Did you two solve anything?"

"Solve anything?" Noel felt his voice was louder than necessary. "Solve anything?" He looked at Beth. "What do you say, sweetie, did we solve anything?"

The minute Beth got home she went over to Aunt Phoebe's and spoke to her privately. First she told her what her mother once told her—that if you ever need help, big help, and for some reason I'm not about, speak to Aunt Phoebe. If it can be done, Susan told her, Phoebe will get it done. She might steamroll over anything in her way, but she will get it done. Then Beth told Phoebe about her father. She told her everything she knew, and everything she imagined, and mostly she told her what he had been doing to her.

Later that day Mrs. Bloom was talking to Dr. Reed about the Roths, specifically Noel and Beth. "Like lovers, the two of them; especially Beth. It's so obvious, it's painful to watch. They had a lover's quarrel, made up beautifully, and left solving nothing."

"I think," Dr. Reed said, sucking on the unlit pipe that was in his mouth eighteen hours a day, "that you are pushing them too fast."

"Too fast! Roth is ready to self-destruct. He told me that himself. He told me he made an entry in his diary to that effect."

"His diary?"

"Yes. It was my suggestion."

"How long has he been doing that?"

"Three weeks."

"I'm surprised you haven't told me this before, Frieda." His voice had a disapproving ring.

"Haven't I?"

"No. I think you are manipulating me. I think you are preevaluating the Roth material and feeding me what you want."

"Doctor! That's absurd. Let's please drop this line of questioning."

"It seems strange to me that you haven't told me about something as significant as Roth's starting a diary."

"It must have slipped my mind. I apologize. That's ridiculous. I don't even apologize. You have put me into an unfair position. Can we please get back to Roth? He told me he made an entry in his diary called 'Out of Control.' He makes this strange comparison between himself and Nixon. He said that he and Nixon, and here he used a very dramatic phrase, were like *two innocent gangsters* strapped into the front seat of a car that was speeding downhill and neither was capable of doing anything about it. He keeps referring to that; and there is something else, a new development—"

"Strapped?" Dr. Reed interrupted. "He used that word?"

"Yes."

"Powerless? Downhill? He used those words?"

"Yes."

Dr. Reed was sucking on his pipe furiously. "Interesting," was all he said.

"If this isn't enough, the latest development is that Roth is convinced he is being followed."

"Predictable. When did he tell you this?"

"This week," defensively. "Just this week. What do you make of it?"

"Predictable. If we had ten bucks for every patient who comes in here thinking they are being followed, we wouldn't have to be involved in those damnable fund-raisers; speaking of which, you never answered my note about next month's charity ball."

"My mail, opening my mail is one of my poorer activities."

"I bring it up because two of the board members mentioned your absence the last two years. I'd like to hear from you as soon as possible about that."

"Yes, of course. I will check my calendar—"

Dr. Reed stood up, signifying an end to the meeting. "Next week?"

"Yes, next week."

"Stop worrying so much about Roth. We both know what he's into."

Nevers. Nevers had a favorite position. With Noel flat on his stomach, she liked to lie on top of him. It had a lot of variations, but the basic position always remained the same. When they were like this, she whispered into his ear describing in detail the things she was going to do to him. She cajoled him to such unexplored dizzy sexual heights, that twice Noel had an orgasm in the bed sheets without her touching him. Nevers was furious. The first time she called in Melonie and humiliated him beyond belief for his lack of sexual control. When it happened again, she told him she was going to teach him a lesson, and she strapped on a small dildo that she slowly inserted into his rectum, not moving while she verbally castigated him, and then without warning, quick penetrating thrusts, causing Noel to howl in anguish, begging her to stop, but she wouldn't hear of it, just slowing down, giving Noel a moment to recover his senses, to assemble his thoughts, and all the time cooing into his ear, telling him that she was going to *fuck* him this way until *she* came, and then when the pain was ebbing, those hard fierce thrusts again until minutes later, Nevers, screaming in pleasure, burying the dildo far inside of Noel, had an orgasm.

After, Noel felt violated and debased in a way he had never felt before, emotionally spent, yet, oddly, crazily, wanting more. Confused by a million senses that he didn't recognize, trying to recover

174

some form of stability, but Nevers, not giving him a chance, began to whisper in his ear again. She asked him how he liked what had happened, and before he could answer, she told him that the next time he couldn't control himself she was going to whip him. When she talked to him this way, she whispered, sometimes so quietly that Noel had to strain to hear every word. She licked and sucked his ear, the back of his neck; she ran her fingers along his flanks, causing him to jump with pleasure. She rubbed her groin into his buttocks, sometimes coming that way, and then, telling him not to move, she would lick and suck the spot where she had just come. At moments like this Noel's mind would slip into areas where it had never been before. She told him that she wished she were a man so she could fuck him with a cock and come inside of his ass. She told him that someday she was going to make him suck a man's cock, suck him off until he came inside of Noel's mouth; that she was going to take him to a gay bar and prostitute him to a man of her choice for one hundred dollars. She told him that she was going to make a whore out of him, and the only way she would ever fuck him in the usual sense would be with Noel on top and Melonie whipping his calves and buttocks, until she, Nevers, came, and after, with his cock and balls still swollen, he would bathe her and thank her for having him whipped, and then she would send him home.

For Noel, whose only previous bizarre sexual experience was taking some eight-millimeter home movies of his wife playing with her breasts, it was a situation without memory.

By the first week of November, six people knew that Noel was doing something that he shouldn't be doing, but no one knew what, or what to do about it. Phoebe and Phil knew; Mrs. Bloom and Dr. Reed knew; and Beth and David knew. Dr. Reed was positive that Noel was having some kind of a homosexual relationship. Mrs. Bloom didn't accept the homosexual theory; never did, despite Dr. Reed's urgings. Beth was sure her father was seeing another woman and, interestingly enough, conjured up visions of what this woman looked like that were pretty close to the mark. David, David didn't think about it. Of them all he didn't seem to care, and didn't understand what all the fuss was about. His father was spending more time with him than ever before, and if he wanted to go out a few nights a week—big deal.

With Noel's help, the downstairs playroom went through what Noel called the fourth transformation. Susan's studio was dismantled, and they made a workshop out of it for David. David was thrilled by it. For a couple of hundred dollars, all under David's supervision, they outfitted it with drills, bits, coping saws, angle saws, hammers, more saws, screwdrivers in every possible shape—enough assorted carpentry equipment, Noel thought, to easily build an apartment house. Noel couldn't hammer a nail in without smashing a finger, and it pleased him to see the dexterity with which his son used a coping saw. I guess, Noel thought, thinking about *his* basketball talent as a youngster, my prowess as a dribbler is going to skip a generation. At first David built simple things, cubes and basic carpentry, getting used to the tools. He had a natural flair for it and in just a few days began building an intricate three-story dollhouse from plans he had cut out of a magazine.

"What are you going to do with it when you're finished?" Noel asked.

"Bring it up to the Center for the nursery. I told Mrs. Bloom about it. She thinks it's going to be terrific."

"I bet she does. Those psychos up there will wreck it the first day."

"Maybe. If they do, okay. I understand that. But maybe they won't. I know some of those kids. I'm using these bolts so it won't just fall apart if one of them kicks it."

Noel had seen the children who went to the Center nursery. Three- and four-year-olds, some looking as normal as any kids, but others with such a vacant look about them that it made him anxious. "You know where your workbench is, David, well, before you were born I had this old black-and-white TV down here that I used to watch. Only me, nobody else would ever watch it because there was something wrong with the vertical and it made everyone look twelve feet tall."

"How come you never fixed it?"

"Ah, I don't know. I guess I just didn't give a damn. It wasn't so bad, looking at all those stretched-out skinny people. Wilt Chamberlain was twenty feet tall."

"Who?"

"Wilt Chamberlain—don't tell me you've never heard of him."

"I don't think so."

"Jesus. I've got a son who never heard of Wilt Chamberlain."

"Who was he?"

"Forget it. A basketball player. Anyhow," Noel said wistfully, "it wasn't so bad looking at all those tall people. It wasn't like some were tall and some were short. They were *all* tall. One day your mother dumped the TV and bought me that pool table with the ping-pong top. You remember that?"

"Kind of," David said, studying the plans for the dollhouse. "It's kind of fuzzy."

"David, for chrissakes, that was only a couple of years ago. Let me see, that was only five years ago. You were six."

"I really don't remember it so well."

"You don't remember five years ago? You don't remember playing pool with me and Beth?"

"Not really. Do you remember when you were five?"

"Daverino, when I was five was thirty-one years ago. I've had all these years to forget. When you were five was six years ago."

"I suppose I'm blocking it for some reason—"

"Blocking it," Noel faked a moan, "when most kids are out going one on one, my kid is blocking out his childhood. Thank you, Madam Bloom."

David smiled. "She's not so bad."

"No, I suppose not. I gotta go. Go to sleep early."

"You going out?"

"Yup."

Don Zacharia

"I don't mind."

Noel leaned over and kissed him.

"Don't tell Beth, Dad, but after I'm finished with the dollhouse I'm going to make her something. I don't know what yet, but something."

"Hey, that's nice. That's OK. See you, Daverino."

Noel left thinking David should become an architect when he grew up. Better an architect than a mother-fucking retailer.

QUESTIONS AND ANSWERS

Melonie and Noel were sitting around Nevers' apartment waiting for her to come back. It was Wednesday evening and Melonie was pissed because Noel had insisted that they watch a Nixon press conference. The President, under a barrage of hostile reporters' questions, said, "The tougher it gets, the cooler I get." Noel liked that. The President lashed out at the press, saying, "I have never seen such outrageous, vicious, distorted reporting in my twenty-seven years of public life." The President also spoke about the new special prosecutor, but didn't name him, and defended once again his firing of Archibald Cox.

Melonie was nude, but Melonie being nude or Melonie being dressed was pretty much the same thing. They were both drinking beer and eating cheese and salami. Melonie had her feet on the table and was balancing a glass of beer on her stomach.

"Look at dat."

Don Zacharia

"I'm looking. I'm looking."

"I bet you can't do dat. You need a flat stomach to do dat and you need to be able not to breathe. I can hold my air for twenty minutes. Look—de glass ain't movin' a touch."

"I can't see your belly button."

"You got a thing 'bout my button. What's dat word you and Miss Nevers use?"

"Fetish?"

"Yeah, fetish. You got a fetish for my button. You stare at it like you never seen none 'fore."

"Melonie," taking a piece of cheese and a slice of salami, "you've got the most gorgeous belly button in the world. It is like a dark, disappearing, mysterious, illusive painting."

"You crazy, Rothman, anyone ever tell you dat?"

"I've got a lady whose name is Bloom I'm paying five hundred bucks a week who occasionally hints at that."

"Can I asks you a question?"

"Shoot."

She pointed a finger at him and pulled an imaginary trigger. "I likes you Rothman."

"I like you too, Melonie. What's the question?"

"Why you like that fuckface so much?"

"*Who?*"

"That fuckface Nixon. Why you likes him so much? Why you listen to everything he sez? Read everything he writes?"

It wasn't the question Noel expected. "That's pretty complicated."

"I ain't stupid."

"I know that." They had finished their beers and Noel got two more. "OK. I feel that Nixon is not as bad a person as he is being made out to be. I feel that he got caught up in a web of incidents, not all of them his own doing. And I feel he is out of control of the situation. And the press—did I mention the press? The press is taking advantage. The press wants to sell newspapers—"

"I sorry I asked," Melonie interrupted.

"Well, let me ask you a question. Do you like him?"

"No."

"Why not?"

"He has a fuckface. Those fucking jowls hangin' down to his kneecaps."

"Is that the only reason? That's a reason to like or dislike some-one? Is that the only reason?"

"I don't trust him."

"Why?"

"Shit, Rothman, once you get goin' you ask dumb-dumb ques-tions. Ain't no reason why you don't trust someone—you just don't. You'se so stupid you'se don't see dat? I trusts you'se and I don't trusts him."

"Oh," Noel said, admiring her logic. "Is that it?"

"Is what it?"

"Are there any other reasons?"

"I'ze bored with you, Rothman. You start in sumpin', you one bor–*ring* fuck."

"OK, OK, let's change the topic. You want to play some five hundred?"

"Dere is 'nother reason."

"Yeah. What's that?"

"He don't like me so I don't like him."

"What do you mean—he doesn't like you? How do you know that? Did the President call Melonie up on the phone and tell her that?"

"You stupid. You nice—but you stupid. You think he likes me? You think dat fuckface walks into dis room and sees me he gonna say, I like dat Melonie, or he gonna jackass it outta here the second his eyeballs sees my nigger snatch?"

"I guess you're right," Noel laughed.

"You guess I'm right! You'se better well know I'm fuckin' right and if he don't like me, you gotta give me one spectible reason I supposed to like him."

"Melonie, that's the best political analysis I've heard in two months."

"My turn."

Don Zacharia

"Your turn for what?"

"My turn to ask you a question."

"Shoot."

"I gotta think it out." She casually scratched her groin. "How comes you here?"

"Here?"

"I didn't ask dat so good. Listening to that lying fuckface makes my brain fuzzy. How comes you lets Miss Nevers do the things she do? How comes you let her whip your ass and tie your nuts up and you still go suckin' after her?"

"Oh, Melonie, I'm not sure I can answer that. If I knew the answer to that maybe I wouldn't be here. Maybe I'd be in my store taking inventory of men's slacks."

"Dat ain't the question."

"I thought it was."

"I understand dat part, de whippin' and shit—"

"You do? I wish you would explain it to me."

"I understand it, and don't understand it, but dat ain't de question. De question is—how comes you pay her? Dat's de question."

"I pay her because she asks me to. If I didn't, she wouldn't see me. You know that."

"Dat's the answer?"

Noel nodded.

"Dat's de dumbest fuckinist answer I ever heard. You crazy Rothman. You needs yourself a doctor. Your brain cells screwed up. You don't pay someone to whip you; someone pay you. She should be payin' you. Dat's so fuckin' simple I can't even say it right. Rothman, lemme give you some advice; you should jump your white ass outta here and get you a Jew doctor."

"Come on, Melonie, it just isn't like that."

"Yeah, what's it like if it ain't like dat? If it ain't like dat, my fuckin' eyes been seein' a mir-age the last month. If I don't see yuh diggin' in your pockets comin' up with all dose Ben Franklins after you gettin' your ass whipped, den I needs the eyeglass doctor. Get me another beer, Rothman."

Noel got two more beers. "Let me turn the question around—"

"Shit—"

"What's the matter?"

"You talk funny. What dat's sentence supposed to mean? 'Let me turn da question around.'" She tried to mimic Noel.

Noel laughed. "OK, OK. How come you are here? How come you call her Miss Nevers?"

"She pays me. You pays her and she pays me. Dat's de American way. How come you asks a question when you knows the answer 'fore you asks it?"

"Is that it? Is that the only reason?"

"I can't think of no other. Here I'm sellin' my snatch on the street gettin' my ass busted every other day by Mr. Fuckface and dis lady comes along, buys me clothing, buys me Heinekens, supplies me with toads, give me five Ben Franklins a week, and all she wants in return is for me to call her Miss Nevers and do what I used to do for a George Washington, and you wanna know *how come?* Sometimes when I talk to whiteass like you I wonders how comes you where you is and all dose niggers is where dey is. You stupid? You always been so stupid or it just happened since your wife got her head knocked off?"

"Come on, one more question."

Melonie pointed a finger at Noel and pulled the trigger. "Shoot, Mr. Questionman."

"Are there any other men Nevers sees?"

"What's you think?"

"I think there probably are."

"Dat the first thing you got right today. Sure dere's other men. You think she's in love with you?"

"A lot of other men?"

"Shit. I thought we finished with dat question. Dis is a mul–tip–le question, right, Rothman?" Melonie slapped her thighs and then pulled on both of her tits, pleased with herself. "I'm studyin' my words like Miss Nevers tells me. Mul–ti–ple—mil–tit–ute or some-thin' like that. What's the fuckin' difference?"

Don Zacharia

"You didn't answer."

"No. Dey ain't a lot of men. Dis ain't no whorehouse. Dis a place where crazy white people come to get their asses whupped. Dere's you and a couple more. Miss Nevers very particular."

"Oh, what are the others like?"

"Like you. Dey all white. Ain't no black mother-fucker comes up here to get his ass whupped. Dey too fuckin' smart for dat. If it makes you feel any better, she sees youse de most. She likes you."

"How do you know that?"

Melonie stared at him. "I gettin' tired."

"Just answer that and I'll play five hundred with you."

"The same way I know Mr. Fuckface President of dese here U.S. of A. don't like me, I know Miss Nevers likes you."

"She never said it out loud, did she? She never verbalized it?"

"I can't take youse no more."

"OK, OK, get the cards. How much do I owe you?"

"Plenty. Eight Ben Franklins and four George Washingtons. Hey, Rothman, instead of five hundred, let's do somethin' different."

"OK, what?"

"Lemme give you head, Rothman. Lemme spring you. I give you head once, just once and youse cured from dis shit. Miss Nevers won't ever allow me to give you head. How you stand dat—you suckin' me and you suckin' her and then she sends you home sometimes your stick so big for a white man I can't believe it. I get a vision of you yanking off in your car and so much gism comes outta you, you gotta put the windshield wipers on. Why you let her do dat?" Not waiting for an answer, "You like it? You like goin' outta here with your white stick bangin' up against your ankle?"

"Thanks for the compliment."

"Lemme give you head, Rothman. Takes your pants off and lay down and I'll do stuff to you your body don't know about. I give head better den anybody in New York. Dat's a known fact. You go out into de streets and asks who gives de best head in dis mother-fucking city, you know what the answer gonna be? It's gonna be

184

Melonie. Melonie don't work de streets no more, but some stud once told me I should insure my mouth. I likes givin' head better den anyting. I dream 'bout dat. I dream 'bout it at nighttime, and during de day when I gets bored I think bout de dream and sometimes de dream is so real it's hard for me to tell where one thing ends and one thing begins. You understand me? If you do, you good, cause just talking 'bout dis dream makes my mouth confused. I dream I got a man, he ain't got no face, no legs, no arms, no nothin', just this giant cock. It's de biggest cock in the whole world. It's de size of de Statue of Liberty. It's black. Dat's all dere is. Dis black Statue of Liberty cock and I'm givin' it head. I start at de bottom like only Melonie knows and works my way up. It takes a year for me to bring him off but when dis cock starts shooting, it shoots for three years and all New York has to wear galoshes and umbrellas cause the sky is raining my man's spink. Ain't dat something?"

Noel was laughing so hard at Melonie's story that tears were coming to his eyes. "Melonie," he finally said, wiping his eyes, "that's some wonderful dream."

"You think it's funny?"

"Well, I don't think it's unfunny."

"What you say, Rothman, takes your stick out and Melonie will take you down the road to bliss."

Noel got up and got the cards and started shuffling them. "Come on, Melonie, gimme a chance to win some of my money back."

Normal. I am the most normal person in the world. I look in the mirror and what do I see? Mr. Normal, that's what I see. Mr. Normal. Normal. Normal. I'm the most normal person in the world. The word abnormal is abnormal to me. My life is the universal standard for normalcy. You want to judge normalcy, judge me: Noelie. I own four extraordinarily successful clothing stores, I belong to an exclusive golf club; I sit in a sauna with other men and it's all right. I live in an exclusive neighborhood. I have two children. I used to have a

Don Zacharia

dog. I used to have a wife. I used to play basketball (and had a damn fine jump shot). I have very normal friends and a very normal friendship with Phil. I have never had VD. I have never had anything even approaching a homosexual relationship. No man *has ever touched me around my genitals (I don't mean goosing and crap like that); I mean* touching *me. I belong to the Chamber of Commerce. I belong to our local Kiwanis and have lunch once a month with my fellow Kiwanians, and before lunch we all stand up and sing "God Bless America." And three nights a week I pay a white woman to suck her toes while a black teenager watches. Why?*

P.W.O.P.

P.W.O.P. In the first week of November, Phoebe decided to force the issue. It was time, she thought. She mentioned it to Phil. "It's time," she said.

Phil scratched his nose. "OK," he said, having no idea what Phoebe was talking about. Their sons were upstairs and they were in the library. Phoebe was absentmindedly looking through a brochure from The New School, and Phil, at Noel's insistence, was reading an article in the *New Statesman* defending Nixon's position on the Nixon tapes. Phil thought it would have been a lot more logical if he were taking the pro-Nixon position that Noel suddenly was championing. Phil had voted loudly and conspicuously for Nixon in 1968, wearing a Nixon button and putting a Nixon sticker on his car that Phoebe scraped off the next day. In 1972 he was disenchanted with the Nixon gang, but still voted for him. Christ, did they fight about it. Phoebe, Susan and Noel would gang up on

Don Zacharia

Phil, trying to get him to change his position, each one taking a different approach, but the more they talked, the more stubborn Phil became. Now, when Phil and the whole nation were doing an about-face on Tricky Dick, to hear Noel constantly defending him was beginning to worry Phil more than Noel's nocturnal wanderings.

"It's time," Phoebe said again, realizing that Phil wasn't listening to her, "for Noel to start dating *women*."

Phil looked up from his magazine. "Phoebe, come on, leave well enough alone."

"It's time." Phoebe waved him away. "How long has it been? Almost three months since Susan's death. Do you know if Noel has seen any woman since Susan died?"

"I don't know," he said, "and what's more I don't think it's any of our business."

"You're wrong," Phoebe said. "I think it's becoming very much our business."

Oh, boy, Phil thought, here we go.

"Noel goes out two and three times a week, sometimes coming home as late as six in the morning. Do you have any idea where he goes or why he comes home so late?"

"No."

"I don't believe you," Phoebe said.

"What?"

"You heard me. I don't believe you."

Phil shrugged. "She doesn't believe me," he addressed the ceiling. "So what else is new?"

"I followed him once."

"WHAT!"

Phoebe smiled. Phil was so predictable. "I said, I followed him once."

"That's despicable." Phil was angry, protective of his friend. Phil was convinced Noel was getting some special piece of ass, a very special piece of ass (go explain that to Phoebe), and for the time being wanted to keep it private. The only thing that bothered Phil was the way Noel was overreacting to everything since Susan was killed, and he hoped to God that Noel didn't come home with a wife one Monday night. "That's really despicable, Phoebe. How would you like it if I started following you?"

"I wouldn't."

"And where did you follow him to, Sherlock Holmes?"

"I lost him. He goes to the city some dumb fucking way through Harlem. I lost him on Second Avenue near One Hundred and Tenth Street."

Phil laughed. He was aware of Noel's tortuous route through Manhattan.

"Where do you think he goes, Phil?"

"To the movies. I think he goes to the movies."

"Don't be wise."

"OK. I'll tell you. He goes to Grand Central Station to the Oyster Bar. You know Noel is an oyster freak."

"I don't believe you."

"She doesn't believe me." Phil spoke to the ceiling again.

"Do you know what I think? I don't think you know where Noel goes. I think Noel is having a homosexual relationship."

Phil looked at her incredulously and then began to laugh. Phil bust a gut. He laughed and laughed and laughed until he was close to tears. Phoebe, having been fully prepared for some kind of a major response, remained calm.

Phil finally stopped and wiped a tear from his eye. He rubbed his stomach where he had strained himself. "A rupture. I think you gave me a rupture. Phoebe, let me assure you of one thing. You can bet your life on it; even better, I'll bet your life on it. I'll bet Mark and Eric's life on it; I'll bet my law practice on it; I'll bet the house and every single fucking penny we have on it. I'll bet my enormous fucking organ on it." Phil stood up and with two hands clutched his groin. "You see this cock? You see this giant cock? I'll bet you this cock, you can cut it off, you can have it, you can stuff it in a jar, nah, it won't fit in a jar, you can stuff it in one of those gallon milk jugs. How's that, I'll bet this giant monster quadruple-size cock of mine that Noel Roth is not now, yesterday or tomorrow having a homosexual relationship. Understand?"

"Are you positive?"

Phil slumped down in his chair. "Did you hear what she said?" talking to the ceiling. "She asked me if I was sure? I'm not sure, Phoebe. I'm positive. P–O–S–I–T–I–V–E."

"How do you know?"

"I know."

"How."

"I know."

"Do you ever talk about it?"

"Talk about it? Phoebe, what do you think we talk about? Do you think when Noel and I get together, we talk about his nonexistent homosexual tendencies? Phoebe, you're full of shit."

"I think you're wrong."

"I haven't convinced her," talking to the ceiling.

"I think Noel could be having a relationship with a man and you wouldn't be aware of it."

"A relationship with a man," Phil mimicked her, "a relationship with a man. Jesus, you make it sound like a piece of shit. What the fuck have Noel and I been having for the past ten years?"

"You tell me."

"Oh, my God. I'm going to bed."

"How about Meyer Meyerson?"

"Meyer Meyerson? What does he have to do with anything? Do you think Noel is seeing *him?*"

"Don't you think there were all kinds of homosexual overtones in that party for Meyerson—"

"Holy shit." Phil stood up.

"You're so close to it you wouldn't see it if it smacked you in the face."

"Phoebe, I have a confession to make."

"Shut up." ·

"Phoebe," Phil put his hands on his hips and began prancing around the room, "I have this confession to make. When you think

I go to court to earn a living, I'm really going to the men's room on Forty-second Street."

"Shut up."

"Phoebe—if only you were a man—"

"There's more truth to that than you know."

"Oh, Phoebe, how can I tell you this—?"

"You think you're such a wise-ass, Phil Radcliff. You think you're such a jock. You think your prick is your sole claim to masculinity. Well, let me clue you in. It's not."

Phil stood up. "I'm going to bed," he said to the ceiling.

"Tell me, darling, tell me, big man, all about it. Do you know what Lois said after she saw you and Noel perform the match trick at the Meyerson party? She said it was one of the most blatant homosexual acts she has ever seen in public. And George agreed with her and so do I."

Phil lifted his leg and farted. "Good night," he said to the ceiling. He slammed the door after him.

The next night Noel came over for dinner. Friday night dinners with Phoebe and Phil had become a tradition since Susan's death, and as far as Noel was concerned, a damn nice one. On Sundays, Phoebe always had Noel and the children over to family-type dinner, chicken or barbecue or deli, or something, but Friday, Friday was *their* night. They would either go out to one of their favorite restaurants or Phoebe would cook at home. Phoebe always arranged everything, and Noel never knew in advance what they were doing. She never allowed anyone to horn in on them. Friday night was just for the three of them, and it was a night each one of them looked forward to.

Before Noel arrived, she told Phil she was going to bring up the subject of dating and she wanted Phil to back her up.

Phil grunted, still smarting from the night before, and then said, "You bring up any of that homosexual shit and I'm gonna slam the shit outta yuh, Phoebe."

Don Zacharia

"Mr. Sensitive speaks a sentence. Slam the shit outta yuh, Phoebe," she aped in a low voice.

Phoebe was into Chinese cooking, and using a wok and buying all the vegetables and meats fresh from a local Chinese grocery store that had recently sprung up in White Plains, she had prepared a gourmet meal.

Phil, clowning around—What kind of wine goes with Chinese?—had opened two bottles of Grand Cru Chablis. Everyone was feeling fine. Phoebe had prepared pearl balls with sweet Chinese sausages, wonton soup, chicken with vegetables, and Szechuan cooked steak.

"Stick," Noel said, calling Phil by his nickname, "this lady can cook." Using his chopsticks, he captured a pearl ball.

"Pal," Phil, having trouble with the chopsticks, was shoveling the food into his mouth directly from the bowl, "you bet your ass."

"Pig," Phoebe cracked.

"It's the way the Chinks do it."

"Boy, is this good, Phoebe."

Phoebe, pleased, smiled.

"She cooks out. Two hundred a week and you can have this rapture every night . . ."

"Generous," Noel said. "Generous."

"Also some occasional indigestion. I should warn you she goes into a green-pepper frenzy that's murder."

"More wine." Noel held his glass up to Phil. "Delicious, Phoebe. I can't believe I'm eating so much."

"You know what they say about Chink food, buddy."

"Yeah, yeah." Noel speared some sausages.

"Phoebe, lookie the way Noelie manipulates those chopsticks."

"I was born of Chinese stock. Phoebe, this is gooood. This is the best fucking meal I've ever had. More wine, buddy."

Phil filled up the glasses.

"Have you ever had a date, Noel?" She said it like that. Just popped it out.

Noel wiped his lips, sipped some more wine and looked at Phil.

192

Phil gave him the eye. "Have I ever had any dates?" Noel repeated. "Have I ever had any dates? I've had some figs—but I haven't had any dates."

Phil broke up, laughing so hard he spit some food out toward Noel. Noel tried to deadpan but Phil's laughter was infectious.

"He had some figs," Phil squealed.

"Would you like some wonton now?" Phoebe dumped some into Noel's bowl without waiting for an answer.

Noel started spooning the soup into his mouth. "Oh, god, this lady is related to Madame Pearl."

"Madame who?" Phil asked.

"Madame Pearl, dummy. She owns a restaurant in Chinatown. What soup! What a delicacy."

"Okay, Jack Benny. I'll rephrase it. Have you slept with any woman since Susan died?"

Noel put his soup spoon down, swallowed a piece of pork he was chewing on, looked first at Phil and then at Phoebe. "Phoebe," plaintively, "can't this wait?"

"Till when?"

"Till later. Till next month."

"Till later, yes, but why not now?"

"Because I'm enjoying myself, Phoebe. I'm having the best time of my life." Phil knocked on the table. "And sleeping with women doesn't go with great Chinese food." Noel winked at Phil.

"Jack Benny," Phoebe said.

Phil opened the third bottle of wine. They were all eating and drinking enormous amounts, and were starting the third dish, chicken and vegetables, Hunan style. No one was giving the slightest indication of slowing down or stopping.

"Have you ever heard of P.W.O.P.?" Phoebe asked Noel.

"It's the next dish," Phil said, with his mouth filled with broccoli. "She makes it with dried figs."

"Knock it off, will you, Phil? Have you, Noel?"

"P—what?"

"P.W.O.P."

Don Zacharia

"Is it a Palestinian organization?"

"Jack Benny. P.W.O.P. stands for People Without Partners. They've been asking me about you."

"Is it like D and B?"

"Come on, Noel."

Phil burped. Phoebe glared at him. Phil held his hands up. "Honey, please. It was involuntary. Now I can first begin to eat. Pass me the steak."

"P.W.O.P. is a group I think you would like, Noel."

"I don't like groups." Noel, for the first time, was beginning to feel full. "What do they do?"

"It's no big deal. They meet once a week in a member's home. Tuesday nights. Mostly divorced people, some widowers, it's all very casual. No pressures. Light drinks, wine, no hard stuff, music, some food. Mostly it's people talking and meeting other people who have similar problems and similar situations who don't want to go to bars."

"And—" Noel put down his chopsticks.

"They want to know if you would like to attend Tuesday's meeting."

"Forget it."

"It sounds like a fuck party to me, Noel," Phil said.

"You go."

"Can I go, Phoebe?"

"Noel is going."

"Ha. Over Noel's stuffed fucking body is Noel going to P—P what?"

"P.W.O.P."

"P.W.O.P. PWOP. Pwop. I love it. Pwop me some more wine, Phil."

"I already told them you would be there, Noel."

"It's a fuck party, Noel. Right here in the suburbs. You lucky shit."

"Let's go into the library," Phoebe said.

They all stood up and headed out. The table looked like thirty people had just had dinner there. Noel pushed his stomach out. "Fifth month," he said.

Phil, sensing it was just the beginning of the evening, opened up two more bottles of Chablis and got three fresh glasses.

"The best meal I've ever had," Noel said.

"The best meal I've ever had," Phil repeated.

"Have you slept with a woman since Susan died?" Phoebe didn't waste any time.

"Phoebe," Noel said, holding his stomach, "why'd you let me eat so much?"

"Answer the question."

"Phoebe, you're a terrific cook, but I'm not really sure that's your business."

Phil tapped his foot on the floor for applause.

"The only reason it's my business is that I don't think you have, and I think it's time, and if you need a little push, I'm the one who's going to give the push."

Noel, clowning, fell off the chair.

Phoebe ignored him. "I get twenty phone calls a week from single women about you. Whether you know it or not, you're the newest and hottest catch in town, and that's where P.W.O.P. comes in. You should feel flattered. It's a display case just for you. All those lovelies parading about."

"P.W.O.P.?"

"Yes. Tuesday night. Dress intelligently. Soon as word is out that you are going to be there, there will be a flurry of activity. Eight o'clock. But if I were you, I'd be late."

"A fuck party," Phil said, "right here in the suburbs."

"This Tuesday?"

"Yes. Barbara Henderson's house in Quaker." She leaned over and kissed Noel. "I knew you'd go."

Monday night
Noel was to get his first caning. "Six of the best," Nevers said.

Don Zacharia

Melonie was to administer it. Nevers, nude except for her high-heeled boots, was showing Melonie how to use the thin, whippy cane. Melonie was nude from the waist up, wearing a pair of skin-tight leather pants that Nevers had bought her that afternoon, and boots. With the cane in her hand, Melonie had never looked sexier. Nevers, as usual, was devastatingly beautiful. Noel was sitting on the couch watching them, nude except for a metal athletic supporter and a two-foot leather thong strapped to each ankle with ankle fasteners. A shiver of fear and sexual excitement went through him as he watched the two women. Nevers had bunched a pair of pillows on her bed, and Melonie, getting the knack of the cane, was whaling the pillows.

"It's not like a whipping," Nevers explained to Melonie. "You're only going to cane him six times, so each one has to be very special. Yes, like that," as Melonie let one go into the pillows. "That's excellent. When you can, side-arm it and use your wrist at the last split second. It makes the cut most pleasant. Something he won't soon forget. Come here, Noel," Nevers ordered.

Noel stood up and shuffled over, the device attached to his ankles preventing normal walk. As always in these situations, he felt his cock hard and strong inside the athletic supporter. His face was flushed, his body tingling. He felt dizzy with anticipation.

"Look at him," Nevers said. "Look at him, Melonie. That's exactly the way a man is supposed to look before a caning." Nevers started her routine. "Do you want to go home?"

"No, mistress." Noel kept his eyes on Nevers' boots.

"If you want to go home, I understand. I'll let you go. Are you sure?"

"Yes, mistress. I'm sure."

"You'd rather stay here and be humiliated and caned?"

"Yes, mistress."

"Look at me."

Noel raised his head and looked into Nevers' eyes. He felt excitement coursing through his body, his heart racing.

Nevers spoke to him in a low, cooing voice, "You're going to be caned by a fifteen-year-old colored girl. I want you to really think about that, baby. I want you to think about it for a full minute; about the implications of it. You are allowing it to happen. You are allowing it to happen. I'm just arranging it, but you are allowing it to happen. She's fifteen and she's a little colored girl and she is going to give you a caning. It's her first, and it's your first. How nice, baby." Nevers came forward and kissed Noel. A long full kiss, pushing her body into his. Finally she broke away. Noel felt uncontrollable passion in his chest and throat. "Now you kiss him, Melonie." Melonie kissed him, holding him close to her, biting his lower lip, and then sucking hard on his tongue and all the time grinding her hips into his. Nevers finally parted them. "All right. Let's start. Lay down on your back, baby. Yes, just like that. In less than ten minutes it will be over." Nevers straddled his face, facing his feet. "Lick my ass, get me ready. Yes. Oh, yes. I remember the first time I asked you to do that, you hesitated. Now look at you. You just can't wait to get your tongue up there. Put your arms straight out." Nevers lowered herself onto Noel's face, imprisoning his arms with her knees and smothering his face with her cunt. "Lift your legs straight up—straight up—just like that." Nevers ducked under the leather strap attached to his ankles so that the strap was now lying across her shoulders. In this position, Noel was ready for the caning. His backside raised straight up off the bed, his legs apart, his arms pinned, his face buried into her groin, totally helpless. Nevers could, either by lowering the strap or just leaning back, increase the stretch of his backside, and particularly his buttocks, making the caning even more painful. In this position it was impossible for Noel to even tense his back muscles for what was to come.

Nevers, sitting on Noel's face, rubbing her cunt into his mouth, pulling on her nipples, was all ready, from the look on her face. "Stop sucking on me," she moaned. "I'm too close." She raised her knees up, leaving her cunt just hanging over Noel's face. "Are you ready?" She spoke to Melonie. "I'm going to come in his face in seconds. Make each one a beauty, Melonie, there's only six—so make each one count. I'll pay you extra if you make it beautiful for us. Start now—quickly."

Melonie measured Noel's ass with the cane. She tapped him lightly one, two, three, four, times. She brought the cane back. The squish that it made before contact was fierce. PWOP—it landed across Noel's lower ass, creating an instant welt. Nevers screamed as her orgasm started, pushing her cunt into Noel's face. Noel's body bucked in pain. "Again," Nevers screamed. Again. Again. PWOP. The cane landed again, this cut above the first, Melonie remembering well her instructions, broke her wrists at impact, causing Noel's legs to leap upward in agony. Nevers, still in the throes of orgasm, rocked back against the strap attached to Noel's ankles, forcing his ass ever further off the bed, giving Melonie more of a target. "Again," she screamed. "Christ, I'm still coming."

PWOP, the blow fell. PWOP, the fourth blow followed it immediately. Nevers was screaming in pleasure, grinding her cunt into Noel's face, holding on to his outstretched legs for support. PWOP, the cane dug into Noel's ass for the fifth time. Nevers was beside herself. "One more," she moaned. "Give him one more. He's sucking my cunt like no one ever has. Each time you cane him, I feel like his mouth is going to devour my cunt, one more one more—" PWOP. The sixth and last blow smashed into Noel's welted ass. Nevers moaned. "Oh, delicious."

Tuesday evening

Noel was more than fashionably late. He was damn late. He soaked in the tub for an hour that evening and then started to get dressed. It took him forever. He was so stiff from the caning that every move was excruciating. Just the merest contact between his underpants and pants against his legs and buttocks caused such pain that at one point he was ready to give up. Nevers had told him that he was going to be very uncomfortable for the next two or three days, and she wasn't kidding. When finally dressed in a brown suit he liked, he looked at himself in the mirror and smiled. If I don't move, he thought, I'm just fine.

As soon as he entered Barbara Henderson's house, he knew he was dressed wrong, but so what? There seemed to be at least thirty people there, more women than men, and most everybody in their thirties. All the men were wearing turtlenecks and blazers. It must be a uniform of the night, Noel thought, and the women were dressed in what appeared to be casual, but wasn't. All the women had scarves around their necks. Soon as he walked in, he was greeted warmly by Barbara Henderson.

"Welcome," she flashed him her loveliest smile, "to P.W.O.P."

"Thanks," Noel said. "I'm sorry I'm late. I was doing some homework with one of my kids."

"It's OK, really."

She held her hand out and Noel took it. A hell of a firm handshake.

"I'm not going to introduce you to anyone. I'm sure you'll meet everyone and I hope you will forget all their names but mine. I'll get you your first drink. White or red?"

"White, thanks." Noel moved stiffly forward.

She handed him a glass of wine. "Cheers." They clinked glasses. "Would you like to sit down?"

"No, no. I'm fine," Noel said, knowing that it would be at least two days before he could sit down without pain.

"Are you OK? You look stiff and anxious. Try to relax."

"Hey, Barbara." Noel winked at her. "I've been exercising with barbells and I think I've overdone it."

"You single men," she chided, "the moment you're single—body beautiful."

"You're not so bad yourself. I bet you look good in a bikini."

"You bet I do." She winked back at Noel. "I look good without a bikini also."

Holy shit, Noel thought, I'm pretty good at this scene.

"Norma Sheer."

Someone was offering a hand to Noel.

Don Zacharia

"I'm Norma Sheer. You're Noel Roth. Hi."

Noel shook her hand. Firm as hell. "Hi."

"Well, I guess I better circulate," Barbara said. "I told you you'd meet everyone. Go easy on him, Norma."

"Welcome to P.W.O.P."

"Gee, thanks. It's quite an organization."

"Watch out for Barbara."

"Who?"

"Barbara Henderson. The girl you were just talking to. She's a shark."

"A shark?"

"Would you like to sit down?"

"No. No. I'm fine."

"You have two children. A girl thirteen and a boy eleven. Right?"

"Yes. That's right. How'd you know?"

"I have a girl thirteen."

"Hey. That's nice."

"She's a gymnast. God, I wish I had her body."

"Well, your body ain't so bad." Noel winked.

"I know Phoebe Radcliff."

"You do?"

"Yes. Just superficially, but I know her. She seems like a fine person."

"Oh, she is that. Can I ask you a question?"

"If you want to sleep with me tonight, the answer is yes."

"Well, Norma. I don't know what to say."

"You could say yes and we could leave this dullsville and have a nice quiet drink somewhere where we can talk. I bet we have a lot in common—daughters the same age—"

"I bet we do. I gotta take a rain check. I promised, really promised my kids I'd be home by eleven."

"You're overcompensating."

"I am?"

"You shouldn't do that. You should try to be normal. I bet since your wife died all you do is spend time with your kids. That's what I mean by overcompensating. It's not healthy, you know. You

200

should act with your children now exactly as you were before. Have you slept with a woman yet?"

"Hey, Norma—"

"I bet you haven't."

"You're the second person to ask me that."

"You better do it in a hurry. Otherwise it will get to be a hang-up. It will get to be a hurdle, and you have enough hurdles in your life without creating new ones."

"Norma," Noel said, shifting his weight stiffly from one leg to the other, "I'm sure you're right."

"Look at you. You're not only stiff emotionally but it has taken over physically. Your body is reacting psychosomatically to hurdles. You're standing like a ramrod."

Everyone stood up and began to clap. Noel turned to see what was happening, starting a shiver of pain in his buttocks. A couple had just walked in, causing the applause. Noel knew they were in the right house because she was wearing a scarf around her neck and he a turtleneck and blazer. He had double-thick glasses on that made his eyes look like bullets.

"Those are the Morrisons, Sandy and Bill. He was P.W.O.P.'s first president. They just got married. They're the third marriage from this P.W.O.P."

"That's something."

"Do you think they look happy?"

"Well, yes. Reasonably so."

"I don't. I think they're going to be P.W.O.P.'s first divorce."

They came over to Noel and Norma. Norma did the introductions. Sandy Morrison smiled at Noel.

"Joel," Bill Morrison held his hand out, "welcome to P.W.O.P."

"Noel, Noel." Noel took his hand. He can't see and is deaf to boot.

"I'm Toby Fishbach." Someone else was firmly shaking Noel's hand.

Norma glared at her. "I'll be on my way. Think about some of the things I've said to you."

"I will. I will."

Don Zacharia

"I'd like to see you again and finish our dialogue." With that she walked away.

"Would you like to sit down?"

"No. I'm fine."

Toby was pretty. Prettier than Norma. As Noel looked around, all the women were OK. None of them could hold a candle to Nevers, Noel thought. I mean, not even a glimmer.

"You seem rooted to that spot."

"What's a shark?"

"Who called who a shark?"

"No one. I just overheard it."

"A shark is what just left you. Norma Sheer. She's recently divorced. Her ego is still damaged. She's out to restore it with as many relationships as possible. Did she ask you to sleep with her? Don't feel flattered. Sharks are promiscuous as hell. You have two children; a girl thirteen and a boy eleven?"

"Hey, right. How'd you know?"

"I have a boy nine."

"Nice. Nice."

"I've been divorced four years."

"Wow. That's a long time for a good-looking girl like you to be single."

"Thanks. I enjoy my freedom. I don't think I'll get married for another four years. I was married at eighteen. Was that ever dumb."

"A lot of people who get divorced jump right back into another marriage."

"That's even dumber. People are basically insecure."

"Do you come here often?"

"Truth?"

"Sure."

"I came tonight because I wanted to meet you."

"Well, thanks." Noel was flattered.

"Noel Roth, I'm Frank Stooper. Welcome to P.W.O.P. I'm the new Pres."

This one seemed more relaxed. Turtleneck and dungarees. He

would be better off wearing something else to hide his stomach, Noel thought. Noel automatically held his hand out and Frank whateverhisname pumped it vigorously. Noel winced in pain. He finally let go and punched Noel in the arm. Noel shivered.

"Nice to have you aboard. We need men of your ilk in our group. I gotta move on. Hey, Noel, baby," he gave him a wink, "if you want some hard stuff later on, I might be able to help yuh."

As he walked by Noel, he gave him another wink and slapped him on the ass.

"ARGGH." Noel screamed in pain. "ARGGH," he wailed, unable to control himself as the pain from Frank's friendly slap was fiercer than the original caning.

"What happened?" Everyone was crowding around him. "What happened? Is it his heart?"

"Noel, what happened?" Barbara Henderson, looking very concerned, asked.

Noel, still shocked from the pain, could hardly talk. He nodded his head and tried to smile. He was holding onto a chair in front of him for support, his legs stiffly apart. "A muscle," Noel finally gasped weakly. "A muscle. I'll be OK." He forced out another smile.

"Jeez, fella," Frank the pres said, "you better get yourself checked out."

"Psychosomatic," Norma Sheer said, pointing a finger at Noel just to make sure that everyone knew who she was talking about.

"I'll be OK." Noel waved to everyone. "Would you excuse me if I left now?" Noel said, speaking to Barbara. "This muscle is killing me. . . . "

"Of course. We'll call you and let you know where the next P.W.O.P. is."

"Thanks. Thanks again."

"I'll walk you out," Toby Fishbach said.

"Shark," Norma muttered under her breath.

When they were outside, Toby pressed something into his hand and kissed him lightly. "Hope you're feeling better."

"See yuh," Noel said, struggling into the front seat of the car.

Don Zacharia

"You look like a hundred and eight."

"I'll be OK. Take care of yourself, Toby." Driving home, he looked at the note she had passed to him. It was a phone number with a short message. "Call me sometime—Toby."

THE CEMETERY

Why is that guy following me? Bloom doesn't want to hear about it. Every time I bring him *up, Bloom brings up Susan. She wants to know, How do I feel about Susan? Ha, ha, loaded question. I don't know what to tell her so I tell her a lot of different things. I tell her I feel hurt (she loves that), I tell her I miss her (she doesn't believe that), I tell her I feel Susan is still alive (she dislikes that), I tell her I'm humiliated by it all (she grimaces at that), and I tell her I would like to hit Susan (she's not crazy about that). I tell Bloom a lot of things. Why not? You have to say something three hours a week. While I talk to her, I put my Noel Roth suffering act on. I cross and uncross my legs—I crack my fingers—I blink all the time—I start a sentence and stop it—I stumble over Susan's name—Bloom eats it up.*

• • •

Don Zacharia

On a Sunday early in November, Noel, Beth and David went to the cemetery for the first time. The week had been cold and rainy, but that morning the sun broke through the clouds, and when Noel listened to the news, the weatherman spoke of Indian summer and temperatures reaching into the high seventies. It was Beth's idea to go, and Noel, who was trying very hard to pacify Beth in every way, said yes, even though he was dreading the day. Both Mrs. Bloom and Phoebe had also been after him to go to the cemetery with the children, but Noel, who had a difficult time opening up the *mail* from the cemetery, had postponed it as long as he could.

"I don't blame you," Mrs. Bloom told him. "I don't blame you a bit. But I think for Beth and David you should go there."

"Why? What's so important about it?" He defended his position. "We know where Susan is. We know she's there. Nobody moved her. No one is kidding anyone about Susan's whereabouts. Beth and David don't think she's on an extended bus trip up there in the sky."

"Why make issues where none exist, Mr. Roth? Why make your life more complicated than it is already? Why create additional problems? You have your share to start off with. No? Your children want to go to the cemetery with you. Under the circumstances, to use a phrase your son just taught me, it shouldn't be such a deal."

Noel was sitting with Beth on the front steps of their house, waiting for David, who at the last minute said he wanted to cut some ferns to bring to the cemetery. Beth and David had been getting along a little better, less snapping, but a long way from peace.

"How's business?" Beth asked.

"How's business?" Noel smiled at her. "Business is fine. How's school?"

"How's school? School is fine."

Noel faked a snore and they both laughed. "Let's go, Daverino," Noel called out.

David came back holding the ferns and sucking a finger. "I'm bleeding. I stuck myself."

"Let nurse Beth look at it."

He showed her his finger.

"Amputation," she said.

"Let's go, you two characters."

The ride up to the cemetery was pleasant. They opened all the windows in the car and Noel wished he had a convertible. Beth and David sang songs they had learned in camp about Vietnam, Blacks, lost loves and lost causes.

"Do you know the first car your mother and I owned was a 1953 Oldsmobile Ninety-eight convertible? Jesus, what a car. It was flamingo pink and as long as a street. We bought it used for six hundred dollars from some thieves in Larchmont. You couldn't believe the color. It was very snazzy. Leather seats, speakers in the back, Hydramatic—"

"Hydra what?" Beth asked.

"Don't ask. Forget it. It's what they used to call automatic transmission. Anyhow, driving home, your mother was driving, we had the roof down, natch, and we were gliding down the old Bronx River Parkway with her hair streaming behind her. I don't think we had the car more than ten minutes, when all of a sudden there's this clunk, clunk, clunk. Your mother stopped the car; everything seemed OK. We got out and looked. There was no flat, nothing was hanging from under the car. I opened the hood and the motor was as clean as a whistle. There was water in the battery cells and all that. Everything was terrific except the car wouldn't go forward. It would only go in reverse. We switched seats and I drove all the way home backwards. We were living in the apartment next to Phil and Phoebe. I was driving and your mother was standing up in the back directing me and waving other cars out of the way. Can't you just see it? This pink convertible, it had to be as big as a battleship, flying down the highways backwards with your mother hysterically waving her arms. We didn't meet one cop. When we got to the apartment, your mother had to put Noxzema on for windburn."

"What was wrong with the car?" David asked.

"The transmission. You buy a used car and buyer beware. Ten minutes after we bought it the transmission went." Noel made a noise with his lips. "Hotshot lawyer Phil called up and threatened them with everything short of the Supreme Court, but those guys were pros. They said they also owned a garage that fixed transmissions, but I told them to shove it. It cost three hundred bucks to fix but we had that car for four years. It was a beauty."

"Do you know what happens in three years?" Beth asked.

"You'll be three years older," David cracked.

"Ha, ha, my comedian brother. Do you know what happens in four years?" she asked Noel.

"I'll bite."

"I can drive."

"Oh, spare me." Noel faked a groan.

"Will you teach me?"

"Sure."

"Will you buy me a car?"

"Now wait a minute."

"I don't mean when I'm sixteen or seventeen. When I graduate high school, for a graduation present. If I graduate high school with an A average, will you buy me a car?"

"You got yourself a deal."

"You promise?"

"I promise." Noel crossed his heart.

"A smashing car?"

"A smashing car."

"A smashing convertible car?"

"A smashing convertible car."

"You're a witness, Dave."

"How many years will that be?" David asked.

"Five years. 1978." Beth's eyes glistened.

"I wonder what everything will be like in 1978? I'll be sixteen. Will you teach me how to drive also, Dad?"

"I'll teach you in my smashing convertible," Beth said.

They had a hard time finding Susan's grave and had to go back to the office for directions. "There's not too many different-looking

The Match Trick

landmarks," Noel said as they were searching about.

"What are those?" David asked. They were driving down a row with buildings that looked as if they could withstand an A bomb.

"Those are called mausoleums. Pretty impressive, huh? I think they are a thing of yesterday. I don't think people are building them anymore."

"What do they do with them? I mean, do people live there?"

"Come on, David." Noel glanced at him. David wasn't kidding. "People—like I said, years ago people would get buried in there. I mean, instead of just being out in the open, they have a roof over their heads. Did that guy say we should make this left or the next?"

"Are they buried above the ground or are they buried below the ground?"

"David, I just don't know. I really don't know." He stopped the car. "Where the fuck are we?"

They finally found the gravesite, high on a hillside with a lone tree above it. The view was extraordinary. Beneath them the entire Hudson Valley opened up. Noel was uneasy, but nowhere near as much as he thought he would be. His memory of Susan's funeral and burial was like memories of certain dreams; when all you can remember is the fact that you dreamed, but not the substance. Noel knew he was there, but that was the beginning and the end of it.

Nothing looked familiar to Noel. They all read the small, simple stone that was right below the tree. Susan Golden Roth—September 29, 1937–August 23, 1973. Noel studied the tree above the grave. It didn't look like it would make a severe winter. He made a mental note to speak to someone about it. Perhaps they could insulate it from the wind and cold. A single-engine plane passed by overhead, its motor reminding Noel of something. But what? David scattered the ferns about, dropping them in clumps here and there.

"What do we do now?" he asked.

"Anything you want," Noel answered.

"I'm going to explore."

"Oh boy," Beth said.

"Don't get lost," Noel called out to his disappearing son.

209

"Don't worry. Don't worry."

Noel and Beth stood silent. "It's not so bad up here," Noel finally said.

"No, it isn't."

"The view is extraordinary."

"Yes. It is."

"You can see to the Hudson River. Look—"

"Yes. I see."

"With a view like this they should put up a split-level—"

"Daddy, why do you always have to make a joke?"

"I'm sorry." He put his arm around her and kissed her cheek.

"You are pretty funny, though."

"Yeah, most of the time."

"But not all of the time."

"I'm going to speak to them about the tree. It doesn't look none too sturdy."

"I did something very immature."

"Oh. That's OK."

"I wrote Mother a note." She reached into her pocket and pulled out a tightly folded note. "I would like to leave it here. I know it's foolish. I mean—" Beth was struggling for words.

"Hey," Noel cut in, "it's OK. You don't have to explain that."

Beth, kneeling at the side of the grave, dug a shallow hole and placed the note into it. She scooped some dirt back into the hole and placed a few rocks and leaves over it. "I'll wait in the car." She stood up.

"I'm ready," Noel said. "Let's go. Where's David?" They both walked toward the car. "David," Noel called out. "David—do you see him?" he asked Beth.

"No."

"Whoooo—" David jumped out from behind a tombstone with his hands stretched out and his face screwed up—"whooo." He broke into a giggle. "Beth," excited, "you won't believe it. There's someone down this hill who's two hundred and forty years old."

210

PARANOIA

Paranoid. I am becoming paranoid. The other morning when leaving Nevers there was that man standing across the street smoking a pipe. It was four o'clock in the morning. I caught his eye and he turned his head. It is the second time I have seen him in the same spot. That in itself is circumstantial. Yet, the man somehow looked familiar to me, but I couldn't place him until now. He is the same man who was on the ferry when I went to Fire Island with the children. I have seen him before, before that, other places, other times, outside of the ferry and twice in front of Nevers. I think sometimes he is in front of the Center watching. It is not easy because he doesn't always look the same. Jesus, I am paranoid. I am nutsville. I must tell this to Bloom. I am going off the deep end. Christ, how do I get out of this? Oh, I wish I could talk to Bloom about Nevers, but I am not ready for that. I don't think I will ever be ready for that until I can break away from her. When will that be? Will it

211

Don Zacharia

ever end? The more she debases me the more debasement I need. The more she humiliates me the more humiliation I need. Perversion begets perversion. I am sinking into a mire of shit. I can not even write about what Nevers does to me. Thinking about it makes my hands jump; my eye flinches; my skin itches. I urinate fifteen, twenty times a day. I need help. I am being followed. Maybe? If I see that man with a pipe again I am going to ask him for a match and see what he does. Maybe I will never see him again. Maybe he doesn't exist. The other day I thought Phoebe followed me into the city. I wonder if there is a relationship between the man with a pipe and Phoebe. Sometimes the man with a pipe looks like Dr. Reed. I think if I told this to Bloom she would have me committed. I am cracking.

In the month of November, Noel's paranoia got so bad he began seeing his therapist three times a week. Besides that, he saw her once a week in the family session; Beth saw her twice a week, and David saw her once. "It would be a lot easier," Noel mumbled to Mrs. Bloom one day, "if we moved the fuck in."

Mrs. Bloom listened while Noel talked. He talked randomly, without order, about anything and everything except Nevers. He talked in nonstop sentences, covering a landscape of related and unrelated words and ideas. Sometimes in the same sentence he would skip decades, going from a high-school basketball game to a recent business decision, never finishing either story.

"I am paranoid," he told Mrs. Bloom. She nodded her head. He told her again. He told her all the time. "I am paranoid." He wanted to shout at her, shout, but he whispered. "There *is* someone following me." He lowered his voice to a level where Mrs. Bloom had to strain to hear every word. "He follows me all the time. Do you believe me?" He stared at her; waiting for a response. None came. "You–don't–believe–me. I can tell by the shape of your eyes. It doesn't matter if you believe me or not. That's not true. It does matter. I will tell either way. Do you want to close your ears? You can't because you are responsible for me, and if something happened to me, wouldn't you feel like a piece of *shit*. Let's say there is someone *really* following me and he knocks me off, wouldn't Mrs. Bloom feel like a piece of *dung*. You would wake up in the middle of the night thinking someone had cut into your stomach. The man who follows me follows me all the time. *All the time.* At different times the man who follows me looks different, but I am not sure of that. Sometimes he looks familiar, and sometimes he doesn't look familiar. Sometimes he has a beard, and sometimes he doesn't have a beard. Sometimes he wears a cap, and sometimes he doesn't wear a cap. I don't think they are different people, but I don't like it when he puts his beard on. It scares me. I am more comfortable when the man without a beard is following me. The man with a beard looks like a killer. Do you think someone is out to kill me? Could there be a contract out on my life? Ha, ha. What a gag. The crazy thing is I know him. I know I know the man who is following me. I can't tell you who he is, but I know him. Who could it be? Sometimes I think it is Dr. Reed but I know that is too bizarre. He smokes a pipe all the time the way Reed does. Once, when I spied on him, I saw him lighting his pipe over and over and then he stopped lighting his pipe and put a roll of film into his lighter.

"Mrs. Bloom, I am really nutsville. You have to help me. For chrissakes, just don't sit there, help me, help me. I am going under."

Noel at thirty-seven. Despite his troubles, Noel celebrated his thirty-seventh birthday twice. On Sunday, Phoebe gave him a small party at her house; just Phil, Phoebe and the children. Phoebe got him two bottles of Château d'Yquem, Beth and David a gray tie and a blue button-down shirt, Mark and Eric the Arnold Palmer book *My Game and Yours,* and Phil bought him a lifesize inflatable doll that was called "Your Personal Sex Goddess." When the kids left the room to watch a TV show, in between at least a thousand gags Phil blew the doll up and presented it to Noel.

Don Zacharia

Noel did a quick, suggestive dance number with the doll, gracefully swinging around the floor, Phil and Phoebe shouting instructions about what to do next, and then in the middle of the number, stopped and tried to drop-kick the doll to Phil.

Phoebe intercepted it. "God, Noel, look at those bozookos."

"They had one I didn't get that had a lot of other features." Phil winked at Noel. "One that urinates." He made a face. "I didn't think that was your bag, buddy."

"Just what I've always wanted," Noel said. Sitting the doll on his lap he kissed her nose.

"Give her a spanking," Phoebe said.

"Ha, ha." Noel smiled at Phoebe. "Ha, ha."

"We are moving into a very kinky era," Phoebe said, "S & M and B & D are going to engulf the U.S.A."

"Watch this." Noel, eager to change the subject, tried a hook shot with the doll and floated it across the room to Phil. Phil grabbed a foot and skimmed her back to Noel.

"Now, boys," Phoebe said, "no ball-playing in the house."

Later, with the doll sitting between Phil and Noel, Phoebe brought in a cake, and Noel, to scattered applause, blew out the candles.

Noel spent the next day with Nevers and Melonie. They had a birthday lunch at a small New York restaurant in midtown. After lunch the waiter brought over a tiny cake with a single candle. Noel was pleased. He blew out the candle, and they both kissed him.

"Happy birthday," Nevers said. "Happy thirty-seventh."

"I think," Melonie said, "when my daddy was your old age, he died."

"Wonderful," Noel said. "I feel just wonderful."

When the bill came, Nevers insisted on paying.

After, the three of them cavorted down Madison Avenue. Nevers was wearing beige glove-leather pants, a man-tailored yellow silk blouse and a tweed blazer; Noel, a gray suit and the blue button-down shirt and gray tie his children had just gotten him, and Melonie, designer jeans tightly tucked into her boots and a red cashmere turtleneck sweater. Flanked on either side by Melonie and Nevers, they caused more heads to turn than the Easter Parade. The three of them window-shopped, walked in and out of a half a dozen stores, crisscrossed in the middle of the street, held hands, kissed, skipped through three red lights, and in a dressing room on Sixty-eighth Street, Melonie gave Noel head while Nevers, trying on a dress, looked on.

"Happy birthday." Melonie mumbled.

"If you come," Nevers whispered, kissing his mouth, "I'll take you home and use that bitchy cane on you again."

They left the store, buying nothing, with Noel hunched over. Noel felt like a million bucks.

At the corner of Sixty-eighth and Madison, Melonie and Nevers hooked their arms around Noel's waist and tried to lift him off the ground and carry him across the street. Both girls were having a good time, giggling and laughing out loud. Noel was sort of protesting. Halfway across the street Noel recognized Sergeant Walter Rudd.

"Mrs. Bloom—" Noel, as uncomfortable as ever in a chair for a six-year-old, stretched his legs out into the room—"I have a question to ask you." It was the day after Noel's birthday party with Melonie and Nevers.

She nodded. Mrs. Bloom had been seeing Roth three times a week for almost a month and was used to his fencing.

"If you were seeing a patient who you diagnosed as anxiety-ridden and one of the symptoms of his anxiety was chest pains, and one day sitting in this dumb chair he rolled over dead from a massive coronary, one of those permanent knockout jobs, down for the final quick count, and this patient of yours who you were treating for psychosomatic chest pains is lying dead in your nursery, not a twitch, what would you do?"

Don Zacharia

"I would call a medical doctor."

"Mrs. Bloom. You know *goddamn* well I don't mean that. How would you feel about your diagnosis? Looking there at this dead patient stretched out on your *goddamn* floor, would you still tell him it's psychosomatic?"

She smiled. "You're getting at something, Mr. Roth."

"You didn't answer my question."

"Your question is rhetorical. What do you want me to say? That it can't happen? Of course it can. But I can assure you that for every person being treated for anxiety who *actually* has a heart condition, there are *ten thousand* who are being treated by internists for heart conditions who have anxieties."

"How about George Gershwin?"

"Who?"

"Jesus Christ, don't tell me you never heard of George Gershwin?"

"He was a composer. No?"

"Yes. He was seeing a psychiatrist for twenty-five years complaining of dizziness and headaches and when he died they performed an autopsy and he had a brain tumor."

"Where is this taking us?"

"It's taking us to me. Me. Noel Roth. Mr. Paranoia. Supposing somebody really was following me? Supposing there really was someone out there who was tailing me? Supposing your paranoia has a face?"

"It is not *my* paranoia," she interrupted.

"Oh." Noel tried sitting straight up in the chair, but it was impossible. "These fucking chairs— You never answer my questions. Supposing *my* paranoia has a face? Legs? Arms? What would you say?"

Mrs. Bloom took a deep breath. "I don't know what I would say. I would want as much as you to know why a man should be following you."

Noel got up and went to the corner of the window and looked out. "Let me show you something, Mrs. Bloom. Look, come here.

216

I want to show you something." She joined him at the window. "You see that man across the street leaning up against a car? The blue Chevy? The man with a pipe in his mouth and a windbreaker on?"

"Yes."

"I'm going to leave now. I'll see you tomorrow." At the door Noel turned back to Mrs. Bloom. "That's the man who is following me."

Mrs. Bloom studied the man across the street. He looked frighteningly like the man Roth had been describing. Roth got into his car and drove off. The man with a pipe got into the blue Chevy, made an illegal U turn and drove off in the same direction as Noel Roth. Frieda took a deep breath.

The next day, five minutes before Roth was due for his appointment, Frieda Bloom stationed herself at the window. Noel Roth arrived, put some coins in the meter, and headed toward the center. He looked very cheerful. A moment later, the same blue Chevy pulled into a spot in front of the delicatessen and the same man with a pipe got out.

"Hi. How's Mrs. Bloom today? What's new in the world of Freud and Jung?"

Mrs. Bloom, back at her desk, stared at Noel.

"Are you OK? You seem upset." There was a mock quality of concern in his voice.

"Mr. Roth, you are being followed." Her voice seemed lower than usual, as if she were telling him something she didn't want other people to hear.

"Yes. I know."

"Yes? You know? Is that all? Is that all you are going to say?"

"What do you want me to say? I've told you a hundred times. Jesus, I've told you a thousand times I'm being followed. I think we should talk about other things today," Noel said smugly.

"The man who is outside today is the same man who was outside yesterday."

Don Zacharia

"No kidding."

"He is very much like the man you have been describing to me."

"Well, what do you know about that."

"Stop playing games with me, Mr. Roth. You are playing games with me."

"You piss me off."

"Mr. Roth!"

"You piss me off. How many times have I told you that I was being followed and you sat there with that pissy expression like I was ready for the loony bin."

"I am not aware of that."

"Well, start looking at yourself in the mirror when you talk to patients. You are not aware, my ass. It's the same goddamn thing with Nixon—"

"Nixon! Please, let's for once keep him out of this. What is going on is enough for me. No more games. Why is that man following you?"

"I don't know."

"That's no answer. You must have some ideas. For three months a man has been following you—you must have some idea—"

"Are you grilling me? For the last month you have made me feel like a certifiable screwball, and *now you are grilling me?*"

"It's—it's most unusual. I think we should for the time being deal with the very real problem of who is that man. Why is he following you? Is he dangerous?" She paused. "Have you thought about going to the police?"

"Hey, now, that's not a bad idea at all!" Noel's eyes danced in anticipation. He got up and walked to the window and stared out at Rudd. "Mrs. Bloom, that's a *damn good* idea. I want you to come here. I want you to stay at the window and watch me. It's going to be a couple of minutes before you see me again, so don't be alarmed. I'm going to go out the back door, walk all around the block, and see if I can sneak up on that crazy bastard. You stay here. Two things before I go. I'm sorry I lost my temper before—"

The Match Trick

"Mr. Roth, I don't want you doing this."

Noel was halfway out the door: "The other thing, Frieda, this guy, this guy across the street with a pipe, this nut who has been following me, his name is Rudd, and . . . and he carries a gun."

Noel left a concerned Mrs. Bloom.

She stationed herself at the window. Rudd was leaning up against the hood of his car, studying the passers-by. A few minutes slipped by before Mrs. Bloom saw Roth. He had circled the block, and was now walking stealthily, keeping his eyes on Rudd all the time. He sneaked up behind him and ducked into the delicatessen. Mrs. Bloom, feeling her breath coming in short gasps, couldn't understand what Roth was up to. The thought of calling the police crossed her mind. It seemed to her that Roth was in the delicatessen forever. He finally reappeared holding a large bag against his chest with his left hand. He stopped on the sidewalk directly behind Rudd. He stared at his back and then looked up at Mrs. Bloom, and with his right hand blew her a kiss. Mrs. Bloom, without realizing what she was doing, blew Roth a kiss back. She watched, aware that her hands were suddenly ice cold as Noel quickly walked in front of Rudd and pinned him to his car. The upper half of Rudd's body was bent backward over the hood, and Noel was shouting at him. Mrs. Bloom heard Noel's voice, but it was difficult to pick up words. His left hand still clutched the bag to his body, but his right hand was beating a tattoo into Rudd's chest. Noel suddenly reached into the bag with his right hand.

Frieda's breath stopped. Oh, no, she thought. Oh, no. He pulled a hot dog out of the bag and held it in front of Rudd's mouth. He stuffed it into Rudd's shirt. He pulled out another hot dog, another, another, another, stuffing them into Rudd's pants, into his pockets, inside his windbreaker, down his shirt again. For a moment he stopped and waved a finger in front of Rudd's nose and licked what must have been mustard off of his finger. Mrs. Bloom lost track: twenty, thirty hot dogs. Finally Noel pushed one into Rudd's mouth, opened up the car door and shoved Rudd in. He slammed the door shut and then reached into the car window and pulled

219

Don Zacharia

Rudd's beard off, holding it up in the air like a scalp. Before Rudd could drive away, Noel started yelling at him again, and Mrs. Bloom twice caught the words "maniac fuck" but that was all. Just when Mrs. Bloom thought it was all over, Noel reached into the car again; she thought Noel was going to strangle Rudd, but in a moment the hand that went into the car came out holding two hot dogs. Rudd started up the car and, with a hot dog still in his mouth and two or three sticking out from his neck, made a wild U turn and sped off.

Noel crossed the street, took the steps three at a time, and bounded into Mrs. Bloom's room. "Did you see that?" He was out of breath.

"Yes," Mrs. Bloom said, fighting to gain her composure.

Noel sat down in a regular chair. "You look different from this angle." He began wolfing down a hot dog. "Crazy bastard." In between bites, "The man should be put away—maniac—crazy—bastard—I kept telling you I recognized him. Rudd is the moron cop they sent over to my house the night Susan didn't come home. He spells all the time—I'm not kidding. He spells out every other word. Just my luck—the craziest cop in the whole fucking world decides to follow me for kicks. The man should be put away. He told me he liked following me. Here, I got a hot dog for you."

"Just a bite. Just a quarter."

Noel broke a hot dog in half and gave it to her. "Come on, it won't kill you."

She took a bite. Her eyes moved upward. "I had forgotten how good they are."

"I'm s–t–a–r–v–e–d."

THANKSGIVING

The whole thing was Noel's doing. He did it, and he undid it. Just days after his emotional, tumultuous fight with Beth at the Center, their tearful reunion and his promise to his daughter about going away together, he personally made arrangements for all of them to spend Thanksgiving weekend at an inn in Vermont. "It's my treat," he told Phoebe and Phil, "and I don't want an argument." He didn't get one. Everyone was pleased: Phil, Phoebe, the children, Dr. Reed—only Mrs. Bloom had some reservations that she kept to herself.

"We're going away," Noel said to her in a singsong voice. It was a week after his confrontation with Rudd, and things, Noel felt, were getting back to normal. "Doesn't that make you happy? Doesn't that please you? How come I don't see you smiling when everyone else is? Don't be such a sourpuss. I feel terrific. I look terrific. Business is terrific. Noelie is doing his old tap dance again.

Don Zacharia

You want to feel sorry for someone? Feel sorry for Nixon. Feel sorry for Rudd. Poor bastards, I wonder what they're doing Thanksgiving. I'm going to be with my kids and best friends. You know what I think you're afraid of? You're afraid of losing a customer. Don't worry about it, Mrs. Bloom. Let me tell you about retailing. There is *always* another customer. Everything's perfect. Perfect. I'm going away Thanksgiving with my family and friends. What could be better? I'm so happy it's scaring the shit out of me. Everything is perfect. The only thing that isn't perfect is you. You want me to be honest with you? You've changed. Ever since I've been sitting in this grown-up chair, your attitude toward me has changed. I'm going to be really honest with you and say something you won't like, but sometimes you give me the creeps. I mean, just what the hell is it you want from me? Why do you keep staring at me like there is something wrong? Everything is OK now. I am very, very, very happy, and very, very, very normal. Goddamn it."

"When I whip you, what do you think about?"

Nevers, Melonie, and Noel were having dinner in a restaurant in Greenwich Village. Noel was sitting next to Melonie, with Nevers across from them against the wall, on display.

"Who ever thinks?"

"That isn't true. I know what you think about."

"Yeah. What?"

"Slides me the A-1, Rothman."

"Your dead wife, Susan."

"I'z crazed 'bout A-1."

"That's ridiculous."

"What do you think about?"

"Not Susan."

"You're not convincing me."

"It's the best I got."

"When you eat me do you think of Susan?"

"No. No. *Definitely* not. *Absolutely* not."

222

"You're lying. I'm sure of it. After you eat me you rinse your mouth out. You're coy about it, not wanting me to know. That's nice. I love that. Did you do that with Susan?"

"I rinse my mouth out all the time; one hundred times a day." Noel was on the defensive.

"Do you remember the movie *Carnal Knowledge?* There is a scene where Jack Nicholson is showing slides of all his old girlfriends. Each slide is shown for a fraction of a second, all in a sequence that means something only to him, it is a very subliminal effect. That's what I think happens to you when I am whipping you—fragmented pictures of your dead wife Susan blink through your eyes. And you know something, Noel, it pisses me off."

"The two of you ain't eatin'. You'se pickin' at your food talkin' all dis bullshit."

"Can I ask you a question?" Noel said, ignoring Melonie.

"Sure, Noelie." Nevers played with her hair.

"Why is this coming up now?"

"It's coming up now because I feel like bringing it up now." Nevers leaned across the table and pinched Noel's cheek, hard. She sat back and patted her lips with the tips of her fingers. "You're sick, Noel, really sick. Do you know that?"

"No kidding." Noel rubbed his cheek. "I just finished telling Bloom how healthy I was. I told her I was Mr. Normal."

"You tell dat Jew doctor 'bout us yet?"

Noel shifted in his seat.

"He hasn't." Nevers didn't give him a chance to answer. "He's embarrassed by us."

"Let's change the topic."

"You need a lot of help, Noel. You can't talk about us to your Bloom, and when I whip you you think about your dead wife."

"I'd like very much to change the topic."

"Your foods gettin' ice cold, Rothman."

"Do you know what I want to do?" Nevers touched Noel's face where she had pinched him.

"I'm afraid to ask."

"I want to spend Thanksgiving at your home."

"Oh, Jesus!" Noel dropped his fork on the table and stared at Nevers.

"I want to whip you where you slept with your wife. Did Susan have her own bed or did you share a bed? It doesn't matter. And besides," she added, "as a special treat, I want to make you a turkey."

"Nevers," Noel said, in a voice as firm as he could make it, *"that's out of the question."*

"How do you feel about it, Melonie? Wouldn't you like to spend Thanksgiving at Noel and *Susan's* home?"

"It's gonna be my first Thanksgiving."

"See? It's going to be Melonie's first Thanksgiving. I'm going to make all your fantasies come true, Noelie. I'm going to do things to you in your home—" Nevers let the sentence hang. "Lean over the table," she ordered Noel, "I want to kiss you."

Noel, conscious of a pulse beating in his neck, moved his head toward Nevers. She kissed him gently, her lips barely touching his.

"It's going to be a real family day," Nevers murmured. "I'll be your Susan."

Noel became aware of an ache in his right eye.

"Rothman, I think Miss Nevers right on."

"I can't," Noel whispered. "I just can't."

"Noel, I want to have Thanksgiving at your house, and I'm *not kidding.*"

Noel waited until the last minute. They were supposed to leave Wednesday afternoon for Vermont, and Noel waited until Wednesday morning before he told anyone. He told David first that he wasn't going to be up in Vermont until Friday, and then Beth, who stormed out of the house over to Phoebe's. Phoebe was stunned by the news. She tried to reach Phil but he wasn't in the office. She called Noel, but he refused to talk to her about it. She called Mrs. Bloom and told her what had happened and asked if she would call Noel, but she refused. Mrs. Bloom tried to calm Phoebe: "It's not the end of the world." Finally Phoebe and Beth went for a walk and waited for Phil. When Phil came home and found out what was happening, he stormed over to Noel's, but before he could get started, Noel stopped him short.

"No preaching, pal. Not this time. I know what you want and the answer is no. Remember, I went to the Concord with you when you asked me. Without going into it, because I won't, I've got something I have to do."

"Noel, listen to me," Phil said. "You can't do this. Do you hear me? Do you understand me? You just can't do this, not without an explanation. You can't do this to your children, especially Beth."

"She'll work it out. She'll work it out with Bloom."

"Cut it out," Phil said angrily. "Cut that shit out. You're coming—"

"Here we go again—you're not listening to me, Phil. It's OK. I'm OK. It's different this time. When you came into the woods and led me out, that was fine. I needed to be led. But I'm OK now. You hear me? I'm OK. It's only one day. It's not going to kill anyone. Everybody will survive. It's not life or death. Who gives a shit about Thanksgiving? I'm not a Pilgrim. I'll be up there first thing Friday afternoon, and in thirty minutes everyone will have forgotten that I wasn't there the whole time."

"Why, Noel? Just tell me why, and I'll leave."

Noel took a deep breath. "I can't tell you. Not now. I will—another time—I promise. I can't now. Look, everybody is very hysterical. Beth, Phoebe. I'm going to ask you to do me a favor. Calm them down. Tell them that it's all right. Tell them that I'm OK. I know what I am doing and I'm doing what I want to do."

"A woman?"

"Well, it's not an elephant."

"What's the big deal, Noel?" Phil was pleading, "I mean, what the fuck is the big deal? Bring her along. Does she have one eye? Is she a midget? For chrissakes, Noel, bring her along."

"Phil, please, a favor. Look at me, Phil. I'm OK. I'm just doing what I want to do. Do me a favor. Take care of my family. I just have to do what I have to do."

Don Zacharia

I am, Noel thought, when Phil finally left, full of shit.

An hour later, everybody except Noel left for Vermont. It was a quiet trip to the country.

On Thanksgiving morning Phil was doing his best to keep everyone's spirits up, despite Noel's conspicuous and, to use Phoebe's term, unconscionable, absence. The inn was located in the middle of two hundred sprawling acres, and the innkeeper had made a great attempt to create a totally self-sufficient unit. It had a small farm, chickens, hogs, cows, a hothouse and its own power plant. They spent the morning exploring, walking down well-marked trails to bird and fish sanctuaries. David climbed a tall tree, with Mark and Eric shouting encouragement, and on the way down skinned his knee. Most of the morning, Beth and Phoebe walked with each other, Phil trailing behind. They didn't talk about Noel. Phoebe was so angry and depressed that once she started to cry. She turned away from Beth, not wanting her to see her tears.

When she and Phil were alone, she told him that when she got back she was going to do *something* to Noel. "Don't ask me what," she said. "I want to get even with Noel for what he is doing to *me*." A moment later she hissed, "I'd like to slap Noel in the face. Hard. Twice."

As things turned out, Noel saved her the trouble. It's like what H. R. Haldeman once told a tearful Rose Mary Woods: "When the soup is boiling in the pot, everything will work out."

On Thanksgiving morning Noel was in his bedroom with Melonie and Nevers. The three of them, having what Nevers called breakfast, were gorging themselves on ten dozen cherrystone clams.

Noel wasn't exactly gorging himself. Noel was lying flat on his back and Nevers was sitting on his face, her cunt in his mouth. Melonie was facing Nevers, sitting on Noel's groin, his cock carelessly inserted into her cunt. As absentmindedly as peeling a carrot, every now and then Melonie would make a languid series of up-and-down movements. The two girls were having a good time, eating the cherrystones and then piling all the empty shells on Noel's body: a stack over each nipple, and a stack over his belly button.

"What a lovely Thanksgiving," Nevers said.

Melonie was trying to see how many empty shells she could stack up before they fell over. She kept getting the stacks to a certain height, and then they would fall. "Don't move a muscle, Rothman," she said. "Dis is gettin' frust–rat–in'." She giggled, pleased with her new vocabulary.

The television was on to a station Noel wanted to hear, and David Susskind was moderating a program about the troubled Nixon White House. There were four panelists, but only one of them, Sheila Blackstone, was a Nixon defender. "President Nixon," she was saying, "as the Commander in Chief of this nation, has every right to withhold tapes if their exposure in his opinion would be a violation of American security."

Noel nodded his head vigorously up and down in approval of Sheila Blackstone's statement. Nevers moaned with pleasure. The stack over Noel's belly button fell over. Melonie wrinkled up her nose and started over.

Every now and then Nevers, being the classy woman that she was, supporting herself on her knees, would lift her haunches off of Noel's face and slide a cherrystone or two into Noel's mouth. "Eat that, you turkey," she would say, sitting herself back down on his mouth.

After breakfast, Noel thought he smelled gas. He and Melonie were alone in the bedroom, both still nude, watching a college football game. Nevers had gone downstairs to "start the turkey and take care of things in the kitchen."

"I smell gas," Noel said. He sniffed the air once, twice, three times. "Do you smell gas?" he asked Melonie. She looked at him like he was crazy. "Nevers," he called out. "Nevers," he went to the bedroom door, "are you in the kitchen? Is everything OK down there?" Noel sniffed.

"I'll be upstairs when I'm *finished*."

Noel thought her voice had an edge to it. He went back into his bedroom and sat down. Melonie, bored by the football game, was painting her toenails bright red. She had the heel of her foot balanced on the morning paper, the morning paper that Noel had yet to read, and every time she finished coloring a toenail, she would rip a piece of the paper off and wad it between her toes. Nevers came into the bedroom. She was wearing a tailored blue suit and checkered apron. The whole situation made Noel flinch. How out of context, he thought.

"Do you smell gas?" he asked her.

"Yes. It's your stupid oven."

Noel started to put his pants on hurriedly. "Do you know what you are doing downstairs, Nevers? I mean, have you ever cooked anything before? I get very nervous when I smell gas. Very, very, nervous."

"Is de house gonna explode?" Melonie was excited. "Barooom!"

"I put the turkey in *your* oven an hour ago at three hundred but *your* thermometer is only registering one hundred and fifteen. When was the last time somebody used your oven?"

"I don't know." Noel sniffed again. "What's that got to do with smelling gas? I have this fear—"

"Oh, shut up." Nevers definitely wasn't happy. "I've been slaving away downstairs in that absurd kitchen where nothing is where it's supposed to be, and to top everything off, your oven doesn't work the way an oven is supposed to. How anybody ever cooked anything in there is a mystery."

Nevers' voice, Noel thought, had a plaintive ring to it that he didn't recognize.

"Barooom! De house gonna blow up?"

"Melonie, that's not funny," Noel said.

"Funny, funny, funny." Nevers put her hands on her hips and stared angrily at Melonie. "You two are up here playing your kiddie games while *I'm* doing all the work. Noel, if your oven spoils my turkey, spoils my day, I'll do something—something you'll be sorry for."

She's going to cry, Noel thought. Any minute Nevers is going to cry because of my stove.

Nevers crossed the room and snapped off the television.

"Hey," Noel protested, "watching football on Thanksgiving is a hallowed American tradition."

"Not in *my* home," Nevers shot at him.

For the first time, Noel wished he were in Vermont.

Melonie, finished her toenails, stuffed the rest of the newspaper into a wastebasket, and walked around the room on her heels, her toes apart and off the carpet. She sat down on the couch next to Noel and opened up a photograph album that was lying on the coffee table.

"Who's dat?"

"That's Susan." There was a page spread of Susan.

"She's pretty," Melonie said.

Nevers came over, hands still on her hips, and stared down at the pictures. "She didn't get dressed up too often."

"No. She didn't. I don't know. She did sometimes."

Melonie turned the pages. There were pictures of Susan, Beth and David at various times of their lives.

"How come de ain't no pictures of you, Rothman? You too ugly? You breaks the camera someone takes your picture?"

"I was taking them. You want to see some pictures of me?" Noel got up, walked across the room, opened up a desk drawer and came back with a worn photo album. He sat back down and carefully opened it on his knees to a picture of himself when he was about ten. It showed Noel with a crewcut, stripped to the waist, fists clenched in front of him, ready to fight.

"Dat you?" Melonie said with a huge grin.

"Dat me. Skinny mother-fucker."

"Holy shit!" Melonie studied the picture. "You shows me dat picture and fer a million bucks I don't figure dat's you."

"That's ridiculous," Nevers said.

Don Zacharia

"What's ridiculous?"

"That picture of you. It's ridiculous."

Noel shrugged. "I mean—what the hell—what's ridiculous about it?"

"You look—you look—you look ridiculous. Turn the goddamn page."

"I likes it. I think he looks sweet. Just look at dat face. It's sooo sweet." Melonie leaned over and kissed the picture. "You skinny but you sooo sweet." She kissed the picture again and removed it from the page. "Can I have dis picture for my scrapbook?"

Noel didn't answer.

Nevers, agitated, reached down and flipped the pages. She stopped at a picture of Noel in a basketball uniform. "You *did* play basketball."

"Of course I did. Did you think I was making all those stories up? Here, look, that's Meyer Meyerson, and look here," he turned the page, "that's Meyer and me right after we won the League championship."

"I can't believe you played basketball. You're so short."

"*I am not so short*. You make it sound like I'm four foot seven."

"You are not four foot seven but you are SHORT. You're too short to have *ever* been a basketball player except in a midget league."

"Oh, yeah, look at this." Noel's anger showed as he pointed to a faded picture of himself holding a basketball in one hand, and the other hand with one finger pointing up in the classic "I'm number one" sign. "For your goddamn information, that picture was taken by Meyer Meyerson right after I made fifteen baskets in a row, which is *still*, twenty years later, the *all-time county record*."

"You're full of shit, Noel. I don't believe you for a second. I wouldn't believe you if I saw it with my own eyes. Nobody in their right mind would believe that. Fifteen baskets in a row! Ha. What fantasies you have, Noel. What imagination. What a line of crap. What *bullshit*. I'd rather watch my turkey cook than listen to this shit. It's all very bor-*ring*. We're going to do something later that's a lot more fun. You have such a wonderful imagination, we'll really let you use it. We're going to have a family game. I'm going to be Susan, Melonie is going to be Beth, and you're going to be our little basketball player. We'll see how you like that!" Nevers turned and stalked out of the room.

Noel felt a rope around his neck. He sat back down on the couch. The photo album was still open to the picture that Meyer had taken. Noel stared at it and shook his head. My legacy, he thought. This is what I have. Susan, Meyer, both dead. Nevers in the kitchen and a black teenage girl in my bedroom who has my morning newspaper stuffed in between her toes, and I have this picture, this memory. I made fifteen baskets in a row. Twenty years ago. Big deal, Noel Roth. Noel closed the album.

Melonie put the television back on. "Don't bother me none you wanna watch dat game."

"Thanks. I'm not even sure who is playing anymore."

"You do Melonie a favor?"

Noel shrugged. He wanted to tell Melonie to leave him alone, to go downstairs and see if she could help Nevers, but he didn't say anything.

"You give Melonie a little smile?"

"Come on, Melonie, I don't feel like smiling right now."

"A teeny little teentsy bitsy witsy smile. For Melonie. Come on, Rothman." She smiled encouragingly at Noel, flashing her lovely gold tooth at him.

Noel closed his eyes, opened them, looked at Melonie, looked at the TV and then back at Melonie. "Melonie, I really don't feel like smiling. Let's drop it. Maybe Nevers could use some help."

"Not until I gets a smile. I knows dere a smile buried back dere. When you smile, de whole world smiles back at you. Dat's a lie, but dat's a song." Melonie stood up. "You know three things, Rothman, I like you, I mean dat, sin–cere–ly, even if you a little weird; I like dat 'bout Rothman makin' all dose baskets, and Melonie gonna make you smile or die tryin'."

Melonie walked over to where the cherrystone shells remained. She placed one in each eye socket, squinching her eyes down around them, and one in her mouth. She started walking toward Noel, parts of the newspaper still stuffed between her toes, nude, arms outstretched in a Frankenstein pose, shells in her eyes and her mouth, and making what can only be described as a mooing sound.

Noel bit his lip and held out for about ten seconds, and then broke out in laughter. Melonie, pulling the shells from her eyes and mouth, was pleased. She smiled at Noel, flashing her gold tooth at him again. "Seeee. I make Rothman smile." Her eyes twinkled at Noel.

"You win." Noel shook his head back and forth. "I wish I had a camera to take a picture of you just then. You would have died if you could have seen yourself."

"You ever play games when you was a kid?"

"Sure."

"You ever play hide and seek?"

"Are you kidding? I was the world champion."

"Blind man's bluff?"

"Well, to be honest with you, blind man's bluff was just a secondary sport for me. I was OK at it, but hide and seek is what I was all about."

"You wanna play?"

"Which one?"

"Combination of both. You put dese shells into your eyeballs, I do de same, and we see who can find who. Come on, Rothman, let's have some fun. So far dis day one bor-ring day. I mean, I thought holidays were fun days."

"Melonie," Noel stood up, "it's unfair competition. You don't have a chance."

Noel and Melonie stationed themselves at opposite ends of the room and covered their eyes with the shells. Melonie put one into her mouth. "Ready or not, here I come," Noel sang out.

Melonie mooed.

"Ring around the posie, pocket full of rosie, ready or not, here comes ROTHMAN." Noel began to move across the room toward Melonie. He made a quick grab but missed her.

"Moo, moo."

"Rothman gonna get Melonie," Noel said.

"FIRE—FIRE—FIRE—FIRE—"

Noel let the shells drop out of his eyes. "What?"

Nevers burst into the room. She was a mess. Her face smudged, her hair astray, gravy and water stains over her suit.

"What did you say?"

"Fire," she gasped, "your kitchen is on fire."

"*Jesus*—" Noel started for the door, stopped, grabbed his pants and began running down the stairs with Nevers and Melonie behind him. "What the fuck happened?"

"You have to call the fire department," Nevers screamed.

"I can't call the fire department—"

Noel burst into the kitchen. Flames were leaping out of the oven, curling around the woodwork and cabinets above it. There was a bunch of wadded burnt-up towels smoldering in the sink.

"I tried putting it out." Nevers was hysterical. "It's that fucking stove. Call the fire department," she screamed at him.

"I can't call the fire department, you asshole. I just called them a month ago."

"How dare you call your mistress-goddess an asshole? I'll get you for that," she screamed at Noel.

"My fucking kitchen is on fire. You're burning up my fucking house," Noel screamed back at her. "You can take your mistress-goddess act and shove it."

"Call the fire department," Nevers wailed. "Please call the fire department."

"I can't call the fire department." Noel looked around. Black smoke was beginning to pour out of the oven. Noel dashed out of the room.

"Where are you going?" Nevers cried out.

"Fuck you."

In seconds Noel came back up the stairs with a fire extinguisher. The kitchen was filled with smoke. "Open the doors," he yelled at Nevers. In less than a minute he put the fire out. He opened the stove and let the smoke pour out. "What a mess." Nevers began coughing. Noel put the attic fan on and waited until the house was cleared of smoke, but the smell was awful. "I've never seen such a mess." He pulled the turkey out and dumped it into the sink. "It looks like a burnt rat." He turned the water on and smoke sizzled out of the turkey. "A starving wolf would pass it by."

"It was going to be such a perfect day," Nevers cried.

"Dat was exciting," Melonie said.

Phil and Phoebe, Mark and Eric, and Beth and David were just sitting down to their turkey and more food than any of them could ever have finished. Phil, thinking of Noel all the time, wishing very much that his friend was with them, shook his head sadly. His appetite, usually gigantic at Thanksgiving, was nonexistent. He wished he could just drink and forget the food. "Do you want some wine?" he asked Phoebe.

"All right." She shook her head and forced a smile at Beth, but Beth never saw the smile because she was staring at her father, who was standing in the doorway.

Beth jumped up. "Daddy—Daddy—" She ran around the table and threw her arms around Noel. Noel kissed and hugged her. He walked over to the table with his arms around Beth. "You got room for one more?" David jumped up and kissed his father. Phoebe, her mouth open, was, for the first time in her life, speechless.

Phil stood up and held his hand out to Noel. "What happened to you? You look—you look—"

"I look like I've been in a fire?"

"Yeah. Something like that. But you look great to me, buddy."

Noel reached over. He grabbed a drumstick. He stabbed the air with it four, five, six times. He started to say something but stopped. He started again. "I feel terrific." Beth, still clinging to her father, tried unsuccessfully to brush some soot from her father's face. Noel took a bite from the drumstick. He closed and opened his eyes. He gently disentangled himself from Beth. All of a sudden, he started doing a little soft-shoe, shuffling his feet and slapping his hands together without a sound.

"Daddy, stop," Beth said.

Phoebe stood up, smiling, with her hands on her hips. "Noel, you're driving me *crazy*."

"Dat's a song, but dat's a lie."

"I'm glad you're here," Phil said.

"I'll shoot some baskets with you," David said.

Noel was still doing his soft-shoe. "If only I knew how to tap-dance," Noel Roth said, "I'd put taps on my heels, taps on my toes and I'd do a tap dance for you. I'd do a tap dance for the world. I could have been a star."

It was a wonderful Thanksgiving.

About the Author

Don Zacharia lives with his family in a suburb of New York City. His short stories have appeared in *Epoch* and *The Partisan Review*. *The Match Trick* is his first novel.